The Last Week in August

Ruth Henderson

Biscuit Press

By the same author

The Other Side of the Tide (pub, Biscuit)

High Tides (Red Squirrel Press)

Published 2012 © in Great Britain
By Biscuit Press

All rights reserved
Full copyright is asserted by the Author © 2012

Typeset by Free Spirit Writers, Bridlington
Printed by Jasprint Ltd., NE37 2SH
Cover design by Colin Mulhern

The characters and events in this novel are inventions, and any resemblance to real persons or events is purely coincidental.

'I dedicate this book
to my husband Alistair W. Henderson
for his patience and unfailing support.
Keep a had son.'

CHAPTER ONE

TILLY

Tilly felt like kissing the young man who sat opposite her at his shiny steel desk, empty except for a slim, closed, lap-top computer and a swinging steel balls toy, but she resisted, it would be unprofessional and he might think her a fool, so she sat on her hands nodding like a fool. She watched the balls ticking the seconds off. He smiled at her. She managed to stand and speak. 'Thank you and I look forward to sending our first orders for the Christmas display.'

'Lovely to have finally met.' His teeth glinted. 'I look forward to our continued partnership.'

'Me too.'

He smiled again before bowing his head to his god – technology.

'Goodbye Mr Connelly.' She bent to pick up her Tote-Tilly bag, the sample she blatantly flaunted to the world.

Daring to turn from his altar, he flashed his teeth again. They'd obviously cost him mega bucks and he intended to get his money's worth. 'I thought we'd agreed, me Michael you Tilly.'

'Yes, sorry, I keep forgetting, Michael.' She stepped back. 'Until we meet again.'

'Count on it.' Aiming his two-finger gun, he shot her before blasting his mobile phone.

She let herself out and smiled at his secretary and then at everyone else she passed until she was in her car and on the way home, still smiling. She was euphoric! She, Matilda Maitland, had taken her first and hopefully profitable step into the business world. She, Matilda Maitland, wife and mother of three, was head of Tote-Tilly, the up and coming, prestigious and soon-to-be most wanted range of bags on the market; at least she hoped they'd be and the firm she'd created didn't, as yet, have any employees, but soon, very soon, all that would change.

She drove straight to Adam's factory. She hadn't been in the building for months. Adam had preferred her to stay at home, to be a housewife and mother. The place suffered from a desperation that smothered the windows and blocked the light. She walked around the long wide cutting tables to an area used to store bits and pieces that might come in useful. As far as Tilly could tell these discoloured and twisted pieces of PVC would never be of use to anyone, but if it was cleared and cleaned she would have a workshop for Tote-Tilly.

Finefit was a replacement window and door firm that had thrived under the iron rule of Adam's mother, the driving force behind their success. Tilly had always known that Adam was weak, but it used to manifest itself in boyish charm, an easy going facet of his nature she'd found endearing. However this trait of charm is useless in business and after his mother died Adam hadn't had the faintest idea how to manage Finefit. Tilly had noticed things were bad, heard a few whispers, even been taken to one side by their oldest serving joiner, who'd confided his fears. She'd tried to help, but each attempt to broach the matter had engendered even more denial in Adam who would simply walk away. Even now with the staff on an enforced holiday of three weeks, while he tried to find new orders, he still wouldn't admit the business was in trouble. She had left him, with the children, in the Bay of Pollensa on Mallorca, where he was propositioning all the friends they'd made over many summers holidaying in a beach-front house. Taking one last look around, she locked up. She would return to Mallorca and persuade Adam that allowing her to use the space was a good idea.

In their personal life Adam's lack of application hadn't been so obvious. She had never expected him to help around the house where she organised everything for him, just as his mother had at work: a great life for Adam and she had to admit she had enjoyed doing things her way at home, without having to consult him at every turn. For seventeen years she'd lived the life she wanted, but over the last couple of years restlessness had stirred a latent dissolution. One day she realised that she was the only mother always there as a general runabout for her children and their friends. This was because the other parents all worked and she'd wondered why didn't she work?

She'd left school with few qualifications, excelling only in dressmaking and art so working in a clothes shop had seemed the thing to do without going on to college, which she didn't fancy, so she'd started as a junior in the underwear department of Bewicks store and risen to the giddy heights of sales assistant before leaving to marry Adam. But now, she was an entrepreneur, about to start her own business, and it was a wonderfully liberating, yet scary, experience.

For years she'd made casual carry-all bags as presents for friends and relatives and for special occasions she'd often provided a pretty bag to match an outfit. She'd never accepted money, but now it was different. She needed to step up a gear, several gears in fact, and had secretly negotiated the deal with Michael Connelly, Bewicks' buyer, to supply them with two dozen bags for the Christmas season. Adam thought she was shopping in Palma.

Visiting the factory, instead of driving straight to the airport, had thrown her schedule and now she realised she'd never get back to Mallorca tonight and should ring him. She drove the few streets through Tynemouth to their sea-front home and let herself into the empty house. She settled in, luxuriating in a blissfully quiet bath before pulling on a pair of soft summer pants and a T-shirt. Relaxing with a glass of wine on the back patio, in the evening sun, she checked her list; all the pre-holiday stuff was done. Robert, Adam's father, had been contacted about keeping an eye on the house and factory while they were away and the only thing still to do was sew name-tags on the new school uniforms for the boys. They'd literally burst out of last term's stuff, growing long in arm and leg, becoming gangly overnight. So that was all of August sorted. She'd make a start on September's list after she'd rung Adam. On boarding the plane she'd realised that she'd picked up his phone instead of her own. She switched it on and a list of missed calls flashed up on the screen. She and Adam never read each other's texts or emails or letters, never had. It was a habit they'd got into when they first married and never questioned, it had just seemed the right thing to do, but confronted by a list of calls from someone called Lonore she was tempted.

Who was Lonore? She sounded like a fabric softener. Lonore had left texts. Maybe she'd just have a look at one, but no, she put the mobile down and sauntered around the big kitchen, refilled her glass before wandering into the hall. She picked up the land-line and dialled the number for the holiday home in Mallorca. It rang out hollowly with that sound you just know means the house is empty. She tried her own mobile hoping Adam would use it, but it went straight to voice mail. She left a message. She wandered onto the back patio and sat on a garden chair in the dipping sunlight. She sipped her wine and toyed with Adam's mobile, twisting it round and around in her hand. It trilled and flashed its alarm. Lonore? There was no-one at the factory called Lonore. Probably no-one else anywhere in the whole world called Lonore. Could she be a contact with an order for Finefit? Perhaps it was important. Perhaps it would save the factory. She really should answer it. Her thumb hovered over the button for text messages then moved again to ring the holiday house where the same empty buzz travelled through the ether.

She pressed the button over Lonore's name. The number showed black against the white, clear and a fact. She pressed it. A female voice answered and she knew this woman was involved with Adam. How? She just did.

'Hello,' the nervous voice said.

'Hello.'

'Is this Adam's phone?'

'Yes.'

'Do you work for him?'

'Yes.' Well, that was true. Tilly tried to justify the deceit she was certain she was about to perpetrate.

'Oh, thank goodness. You've no idea. I didn't want to live here. I wanted to live near my mother in Edinburgh for this very reason, in case I was left alone in an emergency, but would he listen? No. And now it's happened. I'm here alone and the water tank has burst.'

Oh good, Tilly thought as she perused her nails. They were a mess, sewing stiff fabrics did that to them. 'Don't you have anyone you can call?' she asked.

'Not a soul.'

Shame.

'Well … there are people whose boys go to pre-school with ours.'

Tilly sheared the edges from two more nails as she scrabbled to stop the phone from clattering over the Cotswold stone flags.

'Hello? Are you still there?'

'Yes.' Tilly croaked.

'Oh good. I was wondering if you can get hold of my husband ...'

This time the phone clattered to the ground and the casing flew off, scattering its innards to the corner by the shed where the boys, her boys, her and Adam's boys, Sean and Harry, kept their bikes, footballs, skate and surfing paraphernalia. Tilly tried to find all the bits, she really did, but she just couldn't seem to remember what she was looking for. Finally she surrendered the cause and found herself sitting indoors, on the bottom stair, cradling the shattered pieces.

After a while her brain stopped singing to itself and she began to hyperventilate. Back in the kitchen she scrabbled about in the drawers for a paper bag. Too late, one long shuddering breath and she stopped shaking. She ran upstairs for a warm dressing gown then back to the kitchen for hot chocolate then back up to her room where she found herself curled up in bed.

Her husband. That was definitely what the woman had said. And their twins! She must be deranged. There must be two Adam Maitlands. Ineffectual and bumbling he was hardly capable of coping with one life let alone two and he wasn't the type to betray anybody, least of all her.

What was she doing in bed! She got up and discarded the dressing gown. After an hour the house looked like it had been hit by a whirlwind. Every drawer was upended, papers littered every surface and still she was no closer to discovering any details of Adam's double life. Half an hour later she was back in the factory using a crow-bar on his desk drawers. After half an hour she found the number. She rang.

Lonore picked up at once. 'Oh thank goodness. I just knew you'd ring back. Did you drop the phone? Have you been in touch with Adam?'

'I've tried, but of course Adam's in er …?' She left the trap open.

And Lonore fell right in. 'Mallorca, yes on business.'

'And no contac …'

'No. He said he'd be moving about, meeting people, getting new orders for Finefit.'

'Yes, exactly.' Tilly was now in no doubt.

'He's so busy, but I have to get some help. The water is still pouring through the ceiling.'

In the background Tilly could hear the voices of small boys shrieking with excitement. Lonore shouted, almost quietly, 'Please be quiet boys and come away from that electric socket.'

Tilly gasped in horror.

'Can you please get me some help?'

'Have you phoned a plumber?'

'I've tried but no-one's in.'

'No. It's Saturday evening.'

'Could you find one for me?'

'I can, but ...'

'You're a saint. The boys are playing in the water running down the stairs. They never listen to me, oh, I do wish their father was here. If you get in touch with Adam tell him to come straight home. We need him.'

'No!' Tilly shouted. 'I don't know your address.'

Lonore giggled. 'Silly me. It's fifty-seven Syon Place. Do you know it?'

'Yes.' Yes I do, Tilly thought. How can I not? It's round the corner from my house!

'Must go. You'll send help?'

'Yes.'

'Bye.'

'Bye.'

Send help! Not a chance. Tilly hoped Lonore drowned in the deluge when her living room ceiling collapsed under the weight of the flood. She slammed the phone down and stalked back into the factory, splintering odd strips of UPVC framing under her heels. She stalked the length of the building and back again. "Their father" that's what the stupid woman had called him. What was Adam doing getting involved with a fabric softener needier than himself? She was furious with him. How dare he spoil her day. Her day! The day she'd made her own. Well she'd soon settle that. She stormed from the factory, uncaring of the direction her feet were heading.

Finefit's factory was between the coastal village of Tynemouth and the fishing port of North Shields, sandwiched between two acres of allotment gardens and the only building of note in the area, The Master Mariners Homes. Built in eighteen sixty three by the Duke of Northumberland, this retirement home for sailors had sat unchanged by the turmoil around it. Other buildings had come and gone, roads re-directed and parks re-located, but its soft yellow sandstone had only mellowed. Normally Tilly admired the ornate Iconic architecture with mullioned windows, shining as brightly as the day they were first installed, but this night her unseeing eyes missed it. She didn't give her usual greeting of *m'lord* to the statue of that generous duke or notice the familiar road, down a steep bank and through the deep arch of Tanners Bank railway bridge, then past her mother's studio and her childhood home, then on to the Fish Quay, where groups of people were speaking a mixture of languages.

On the quay itself lights spilled from bursting restaurants and pubs, the clientele in celebratory mood, singing and dancing, chatting and laughing. Tied up along the length of the quay were old sailing ships in a variety of styles and sizes and people in outlandish nautical costumes were hospitably inviting each other aboard. This was such a strange phenomenon that it finally penetrated Tilly's numbness. Who were all these people? Then she remembered that the Cutty Sark Tall Ships Race was leaving the River Tyne the last week in August and she had planned for the family to return home from Mallorca a week earlier than usual for the event.

She sat down on a bench and concentrated on her problem, or was it Adam's problem? Obviously not, as he didn't seem to be bothered that he had another family and hadn't mentioned it to her. How would it go? "Pass the marmalade pet, oh and by the way, I met this woman and she has two sons, twins, coincidence eh? And well, I rather fancy the boys are going to call me Dad." I think not, Tilly told herself. Somehow she knew her original instinct was right and these boys were Adam's flesh and blood. The boys. Two little boys with an ineffectual mother in a flooded house. Wearily she set off, back up the bank. The three rows of windows in her mother's house were in darkness; she'd probably be having supper with some of her weird friends in one of the restaurants along the quay.

Retracing her steps Tilly reached her car without meeting anyone she knew and drove to Syon Street. It was a quarter to one and the moon was quarter new, obscured intermittently by dark clouds. Looking at the time reminded her that she had a plane to catch at six-fifteen from Newcastle Airport. Hey-ho, here I go. She rang the bell. The door was opened almost immediately by a dishevelled woman in her late twenties. Slim and lithe with masses of curling auburn hair around a narrow face with a generous mouth and big brown eyes; a younger model of herself. 'Lonore?' She inquired.

'Yes, yes, do come in. I'm so glad you're here. We're in the back.' The woman was almost crying, obviously the ghastly events she'd kept at bay all evening were beginning to overwhelm her and she was so young.

Through her tears she smiled at Tilly. 'This is so kind of you, but no-one has come to mend the boiler and I'm hopeless. Was it you who rang?'

Tilly accepted the inevitable. This vulnerable mother of two little boys with no support was not to blame for Adam's infidelity. She might not even know that Adam, adulterous bastard and useless father of five children, was already married. 'Yes it was,' she answered as she sloshed through six inches of water. Up a short flight of stairs to the back of the terraced house, she followed Lonore into a large comfortable room with a kitchen at one end and an informal sitting arrangement around a wood-burning stove directly in front. Curled up together on a battered sofa, like chubby little puppies, were the twins, asleep and the image of her boys at that age. Tilly straightened her backbone. 'I'm sorry, but I lost my mobile. Do you have one?'

Three hours later with the electricity turned off, the plumber been and gone and the water slowly subsiding in Syon Street, Tilly carried one boy and Lonore the other up the stairs in her own house, 11 Sea View, and lay them in Sean and Harry's beds. Wearily Tilly showed Lonore into Beth's room before wandering down to the kitchen. She'd offered no explanation to the grateful Lonore and felt that she'd rather just catch her flight and let Adam deal with the mess, but she knew she wouldn't; she'd been picking up after Adam for seventeen years and old habits die hard. She rang her mobile.

Sleepily he answered. 'Where are you? Do you realise the time?'

'I'm at home Adam.'

'What the hell you doing there?'

'There's an emergency. Can you manage with the kids?'

'What emergency? Is Dad alright?'

'Yes. It's nothing to do with your Dad.'

'What then?'

'It's a friend. Her house is flooded.'

'Bad show Till, you need to come back here. We need you.'

'I suppose you do, but this friend ... who lives in Syon Street ...' She waited, but there was no discernable reaction. 'She's been flooded out. She's all on her own. I've offered her the use of our house till she gets thing sorted.' She detected a slight grunt. 'That's all right with you isn't it?'

He mumbled.

If it wasn't so tragic she'd laugh. 'It's handy for organizing things. She has two little boys.'

'Yes.' He sounded puzzled.

Probably because he thought Tilly had lost her mind. She wondered if she had it all wrong. 'Do you know them?' In itself an innocent enough question.

'Yes.'

'So ... I'll stay for a few days.'

'Tilly?'

'Yes?'

'You're sure you're fine with this?'

'Well yes, there's not much else I can do, is there?'

'You're a brick.'

The swine! He'd chosen to deliberately misinterpret the situation, sliding his infidelities in under a problem she was already dealing with. She would not let it be dealt with in this way. 'This needs to be talked about Adam.'

'Yes.'

'I'll see you in a day or two.'

'Yes, you stay and help your friend. We'll manage till you get here.'

'You're a swine, Adam!'

'Yes.'

'We will talk when I get back to Mallorca.'

'Yes.'

'Is that all you can say.' She yelled at the phone and slammed it into its cradle. It was impossible to talk to Adam, he solved problems by ignoring them, but she'd make him discuss this. He had to acknowledge his treachery, his betrayal, not just of her and her children, but also Lonore and her two boys. Five innocent children now forever burdened by their father's guilt. And now he thought it was sanctioned! As usual he'd passed the problem to her, certain that she'd deal with it. Well not this time buster, not this time. This time she'd make him confront it. She was furious.

She made herself a coffee and wandered about restoring order from her mad search of a few hours ago. Then weary, but unable to sleep, she climbed the stairs to the office above the sun lounge extension, a favourite place for her in the silence of the early morning house, before the kids tore the day to shreds of need. She settled at her workbench in front of the large window and looked out across the North Sea. It lay there in the false dawn, quietly waiting for the wind to send it barrelling along the length of the pier and rushing up the long broad sweeps of sand that fell away from high cliffs and dunes, these recently reclaimed from the formal Victorian layout of paths, steps and flower beds that had cost the council too much to maintain. Tilly was in favour of this sanctioned neglect. She liked things that grew as nature intended. As she sipped her coffee and emptied her mind of problems the sun cracked open the horizon with a shaft of silver light and another day dawned.

CHAPTER TWO

ADAM

The Bay of Pollensa also shimmered in the morning sun, the sea an impossibly imagined blue under a veil of milky silver. Picasso never achieved such a blue. Yachts of every size and shape lined the jetties and millionaire's palaces floated in deep water, pulling at their anchors in the fast current, impatient for more exotic latitudes.

Adam sprawled on a lounger on the narrow beach, smoking. He was annoyed with Tilly. Why did she have to interfere? His life with Lonore had nothing to do with her, but she had to butt in, always telling him what to do, how to live his life.

The drone of the seaplane taking off from the military base at the north end of the bay attracted his attention. Idly drawing on his cigarette he watched it heave itself into the air and bank across to deep water where it dipped down, skimming the waves to fill its tanks in preparation for the first practice run of the day. Hardly ever called on to dowse any flames, the crew, never-the-less, practiced every day to the delight of the tourists who speculated on its purpose. Most favoured the rumour that it belonged to Michael Douglas whose holiday home was a few miles down the coast above Soller. Pollensa Bay was always rife with rumour, as each new intake of tourists discovered its delights and mysteries and solved them to their own satisfaction and the waiters fuelled wild guesses with wilder stories that the new people eagerly passed on to their hotel friends.

On top of the rocky headland a helicopter landed at the empty mansion that also belonged to the military, but was up for sale for sixteen million Euros. It was occasionally used for functions and was now being prepared for a hush-hush meeting. White canvas awnings were being stretched between the stone arches that bordered the courtyard to shield the important guests from the paparazzi. It was known in the supermarket that a secret meeting of European high ranking officers was imminent; there were no secrets from Guadalupa, the owner, before the meeting was five minutes old she would know its findings and be giving her solution to the problem baffling world leaders.

With soft voices discussing their plans for the day, Sean and Harry, Tilly and Adam's twin sons, aged twelve, came tiptoeing from the house. With a pat on his head and a wave away of his tobacco smoke, they made straight for their dinghy. He really should buy them a new one, the rubber was beginning to perish on that old thing they'd had since they could toddle. He finished his smoke and headed back indoors to sort out breakfast. Opening cupboards and drawers where alien kitchen stuff baffled him he finally discovered the cereals. Milk and juice were in the fridge, but he couldn't find any eggs. His daughter Beth walked in, soft footed on bare feet.

'Eggs?' He asked her.
'No thanks.'
'I mean I can't find any.'
'We don't have any.'
'What'll I do then?'
'The supermarket, duh?'

'Mmm.' He studied her. Fine curly hair like a mass of red flames falling around her pale heart-shaped face, her deep green eyes wide and inquisitive, she was a beauty. How had he never noticed it before now? Tilly had been concerned about her, she'd said that Beth was a bit down this summer and had intended to talk to her. Tilly was big on talking.

He sauntered to the supermarket for a few essentials, dithering so much that Guadalupa finally took the empty basket and filled it. Back at the house he called the boys in for breakfast. They had juice and cereal then coped with the dodgy stove to make eggy-bread for themselves and him, before running back out again to mess about in the sea. Beth refused food and conversation and slamming the door of her room left him in no doubt that she'd rather be alone. He climbed up to the first floor balcony to have another ciggy and a bottle of beer, watching the boys from his favourite position in the hammock, only moving to replace the empty bottle with a cold one from the fridge. He decided it would be a good idea to have one of those mini fridges on the balcony. Then he wouldn't have to go downstairs for beer, he'd be able to keep an eye on the boys all day. He sighed and finished his beer, the fourth one; a quick glance at his watch showed it was past eleven. Oh well, no use letting Beth's strop or Tilly's desertion spoil the day. He'd take the boys sailing, maybe around to Formentor.

With a bit of tinkering he got the outboard started and, despite opposing directions from the boys, negotiated the busy harbour before letting Sean take the tiller. It was his turn, and anyway Harry wasn't bothered, he always deferred to Sean treating him tolerantly as the younger twin; which he was, but Sean gloated, always eager to score a point. Adam settled in the stern and thought about his other twins Joseph and Justin. It was going to be hard to give them the education Sean and Harry enjoyed. In fact, it was likely that Sean and Harry would have to change to the local high school because he had no idea where next year's fees were coming from. Joseph was a bit like Harry, considerate and thoughtful, always with his head in a book. Justin wasn't like anybody, he was his own man with lofty ambitions to be a chef, at least they wouldn't starve. Adam thought that it was just as well Tilly and Lonore had met, if the worst came to the worst and he went bust, they'd all have to move into his father's rambling farmhouse up in Rothbury. He looked around him, taking particular notice of all the expensive boats on show. Yes, well, one day. He was confident he'd be able to persuade someone to invest in Finefit before the summer was over.

The boys were managing the little craft very skilfully, dodging dozens of boats milling around in the bay. As they approached the narrow entrance where deep water funnelled through steep cliffs, swift and contrary, Harry was in control. He had a tendency to concentrate on the immediate and was keeping a steady course.

But Sean had eyes everywhere. 'Port, port.' He rebuked Harry. 'Port! You'll hit that ketch under the cliff.'

'I'm skipper. I know what I'm doing.' Harry argued, annoyed with himself for not noticing the little white and green boat.

'Bit of hush boys. Calm heads at sea.' As they accepted the warning Adam relaxed again. He felt a bit tired, must be the heat, it always made him tired. The boys jostled each other for turns at the tiller. Adam had utmost faith in their ability to get them round the headland and safely tied up at the little wooden jetty in Formentor, but they narrowly missed a lone swimmer, who swore at them. Adam swore back. 'Bloody idiot.'

Harry joined in, laughing at his own daring. 'Yes absolute bastard!'

Sean laughed with him.

Adam couldn't help a smile. 'Sean!' He admonished.

'It's what Jack says.'

'Yes, well, Jack says a lot of things and you shouldn't copy him so much.'

'Jack's a hoot.'

'Yea, he's cool.' Harry was determined to back his brother.

'He's an adult and can swear if he wants to. You, on the other hand, shouldn't.'

'OK Dad.' Sean knew the best way to win an argument with his father was to abandon it. He handled the little boat with an easy competence. In front of them, rising and dipping through the green waters came the *Esmeralda*, a huge catamaran filled with tourists. 'Way. Way!' Sean shouted at Zander, who was skipper and showing off his seamanship to the passengers by tacking the big craft to and fro under sail.

Adam eyed Zander, handsome and easy going, a nomad with an easy daring way about him. He'd once wondered if Tilly was having an affair with him, but had talked himself out of such an idea. Tilly was incapable of disloyalty.

'Get that thing out of my way,' Sean shouted.

'I see you.' Turning the big wheel with casual skill, Zander laughed back at him. 'Why don't you come and work for us. I'll show you how to handle a real boat.'

'When I buy my own boat I might give you a job,' Sean countered. 'You're not such a bad sailor.' He was a master at sparing with all the skippers in Puerto.

'Oh-ho, so the little sardine's growing into a shark.'

This banter pleased the tourists who hung over the rails laughing and expectant. Adam knew it would persuade them to give the crew a bigger tip at the end of their trip around the bay.

'Yea,' Sean yelled as he pulled away to tie up at the jetty. 'And I'll get a proper boat with only one hull so you'll have to learn to sail without stabilisers.'

Zander pulled the huge cat about, gliding across the stern of the little rib, sending a swell that pushed the inflatable away from the jetty a couple of feet just as Sean was jumping ashore. He splashed into the water.

Harry howled, laughing as the passengers gasped in horror, before Sean emerged spluttering, to face Zander's big grin.

'Maybe one day you'll be a sailor, bye for now little shark.' And the cat sped out to open water.

After the boys had tied up the boat and were trailing behind

Adam, pushing each other over in the sand Sean bragged, 'He called me shark.'

'Little shark!' Harry reminded him.

'Yes, but shark, better than sardine.' Sean was in heaven.

In the hotel the boys fled toward the pool to meet a brother and sister they'd become friendly with. Adam encouraged them. The father was 'something' in the city and he obviously had money or wouldn't be able to pay the exorbitant rate the Formentor Hotel demanded for one month's stay. Obviously this man was not suffering losses in the crisis-hit banks. Adam thought that if he played the game properly he'd persuade him to invest in Finefit. Somebody had to. Jack had made vague promises but nothing concrete. He'd remind him.

In the bar he quickly scanned the men, nothing meaningful had ever resulted from conversation with women. He was surprised to see Jack in jovial mood with another ex-pat, Max, whose wife had died at Christmas. Adam approached from their blind side, never could tell what snippets of usable information might be gleaned.

Jack was talking, recounting one of his interminable stories from when England still had an empire. 'And he said, I've never had such a great time. Bloody tours, who needs them?' Max laughed dutifully as Jack turned, sensing someone behind him. 'Hello Adam.'

Adam slid onto a stool. 'Jack, Max.'

Max finished the last swallow of his whiskey and moved to go. 'Oh well, got to go. Bye Jack see you tomorrow. Adam.' And stumbling on arthritic hips he left.

'Bloody rude.' Adam said, turning away from him.

'The man is barely holding on.'

'We've all got problems.'

'He needs friends.'

'Got a funny way of showing it.'

'I said friends Adam, and you can hardly call yourself that.'

'Yea well I can't get around to everybody. Spread myself too thin.' He attempted to lighten the mood.

'We were just saying it might be an idea to make a rule not to talk business in the bar.'

'I did want to talk some business. Wondered if you'd given any more thought to investing in my company?'

'Not sure I'm in a position to take chances what with the market so unstable.'

'Yes, but Finefit is an established company and you know how reliable Mam was.'

'Your mother yes. Did I ever tell you about when we met up in Singapore, monsoon season?'

After an hour of Jack's derring-do Adam was no farther forward in his quest for investment. He downed his third whisky and said goodbye. The boys were ready to go, their friends having left to spend the day at the villa of a business partner of their father, up in the hills above Pollensa Old Town.

'Might have bloody well asked us,' Adam muttered. The boys were too far ahead to hear him. Stepping unsteadily into the stern of the ancient rubber dingy he left it to the boys to get them safely home, while he, slipping into melancholy, slept.

He was wakened by Harry's frantic yelling. 'Dad! Dad, wake up.'

Adam felt as if a giant bell had replaced his head causing a deep thud to resound through his whole body. With unresponsive arms he tried to push himself upright, but he'd fallen into the bottom of the boat and great folds of heavy rubber trapped him in inches of water.

Harry was frantic now, tearing at Adam's legs. 'We're sinking!'

Finally Adam realised the obvious. They had been pushed by a steady wind into a narrow gully under the towering black cliffs of the Tramuntana Mountains that stuck out into the deep water channel. A heavy squall pelted them with rain like lead pellets, battering them onto the vicious rocks. Before he could gather his thoughts a rogue wave lifted the rapidly deflating craft and just as swiftly retreated leaving them wedged. Sean was fighting to hang on to the pile of useless rubber and Harry sat on the last inflated pocket. The drenching spray sobered Adam and he grabbed Sean just before he fell into the murderous undertow. All three of them crawled to higher ground.

The boys were freezing cold, shocked and shivering. Adam tried to get them to huddle together, but the rocks were murderously jagged, there was just nowhere to sit. Sean managed to get his fingers into a pocket of his soaking wet shorts that clung to him as if glued so it took about five minutes to extricate his mobile. Stuttering through chattering teeth he called the coastguard, but there didn't seem to be any reply. They became silent and sullen. Confident sailors they blamed themselves for the accident. Adam knew he was at fault. 'Sorry guys. Shouldn't have slept.'

Harry dipped his head so as not to meet his father's eyes.

Adam examined the rising rocks and wondered if a way to the top was possible. He started to clamber along the slippery ridge.

'Dad don't!' Harry's panic-stricken voice stopped him.

The kid was terrified. 'Got to try Harry old man. Can't just sit and wait. Come on, give's your hand. We'll edge our way up.' But Harry sat terrified, unable to move. He was a pitiful sight, drenched and shivering with his legs bleeding from clambering up the mica-loaded rocks, then Sean tried to crawl closer to him, but fell backwards into the water. Adam rose unsteadily on the spray-drenched rock and jumped across the gully. Misjudging the distance he too sank into deep water, his shirt caught on an overhang, the double stitched seams tightening with the wetness. His fingers felt like dead toes as he struggled to loosen buttons that wouldn't budge. Sean was being dragged under the cleft, his head under water and his body lolling about in the waves. Just as Adam thought he'd never get free of the clammy material it tore. He surged toward Sean and managed to pull him clear of the water, but they were helpless, being tossed back and forward by the strong waves. The unrelenting black rocks ripped at Adam's hands and legs, his feet were slippery with blood, but pulling Sean with him he finally managed to clamber above the water-line.

Harry was crying and shouting. Sean was a sodden lump lying over Adam's knees with his legs bobbing grotesquely in the water. Adam forced himself to feel for a pulse.

'Dad. Dad!'

Adam ignored Harry's shout. He couldn't feel any movement in Sean's freezing neck, he managed to slip his fingers into his mouth. It was warm.

'Zander. It's Zander!'

What was Harry shouting about. 'Hang on son.'

'Zander, Dad.' Putting himself at risk of losing his balance the boy was struggling to stand, He was waving.

'Keep still!' Movement on the edge of Adam's vision attracted his attention. My God! That's what Harry was shouting about. The *Esmeralda* was about a hundred metres away and closing fast. The crew were ready in the bows, ropes tied about them and wearing snorkels and fins. Adam tightened his grip on the still unconscious Sean. 'You're alright son.'

It wasn't easy, but the crew were fearless and the toughest swimmers in Mallorca. Competitors in the annual race around the bay they were familiar with the currents and submerged rocks and blessed with cool heads and strong young limbs. Soon everyone was safely on board the big boat and it cut through the swells and dips towards safe harbour. Adam clutched a silent Harry in his arms, immobile, his green eyes wide and fixed on his twin who was being attended to by one of the crew. When Sean finally opened his eyes Adam broke down, sobbing bitter tears.

Zander hauled him away from the shocked boys into the little cabin. 'You bloody drunken fool!' He had no intention of letting Adam off the hook.

'I know. My God, do you think I don't?'

'Lucky for you I was watching. If you ever, ever again get in a boat with those boys after you've been drinking I will personally drown you!' Calm and thoughtful, Zander had never been known to hit anyone, but Adam cringed, waiting for the blow. Instead he felt himself thrown to the deck as the tall man strode aft to help the crew pull the big sail in. Adam was in no doubt that this experienced sailor meant every word he spoke, but he needed no reminder, he was certain he'd never forget that his own actions were to blame for the near death of his precious sons. He staggered to the seats that ran along the hull of the giant boat and slumped there with his guilty misery.

At the hospital the boys were pronounced fit enough to go home. Adam had instructions to keep them warm and not to leave them, any change and he was to bring them straight back. He argued with the doctors, insisting that they'd been through an ordeal that might have repercussions he wasn't aware of, but he knew the real reason was that he was terrified to be responsible for them on his own.

He phoned Tilly, but she didn't answer. This was just selfish. Surely she wasn't going to go all huffy on him. It wasn't as if his other life had ever affected her. He'd always seen to it that she and the older children were separate from Lonore and the little boys. She'd probably gone crying to her mother, the earth mother, Mai, the white witch.

CHAPTER THREE

TILLY

Tilly had indeed gone to her mother's. She was desolate. Half heartedly she kicked a gnarled lump of driftwood and sent it rumbling down the cellar steps.

Her mother came and stood behind her. Tilly felt her hand on her shoulder and moved a step to one side.

'Them as don't like me can leave me alone.' Her mother sang the bars of an old folk song, the words her creed. A widow for almost forty years she lived in an old brewery, on a steep bank leading to the river. A rambling building on four floors she'd bought it cheap from the council when the quayside had been a no go area full of drunks and rats, the one often or not indistinguishable from the other, but ten years ago the area had begun a massive renewal and the government had sunk millions into upgrading its ruined buildings. Mai discovered that all manner of grants had become available and her renovations had taken on a new vigour. The building was now sound and appealing, sought after by estate agents who were sent off with a smile and a song so that Mai could continue to let her rooms to artisans who supported each other with wine and encouragement while she sculpted and carved, smoked weed, drank vile concoctions of her own making, fished and fought mermaids. Women came to sit and marvel at her wisdom and take away a potion distilled from seaweed, potions to make them beautiful, healthy, alluring, fertile, but most of all empowered. Mai promised nothing except a sense of well-being that would, in its turn, engender all of these properties.

'Sorry Mum.'

'Mum!' Her mother scorned the word. 'Time was when Mam was good enough for you. And I taught you better than to disregard the hardships people endured to enable us to retain our identity, but you, you throw it away like a spoiled casting. No good ever comes from getting above yourself.' She turned back to her work, a representation of a mermaid.

Mai had become famous for her statues of the creatures, but

these were not the pretty tail flicking and beguiling fish the public were used to buying on a day out at the coast; these were the products of Mai's fertile mind; sinuous and coiling around themselves and each other it was hard to tell where they began and ended. Each one was subtly different, but all had a malignant twist to their forms because Mai believed that mermaids were intrinsically vile and corrupted. They varied in size, from tiny silver pendants and small statuettes to sit on a windowsill, to life-sized pieces that commanded thousands of pounds from wealthy buyers, but each one had a spell woven into it that she swore would ward off evil.

Tilly sat on a stool covered in paint and plaster and gouged in a hundred places by the chisels her mother stuck in to keep to hand. She studied the piece her mother had returned to. It was a piece of driftwood, almost as big as she was and Mai was a generously proportioned lady with high cheekbones, slanting eyes and tangled tresses of what had once been auburn hair, bequeathed to both Tilly and Beth, but now shot through with silver; her eyes, like Tilly and Beth had a sea green quality that could change with their moods. The statue she studied was a slithering sliding mass of curves and limbs with a pointed face turned away from Tilly and lifted up to see – what? 'What is she looking at?'

Mai Morris stood back with her head on one side. 'Not at, for. She's looking for something.'

'What?'

'Not sure yet, maybe before I finish it I'll know. But see this.' She traced a line from the tip of the wildly tossing hair to a swollen belly. The mermaid was pregnant. 'The sea showed me this; it knows the shape of people. This is a sign of new life.'

'I've got all the new life I can cope with for now, thanks very much.'

'Not this life, not yet, it's a message.' Mai threw a cloth over the statue and focussed her attention on Tilly.

Tilly turned away from her mother's all-knowing eyes that often made her feel uncomfortable. Her mother knew things, could see into the future. All her life Tilly had tried to ignore this mysterious facet of Mai's personality that had underpinned her upbringing, but had never found a hiding place. She had been relieved to marry and finally leave the house on the Quay with its strange prehistoric signs carved into rocks that jutted up all over a back garden that fell into a valley with a stream that dropped underground and then into the River Tyne. She had never been interested in her mother's beliefs and as a teenager had been embarrassed when friends from school showed any curiosity. Mai had never tried to cajole Tilly into accepting it but Tilly knew that Beth was beginning to interest herself in her grandmother's secret magic. She was hoping she'd grow out of it when she went to uni.

'Are you sure about this Tilly? I didn't think Adam had it in him.' Mai mused, with ill concealed mirth.

'You mean he's gormless and useless and you were right I shouldn't have married him.'

'Well, now that you mention it ...'

'You never liked him.'

'That's cos he's a prat.'

'He's been a good husband and father and I love him.'

'Like a brother.'

'I'm not having this conversation with you. You're my mother.' Tilly didn't like the way Mai's intuition had unerringly spotted the problem she'd been ignoring. Sex between she and Adam had been practically none existent lately and, oddly, it hadn't bothered her. And it obviously hadn't bothered him because he had Lonore. 'Lonore! What sort of a stupid name is that?'

'You don't need to use her name to insult her. You've a perfectly good reason. Where is she now any rate?'

'I left her at home.'

'Your home?'

'It's Adam's too.'

'And she has as much right as you to be there. Is that what you're saying?'

'No. No of course not. But ...' Tilly stood and looked out of the window to where an ebbing tide dragged the river through the piers and into the open sea. Her mother followed and stood beside her, slipping an arm around her. Tilly didn't step aside, but she felt her body stiffen even though she needed the comfort. She had always spurned Mai's earth mother support, had schooled herself not to be reliant on it, never allowing emotions that seemed to weaken other women to rise in her body.

'You have to confront him. It's no use railing at yourself. Go on, get a flight and talk to Adam.'

'What do I say?' She breathed in the smell of clay and the salt sea, her mother's essence. It calmed her racing nerves. 'Maybe you can cast me a spell?'

'It wouldn't work for you. You don't believe.'

'I can't bring myself to blame her.'

'No. No it's not her fault. You have to remember that. From what you've said she has no idea that the rat has another family.'

'And how did he afford it? We're barely managing lately, the factory's in such a mess.'

'All the more reason to get back and talk to him. You'll go mad here, speculating.'

'I'm not sure we can afford to sun ourselves in the Med.'

'You'd planned to be back for the race and it's only two more weeks, then you'll all be here and we'll get things sorted out. Tell the woman to come and see me.'

'I don't know.'

'She needs a woman.'

'She has a mother, in Edinburgh.'

'Obviously not a proper mother or she'd be here.'

Tilly pulled away from the arms that had kept her from harm all of her life. Growing up in such a dangerous place as a fish quay where all kinds of men from around the world drank and whored was not an ideal environment for a child, but Tilly had never come to harm, there'd always been her mother and her artist friends to care for her, to teach her caution, but Tilly wilfully denied Mai's comfort, then as now. 'Don't worry Mam. It'll get sorted, but there's not a lot I can do. The fact of it is there. Another set of twin boys. It's not their fault either.'

'Don't sort Adam's mess out for him.'

'No. No. This is something I won't ignore.'

'You give him too much leeway.'

Tilly sighed. 'I know.' She reached around and kissed her mother's cheek, aware that this was not a habit for her. 'Take care.' She said, and eager now to return to Mallorca and confront Adam, she swung away, but Mai held her back.

'You've always had your life mapped out. Been so sure that what you were doing was right and I'm not saying it wasn't.' She hastily interjected as Tilly protested. 'But maybe it's time for a change. It's not set in stone that you have to be a model mother and wife with lists to abide by, there is another way, you can step onto another path.'

'I'm setting up my own business.' Even to her the words sounded petty, childish.

'I don't mean anything so prosaic. I mean follow the woman you're supposed to be, let her in, forget the one you've created.'

This time Tilly did turn away. She didn't want to listen. She had enough to deal with without her mother's opinions on intuitive women.

Back in her own home she felt like a stranger. She wasn't used to mouth-watering smells of slowly cooking food emanating from the kitchen, unless she was responsible for them. Lonore was checking the oven where a pair of plump sea bass simmered in a deep dish and beside her on the bench dozens of little cinnamon buns were cooling on a rack. The little boys were in the garden, daring and commanding each other to jump from the old banana slide. Sean and Harry had outgrown it. She just hadn't had the heart to get rid of the last memento of their childhood.

Lonore was wearing one of Tilly's aprons. She looked up. 'Hope you don't mind. You've been so kind to us I thought you'd appreciate not having to cook dinner.'

'You're staying for dinner?' Tilly said, aware of being unnecessarily harsh. Instantly she regretted the bitchy inflection in her tone. 'I'm sorry … I um …'

'No. I shouldn't have taken it for granted. You're right. We've intruded long enough.' She untied the apron.

'No. Please. You can't go until that house is made safe.'

'We'll manage.'

'No.' Tilly felt her resolve ebb away and she'd promised her mother she'd be strong. 'Have you been there today?'

'Yes. Those men you sent are doing a grand job.'

Tilly pulled her bag off the chair where she'd dumped it. 'I'll just go and make sure they know what's needed. You er …' she gestured to the oven. 'Carry on. It all looks lovely. I won't be long.'

She left the car and walked the few hundred yards to Syon Street. Oh God! She was as wet as Adam. No wonder their marriage had been just jogging along for years. Neither of them had the gumption to admit that it was just a great friendship sheltering three children. It had become too comfortable to want to change it for something unknown. Despite her cold reaction to Mai's suggestion she found herself thinking that something different may be possible, a new way of living, but she had no idea what it might be. Something unknown to even herself tugged at her. She pushed the thought away.

In Lonore's house two factory workers Tilly had rescued from their enforced holiday were busy ripping up the stair carpet. Len glanced behind as she entered.

'Hi Tilly. We'll have to bin this. It's useless.'

'Same for the bedrooms I suppose?' She asked.

Jerry took the opportunity to slide past her to have a smoke at the door. 'Place is a death trap.' He prophesied in his usual lugubrious way.

'Ignore the harbinger of doom. But he's right for once. It's a mess. All the 'lectrics will have to be checked. I think they're OK, but I've sent for Steve to give them the once over.'

Steve was another worker from the factory, the maintenance man.

'Did none of you go away for the hols then?'

'We've not been getting many hours lately, can't really afford it.'

She nodded, feeling guilty for sunning herself in Mallorca while the workers had to stay at home. 'I'll see that you get paid for this, Len.'

'Yea.' He didn't sound very hopeful This made her feel worse. These were loyal workers who'd been with Finefit for years and they were being treated shabbily. 'I'm sorry Len.'

'Not your fault.'

She breathed in deeply and focused. 'Any chance of getting them back home tonight.

Len sucked his lips in and shook his head. 'Too dangerous ... and the bedrooms need drying out, and the downstairs ceilings might have to come down.'

'How long?'

He leaned back against the floral patterned wallpaper. 'Depends what Steve says about the 'lectrics, then if you need a plasterer it'll take months, celebrities they are, the *crème de la crème*, and they don't know what to charge. I should have been a plasterer, millionaires them lads. Nice place this though. Shame. How come Adam didn't come eeself?'

Half way up the stairs Tilly reeled, she clung on to the banister. Did everyone know? Everyone but her.

'Sorry. Didn't mean to shove me nose in. Just thought, like, you know ...' Embarrassed Len stamped on, up to the bathroom. He shouted back at her. 'It'll take weeks to dry this out. The boards've lifted.'

Tilly followed him and they pretended that no allusion to

Adam's affair with Lonore resulting in twin boys had been mentioned. Good at that we are, she thought, not mentioning things. She took in the mess in the bathroom where the cupboard that housed the ancient boiler had been ripped out.

Len kicked the heap of broken tiles and splintered wood that littered the floor. 'Had no choice. This old boiler'd been built around and tiled over instead of moving.'

'It needs moving?'

'It needs condemning.'

Tilly left him and wandered into the bedrooms. They were stripped of their carpets and the furniture was piled up in the middle of all three rooms, but it was obvious that someone was a very nimble needlewoman. Embroidered cushions and curtains were evident along with swags and hand woven hangings for decorating the walls. Walls that flaunted bold hand painted designs in glorious colours. Had Adam lain in bed, post coital and admiring of these patterns? Could it be that Lonore was a mirror image of her? A home-maker and skilful craftswoman. It was all too much. She turned back and confronted Len. 'Can I leave you to it? If you need Lonore she's staying at my house. I have to go back to Mallorca, but we'll all be returning soon.' This had got to be sorted out.

'That's OK missus. We'll hold the fort till you get back.'

'I know. I can rely on you. You've never ever let us down and I intend to make sure that we don't let you down.' She had been hording a small savings account to start her new business, money left her by a vaguely remembered fraternal grandfather, but it probably wouldn't be needed. On the strength of the orders from Bewick's the bank would surely approve a loan. She would go the cash point now and get some money for the men. 'I'll just pop to the hole in the wall. Not be long.'

Lonore had waited to serve the dinner. Tilly sat with her and the two little boys. As they ate they made small talk. They discussed the forthcoming Tall Ship's Race which had the boys so excited they both spoke at once outlining their plans to board all the ships that would be in the river, looking for pirates.

'You can spot them by their tattoos,' Justin solemnly informed her.

Joseph laughed. 'Stupid, stupid, it's their earrings.'

They looked and sounded so much like Harry and Sean that Tilly had to fight back choking tears. Damn you Adam, damn you. How could you do this to the children? She struggled to stop from screaming and then, thankfully, it was time to leave for the airport and her flight to Mallorca.

On the plane she gave some thought to her daughter Beth who was obviously in trouble, but Tilly had no clue as to what it could be. Beth was losing weight and becoming increasingly morose, even obstructive. Tully had tried several times to broach the subject in the past few weeks, but Beth had blanked her, even leaving the room on one occasion, so Tilly hadn't wanted to push it in case Beth shut down completely and they had no common ground left. Whatever was changing her bright happy girl into a sullen rebellious teenager was more than raging hormones. Tilly needed to get to the bottom of it.

CHAPTER FOUR

BETH

Beth sat on the patio, outside the open front door, her back against the already warm stone, mesmerized by the glass like quality of the sea in the Bay of Pollensa, This was the only time it was calm and almost still, during the day it would get rougher and after lunch the wind would get up and combine with the wash from the yachts to whip it into a frenzy. Seas were not to be trusted. They were treacherous, although, with the North Sea you knew where you were. It was always dangerous. It didn't set out to fool anybody. It made no promises of safety. It would kill you. But this Mediterranean stuff lured you in with winking waves and warm promises, then it killed you. Boys were like the Mediterranean.

She thought about the accident yesterday when she could have lost her brothers forever, and her Dad. To lose two brothers and a father was unthinkable. What would life be like without a father? Some people didn't have fathers. If you'd never had a father did you miss one?

The point of land, where her brothers and father had almost drowned rose from the sea. The rocks glinted in the sun, turning the savage stone into a pewter sculpture displayed on a blue satin cloth. She sighed. She couldn't work it out, it was all too much and she had bigger problems to worry about.

She had heard her mother return, from wherever she'd been, in the early hours, and knew something was very wrong between her and Dad, probably his getting drunk and almost killing Sean and Harry hadn't helped, but there was something else. Yesterday her father had refused to tell her where her mother was. Beth was certain he'd known, but he'd hummed and hawed in his usual evasive way every time anyone asked about her, and the house felt nervous and there'd been none of the usual sense of relaxing after Mum had gone to bed. She had waited for the murmured whispers and the final setting to rights, but it hadn't happened.

The patio was flooded with light from the early morning

sun, it caught the shadows on the old wooden chairs and table that sheltered under the spreading fig tree, staggering under the weight of burgeoning fruit. The branches were heavy, much to much of a burden for the groaning trunk, so ropes and chains were woven among them and tied to brackets in the brickwork of the house. On stormy nights Beth imagined that the little tree would rescue its branches from their entrapment, whip out its roots and heave itself onto the beach, from where the possibilities for escape are endless.

This early the beach front was empty, except for a few early risers jogging along the promenade, disturbing the stillness. Beth stepped carefully down the pebble studded steps, crossed the square stones of the pedestrian walk and slid her feet onto the beach, she felt adrift, not belonging. She weaved among the sunbeds. Like the fig tree they too were in chains. Across the bay where the yachts were still sleeping she picked out the boats belonging to their friends Lena, Tony, and Jack. Lena and Tony cared for their boats but Jack and his wife Cloris never used theirs, what a waste. It sulked under a worn tarpaulin, chained to the quay, shackled, confined. Everything was caught fast. There was no choice. She had no choice. She too was tied down, destined to be grounded, not just because she'd stayed out late and was confined to the house, but earthed, clipped, bound forever in a non-stop loop of certain confusion.

The warm sea closed around her, soft and welcoming, deceitful though, not to be trusted. She swam with long overarm strokes, monotonous, obliterating thought from her burdened mind. Out of the safe bathing lanes, beyond the white buoys bobbing lazily in a slight wash from the incoming fishing boats, she turned on her back and floated, inaction giving her time to think. How could she tell her mother? She had no idea how she'd react. They had occasionally touched on the subject over magazine articles or TV programmes about teenagers and their problems. Mum had been adamant it would never apply to her and Beth and convinced her daughter would be sensible, had put it from her mind. Ruminative speculation was not her mother's habit. She was a woman of decision. She had everyone's life mapped out for them, forever compiling lists to festoon the fridge door.

Beth was intended to be a glittering student, excelling at sciences and attending an Oxbridge uni from where she'd leave as a doctor with research grants to cushion her for life. Beth however had no intention of going to Oxford or Cambridge, she had been thinking of Newcastle after a couple of years at college. doing as little of her studies as possible without them intruding into party time. Fat chance now, nobody would want to party with her. They'd all go off and shag each other, and Mitchell wouldn't want to see her again. Mitchell would be like the North Sea, he'd just cut her stone dead. 'Mum!' She yelled across the quiet bay. 'Mum!'

'Can you keep the noise down?'

Beth dropped into the water with the shock of hearing a voice in the empty stillness. Spluttering and threshing she surfaced. She'd drifted close to the yachts without noticing and was now under Jack's Fife eight-metre boat, the *Mirabel*. Shaking wet hair from her face she looked around. From under the worn tarp a girl was solemnly watching her. Tangled black curls framed a full round face with wide brown eyes flecked with gold and full dark lips that curled in question marks, demanding a reaction. Hanging one arm over the mooring rope Beth also demanded answers. 'What the fuck you doing on Jack's boat? Does he know?'

'Who?'

'Jack. Jack and Cloris. This is their yacht, but it's not been opened up yet, probably won't be this year.'

'Good.'

'Who are you?'

'Krista.'

'What you doing on Jack's boat?' Beth asked again.

'Stowing away.'

'No shit!' Beth laughed. The morning was improving.

'The water looks good.'

'S'alright.'

'Think I'll join you.' And the naked, olive-skinned girl slid over the side, where slipping like a sleek seal she dropped into the clear depths.

Beth waited and waited before she surfaced. 'Took your time.'

'I like the water.' Krista dived again and ages afterwards, when Beth was starting to worry, she surfaced about a hundred meters away.

Beth pulled herself onto the jetty. The wooden planks were smooth and warm. She stretched out. Not recalling that she'd wanted to sleep she was surprised when she woke and the sun was higher, well into mid-morning. She sat up, raking her fingers through her salt-stiffened tangles. Krista sat at her feet, dressed now in cut-offs and vest. Beth felt embarrassed. The big dark eyes seemed to be able to see more than just the outward Beth. 'Stop it.'

'Soz, just waiting for you to wake up. Didn't want to leave you.'

'I'd be OK. Everyone knows me.'

'Still ...'

'How'd you get on Jack's boat?'

'The tarp wasn't secure over the stern. Just needed a place for the night.'

'I'm Beth.'

Krista nodded. 'You got anything to eat?'

Beth looked down at her skinny, bikini-clad body; spread her arms in a shrug. 'Not on me.'

'You live here?' Krista's dark eyes searched the houses and hotels along the beach front.

Beth pointed to the three storied terraced cottage in the middle of the Pine Walk. 'That one, with the fig tree.'

'Stuff to eat?'

'Yea.' Beth jumped up and began to walk away, down the jetty. 'Come on.' Walking backwards she watched as Krista pushed under the tarp and emerged with a faded blue back pack that looked like a school bag. 'What you doing here?'

'I've been working, crewing for yachts around the South of France and down the coast of Spain. Ended up here yesterday.'

'Why didn't you sleep on the boat you came in on?'

'Skipper thought my duties extended to his stateroom.' She pointed to a Princess V65 tied up at the far end of the jetty, all flying bridge, gleaming white paint and shiny steel, shaped like an arrow.

'The *Ecstasy*! Olly Thursson! You were lucky to get out intact.'

'You know him?'

'All the girls in Puerto know him, probably all the girls in the Med. None of them will crew for him.'

'Should have sussed by the name, but I was broke and desperate.'

'Where'd you come from?'

'A little place up by Newcastle in England, North Shields.'

Beth stopped dead, mouth open in a surprised O. 'You're shittin' me.'

'Why would I?'

'We live in Tynemouth.'

'Posh.' Krista dismissed the location.

Beth was quick to defend a lowly status as a state school student. 'I did my last four years at Marden and I recognise that bag.' She touched the tattered and faded pack back gripped tightly in Krista's brown hand. 'You go too?'

'Did. Finished.'

'You weren't in my year I'd have remembered you. When where you there?'

'As little as possible.'

'Bummer.'

'I hated it.'

'Yea?'

'The teachers and the other girls. Bitches.'

'Some of the teachers are OK.'

'You get Armstrong?'

'Oh him. What a dork. He got sacked for bullying.'

'Serves the little shit right. He hated me, made my life a misery.'

'It was you!' Beth stopped and put a hand on Krista's shoulder to halt her. 'It was you who wrote all that stuff on the board about him going with prossies and having a limp dick. Wow. You're a legend.' Beth was in awe.

'He deserved it.'

'So you're just seventeen, a year older than me. What do your parents think about you sailing and hitching and all that?'

'I came from Shields to Gib with my Dad, least I thought he was my Dad, turned out he wasn't, so I left.'

'Why didn't you go home?'

'Haven't got a home.'

Beth looked at Krista's face with its well defined features, strong and beautiful in that exotic way of girls with mixed parentage. Silver rings twinkled and danced in her eyebrows, ears and lower lip. Despite her shabby appearance she wore interesting bangles in silver and the bright colours of South Africa, yellow, red and green. Around her neck she wore a tiny pendant on a silver chain; a depiction of a mermaid baby in the womb.

Beth fingered it. 'My Nana made that, same as mine..'

Krista shrugged and tucked it into her vest. 'So, you can buy them anywhere.'

She was assured and yet, there was a guarded aspect to her whole being that could be a bit intimidating. This girl knew how to take care of herself and wouldn't be afraid of boys. She had been sort of relaxed with Beth up to now, but as they neared the house Beth felt a wall go up and a stiffness that pulled Krista's shoulders back, she was arming herself. She was a mystery.

Beth's mother was in the kitchen when they entered. 'Hello girls.'

Beth had been waiting to confront her mother and her feelings of neglect surfaced. 'Where'd you go? You should have been here. Harry needed you.'

'So people keep telling me, but I should be able to feel that my children are safe with their own father.' Her mother was tense, but used to having a house always filled with friends of Beth and the boys she smiled at Krista.

'This is Krista. She's staying.'

'Don't worry I wasn't expecting you to take me in.' Krista turned to go.

Beth hauled her back by the straps on her bag. 'No you don't.' She stared at her mother. 'She's sleeping in my room.'

'Of course, well you'd better have something to eat, you look famished.' She smiled at them.

'Thank you.' Krista said.

Beth laughed. 'What a suck up!' This girl knows the right buttons to push, Mum loves good manners. She took Krista upstairs and took the bag from her, throwing it on the unused second bed. 'You can have that. Is that all you've got?'

'I travel light.'

'Did you get paid?'

'Knaar.'

'You should get your money. How much does he owe you?'

Krista shrugged.

'All bed and no board?'

'He never got no bed off me.' Krista turned on Beth, her pupils narrowing and the gold flecks sparking like fire above cheek bones that had sharpened to knives.

'Jeez, I didn't mean anything, just a thing to say, you know. You want a shower; get the salt out your hair?'

After they had showered, dressed, eaten and were just leaving, her father arrived. The tension between him and her mother was unbearable. Beth knew it was more than just the fact of him almost killing the twins, although that was bad enough. Something was very, very wrong. Beth looked at her mother, hard. There were lines under her eyes and she kept tying her long auburn hair up in a scrunchie, then pulling it out again. She did that when she was worried. There was so much Beth needed to talk to her mother about.

The beach front was busy with holidaymakers wandering and gazing; the newbie's dawdling, getting acclimatised and the regulars who all knew each other, lounging in the cafes, gossiping, catching up. People did that in the Bay. The same families returned for the summer over and over again, but the little girl sitting on the wall of the house next door lived in Pollensa Bay all year round. She hurled herself at Beth, all skinny arms and legs, lank brown hair with pretty slides keeping it tidy, her arms and neck adorned with plastic jewellery she made and sold from a stall on the patio wall. Beth disentangled herself from the little girl, who shrugged and wove her limbs around Krista, who let her.

Beth loved Daisy who was desperate for a mother and attached herself to Beth every summer while her father, Zander, worked at any odd job he could find. Her mother had abandoned her at her birth and her grandparents, Jack and Cloris, who lived in the hills of old Pollensa Town, seemed not to care for her. 'Sozz Daisy, but I'm busy just now, catch you this after.' Beth tried not to look at Daisy's face as she moved on, but she was too late. Daisy's father, called from the balcony above.

'Hi Beth. Can you have Daisy today? I've got a job.'

'Oh hi Zander, sorry can't. This is Krista,' She watched them eye each other and mumble hello. 'Got something important to do. Got to see Olly about some money.'

'Oh.'

Zander was a footloose drifter, ambling through life not thinking that anything might be important and always putting everyone else first, anyone in front of Daisy, but he was the kindest man and Beth liked him. She hated letting him down. She did usually take care of Daisy, but it wasn't a hard and fast arrangement.

Krista spoke to Beth. 'I don't mind if you want to look after her. I can go see Olly myself.'

Beth looked up at Zander. 'We can take her with us, shouldn't take long to get some money out of the shameless old pervert.' She covered Daisy's ears, but she was like an eel and escaped to dance on the harbour wall and shout, 'What's pervert?'

'A person who likes to do things that other people think strange.' Zander explained, he wasn't a father who shirked his duties. He believed in answering the eight-year-old's numerous questions whenever and wherever she asked them.

'Like Grandpa?'

'Your grandfather is not a pervert.' Zander hid his laughter, but Daisy recognised the set of his mouth and soon they were all laughing. 'You'll get me barred from the yacht club.' Zander prophesied. 'Thanks Beth. I don't mind if my daughter is exposed to Olly. He's the one I feel sorry for. It'll be an experience for him to be cross-examined by you three, wish I could watch. I know you'll take care of her, you're a star and you too Krista.' He smiled, narrowing his shy grey eyes at Krista, crinkling the tanned skin of his thin face.

Krista regarded him with intense curiosity.

Beth felt suddenly awkward between them, as if she was intruding, but that wasn't likely, they didn't know each other.

'But Grandad talks all the time and gets on everyone's nerves. Everyone says he's odd.' Daisy would not let go of a good story.

'Daisy, do not talk about my father like that. It's disrespectful.'

This was enough to halt Daisy's merciless baiting and she began to pack up her stall. The little girl knew her father was serious when he referred to Jack as 'his father'.

Beth was certain that the estrangement between the two men had not escaped Daisy's notice, she had grown up with it, but lately Beth would catch her watching other grandparents swim or play catch with their grandchildren. Was the little waif wondering why Jack and Cloris kept to themselves in their villa up in the hills?

'I'm just taking a boat down to Palma. I'll catch a lift back with Tony. He's got to go in and register the entrants for the race.'

'Good oh! Are they all swimming?'

'Yea, the usual crowd, just like always.'

Krista was still staring at Zander. 'Is this a swimming race?' she asked him.

'Yes, across the bay once from Alcudia to the Stay

Restaurant.' He pointed to the restaurant on the edge of the harbour.

'Is there money?'

'Cash prize of a thousand Euros.'

'Can anyone enter?'

'Anyone who can swim across that bay deserves a thousand Euros. It's too hard for mere mortals.'

Krista turned and looked at the sea, studied the distance. 'The currents are strong, but that's the only difficulty.'

'Three miles of treacherous water!'

'Where do I enter?'

'Are you mad! A girl will never do it. Grown men who've swum in this bay all their lives have come to grief.'

'I can do it and I need the money.'

'You have to have a medical.' Zander was in awe.

'So?'

'Well … if you're sure. You need to see Tony and he'll add your name to the list, you're just in time.'

'Who's Tony?'

'Beth will introduce you on the way to see Olly. Wish I could be there to see his face.'

'Wait until I win then you'll see a grown man cry.'

'He won't be the only one.'

'When's the race?'

Beth could contain herself no longer. 'Are you mad!' She yelled at Zander. 'What you telling her all this rubbish for? She can't swim across the bay. She'll drown!'

'No I won't.' Krista's voice was calm and matter of fact. 'I can do it easy. I've swum the Channel.'

'Oh, yea!' Beth dismissed this claim.

'Yea. Look on-line. You'll see me there, youngest contestant, twelve hours ten minutes.'

Beth was caught with her mouth open and silent.

Zander recovered first. 'You're serious aren't you?'

'Yea.'

Beth whooped and jumped onto the low wall, hugging Krista until they both fell into the soft warm sand. Finally she calmed down. She held Krista's head in her two hands and saw mirth in her watchful eyes. 'You're serious. You swam the English Channel. Boy you're going to stir up these macho Mediterranean men. I can hardly wait.'

Daisy jumped on top of them and the three girls rolled about hugging and screaming.

Zander took advantage of the temporary madness to come down and lock up. He stood watching them, laughing. 'Right. Got to go. See you later, about four. I'll be in the middle, on the Waverly.' He pointed to the jetty where the boats bobbed in the now choppy water. Then his gaze strayed to Krista. 'You're quite a girl.' He raised a hand and turned away, loping off in his casual loose-limbed way.

Beth watched Krista chart his progress. 'You're shameless.'

'What?'

'You. You and him. You couldn't take your eyes off each other.'

Krista dusted sand from her clothes and hair, bangles jangling and dark eyes hidden under a sweep of sooty lashes.

'It was like I wasn't here. He fancies you.'

'Don't be stupid. He's far too old.'

'Do you love my Dad?' Daisy butted in.

'No. No I don't.' Krista was calm, still watching Zander make his way through the holiday crowds.

'Yes you do.' Daisy was adamant. 'You love him, you want to marry him,' she sang.

Krista shook her head and walked away.

Beth took hold of the wayward little girl and followed her new friend. 'Stop that Daisy. It's not nice to talk about your Dad in that way.'

'Cloris said he needs a woman.'

'Daisy! Stop that this minute.'

'She did.'

'When did you see Cloris?' Beth sidetracked the conversation.

'We were up to the villa yesterday and I was swimming in the pool and Dad was talking to Jack and when he went to the bathroom Cloris gave me rubber pasta and melted ice cream and she told him he needs a woman.'

This was unusual. Jack and Zander hardly ever spoke and the old man never invited his son and granddaughter to the villa. no-one in the Bay knew why and people had long since given up speculating. Zander was a loving and caring man, but his overtures to mend the breach always seemed to be rebuffed. Jack, it seemed, didn't want a son and granddaughter. Just wait till she told her mother. She turned her attention to Daisy. 'Well that was nice, but best not to talk about it. Come on, race you to the jetty.' And she set off after Krista with Daisy soon in front. Beth was too tired to run.

CHAPTER FIVE

TILLY

As she tidied the kitchen Tilly listened to the boys arguing. It was desultory, not their usual heated exchange. They were sore, cut and bruised and still frightened. She was frightened too, afraid to let them out of her sight. They had an appointment at the hospital at two this afternoon to check their lungs and have dressings changed. They were forbidden the beach and there was definitely no sailing. Thank God for Tony who owned the big catamaran Zander skippered, he had brought a project. He'd told them they must pass a test of the harbour currents and tides, the submerged rocks and wrecks and rights of way. They were now in their room, with a bewildering array of charts and timetables spread out around them. Adam had disappeared early, obviously evading the inevitable.

After the girls left Tilly had stood on the rooftop terrace watching them talk to Zander. Her limbs had done their usual turn to jelly stuff at the sight of him, his loose-boned stance with one hip leaning on the wall and if she went through to their bedroom balcony she would be able to smooth a hand over that hip, ruffle the thin dark hair, that habitually fell over his smooth brow, slide her panting tongue along his mobile lips, tease the smile and explore his body while expectation turned to desire. He was a calm man, thoughtful, in his long fingers he plaited string, his hands always busy he was forever tying knots for Daisy to sell to the tourists as bracelets. Zander did anything that brought him money and she'd do anything to tie herself in knots around him, but it was their secret; a secret they'd harboured for two years when the easy friendship between them had turned to something altogether more passionate. He may have other women when she was back home in England, but it didn't bother her, he wasn't part of her life plan, he belonged in Mallorca..

One afternoon, in the stifling drowsy heat of siesta, Tilly had popped in to tell Zander that she'd just received a phone call from Beth to say that she and Daisy were up in Pollensa Town at Lena and Jazzy's bar. It was too hot to come home and Lena would bring them later. Zander had seemed to listen, but then he'd touched her, wordlessly tracing the line of her jaw, lifting her hot heavy curls from her neck and she'd realised that he'd not heard a single word. She'd just stood there and let him slip the loose dress from her shoulders. In fact she'd let him do lots of things that day. Since then there'd been lots of passionate afternoons, but they never discussed them, never referred to the lust that left them breathless and perspiring, tangled in the sheets in his empty house. She yearned for him now, and wondered if it might just be possible to have a different life, one that didn't include Adam. This thought brought her down to earth. Adam had also thought such a thing possible, or had he? Had he even thought at all?

As if she'd conjured him up she noticed Adam coming back along the Pine Walk. He was the opposite of Zander in every way. Big, blond and noisy, verging on heavy these days, with thick curling hair that grew at an alarming rate, down around his neck and shoulders covering his strong chest and he had pale blue short sighted eyes that gave him a permanently puzzled expression. She used to think this was a look of mystery, now she realised it was because he had very little emotion to display. His gait was erratic, he'd been drinking again. Tilly had always been aware that he liked to wind down with a drink or two, but lately it had got a whole lot more than just two glasses of wine with dinner, whisky was now a regular item in the shopping trolley. Well, drunk or not she was determined to have it out with him now.

When she'd arrived at five thirty that morning she'd woken him, but before she could bring up the situation at home he'd told her about Sean and Harry and then gone back to sleep. Despite her urge to throttle him she'd stalked the house checking and watching her children sleep. The boys flat on their backs, arms and legs spread-eagled in utter exhaustion; Beth curled up in a sheet, muttering and perspiring, disturbed by dreams. Tilly had unravelled her, stroked the thin limbs with a cold wash cloth until she'd finally slept, but still uneasily. She was far too thin and Tilly remembered she'd been sick last week. Beth had said it was a dodgy taco, but was that the real reason? Tilly had felt sick herself, thinking that perhaps her beautiful, funny and clever daughter was anorexic. The horrible realisation had driven all thoughts of Lonore from her mind and she'd sat and watched over her child until morning.

She would have to find a way to talk with Beth about this. A way to help without frightening her away, she'd been so prickly lately. The early morning stillness had given her time to think about how she'd broach the subject of Lonore to Adam. Why did she hesitate over this and feel that she needed to be the one responsible for sorting it out. Guilt weighed her down. It was Zander. Maybe Adam's affair was justified. Did Adam know about them? She thought not, but if he did and she confronted him with Lonore he'd turn on her, using her own infidelity to excuse his affair. Oh what a mess.

Wearily she returned to the kitchen. Adam came in, fiddling with his specs, that hung on a black cord about his neck, handy for strangling. He just stood and waited, always waiting for her to goad him into action. 'Adam we have to talk.' He nodded and sat down at the table, fiddling now with the cutlery she'd set out for lunch. Well he could just fiddle, he wasn't getting any until this was resolved. 'How could you do this to us Adam?'

'I know, bad show, but I'm trying to sort it out.'

'Well that's something. I've had to get the men in from their holiday and set them to work.'

'Did you?'

'Yes. Why is that so surprising?'

'You've never been involved with the factory before.'

'What was I supposed to do, just leave it?'

'No. No. I should have checked things out before we came away, but I thought I'd get orders and then they'd all be back at work. I'm not having any luck.'

'I'm not talking about the factory!'

'No?'

She couldn't believe he was still in denial about Lonore. 'You pig! You unutterably selfish pig! I'm asking about Lonore. Lonore and two little boys who don't deserve this and talking about boys, how are you going to explain their new brothers to Sean, Harry and Beth?' Trembling with anger and guilt she turned away from him, waited. Now it would come. Now he would throw Zander at her. She heard him move to the fridge, listened to the chink of bottles, loud in the midday silence. Whirling she knocked the whiskey bottle to the floor where shards of glass burst into silver and bronze missiles, stabbing her legs and spilling the liquid to pool on the tiles. 'You will not hide in that bottle. I forbid it!' She shouted as if he was a reluctant boy hiding in a cupboard. She shook with relief. He didn't know about Zander, but guilt nailed her to the floor. She couldn't move.

Silence settled on them again, broken only by the murmur of the boys whose occasional raised voices filtered through the house. After what seemed an age her mother's advice for tension filled her mind, breath, drop your shoulders and relax; it came to her rescue, she exhaled deeply then stretched over to grab a paper towel and dab at her bleeding legs. After another minute of silence she turned to look at him just standing there, watching the whiskey run across the uneven floor. She took a deep, calming breath. 'Why Adam?'

'Just happened. She came for a job, but I didn't have any work, asked her to lunch and ...'

'How long?'

'Five years. The boys will be four on the twenty-ninth of August.'

'The last week in August. The week we go back?'

'I might just go ...'

'Yes.' She was so used to organising his world she even finished his sentences for him. 'You should go and see everything's ok for them. Get them back home.'

'The factory, Tilly.'

'It's finished?'

'I tried, but it's a bad time, the market being what it is, people just don't want replacement windows.'

Tears oozed out and ran unchecked down her face. Finally Adam stood up and came to her.

'I'm sorry Tilly. I didn't want to hurt you. It just happened. And I do still love you.' He dried her tears.

Furious at his ability to rationalise everything she yelled at him. 'For Christ's sake Adam will you stop being so bloody nice. You sound like it doesn't matter! Is she the reason you were so careless with the boys? Were you thinking about the other boys and not concentrating on Sean and Harry?'

'Of course not! I'd never put them in danger.'

'But you did.'

He bent his head, watching longingly as the whiskey evaporated, then he stooped and picked up the biggest part of the bottle. It still had a few drops in the dimpled glass; he set it on the bench.

'You were drunk! You'd been drinking in the hotel bar and set out with them, drunk.' She had never struck another human being in her life, but without thinking she brought her hand up and slapped him so hard his head whipped round and her palm was left in midair ... stinging. The violent action did nothing to calm her. She was incandescent with rage. 'You deserve more than that. You should be charged with attempted murder.'

'Tilly ...'

'You are unbelievable, unforgivable! You almost killed our sons, our sons Adam, who you've neglected because you're more interested in Lonore and two other boys; two other little boys who don't know how irresponsible you are. I hope to God they never find out as Sean and Harry found out what an unreliable, drunken, disgusting pig their father is. You could have killed them Adam. My sons could be dead.'

'Well you weren't here ...'

She was stunned. How dare he try to shift the blame! She stepped closer feeling uncontrollable rage swell inside of her, her hands bunched into fists. She wanted to lash out, to hammer some sense into his stupid face, to wipe that vacant expression away. A movement in the doorway attracted her. Sean and Harry stood in the hallway.

'You two fighting?' Harry, hanging over Sean's shoulders.

'Can we join in?' Sean, eager as ever to have a fight.

Tilly couldn't face them. She pushed past and walked out, across the pavement and over the beach where, unknowingly copying the actions of her daughter, she dropped her dress from her trembling body and flung into the water. She swam and swam until she had no breath left.

When she surfaced she saw she was under the bow of the *Brigantia*, a schooner belonging to her friend, Lena Kirkwood, who was at the rail, smoking one of her hand-rolled cigarettes and watching.

'The act of a desperate woman,' Lena mentioned.

Tilly pulled herself round to the ladder and climbed aboard.

'Not the usual way my guests arrive.' Lena helped Tilly to her feet. 'Coffee?'

Tilly followed her to the galley where coffee was always percolating and accepted a dry towel to wrap around her bikini.

Lena poured the hot aromatic goo she called coffee and sat opposite. 'I'm not going to beat about the bush so come on, out with it.' She waited, watched while Tilly simply stared at the coffee. 'It's getting cold.'

Lena's observation was superfluous and mattered not at all to Tilly, who couldn't even remember why she was there. After a few minutes her head cleared and she burst out crying, not exactly crying, she heard a terrible howling and heart wrenching gulps of anguish that sounded so alien she could hardly believe she was responsible. After a box of dry tissues had been reduced to a sodden ball in her hands Tilly managed to speak and tell Lena the whole sorry tale of Adam's second family.

'Shit!' Lena voiced her opinion. 'Wasn't on your list then?'

Tilly shook her head and finally gulped at the refreshed coffee.

'Who'd have thought it? He jogs along doing nothing for years then in one day he goes bankrupt and drowns his kids, gets himself a mistress and two new kids.'

'Well that hardly happened in one day.' Tilly now felt sorry for herself, but was aware that she was sulking. She mopped at her ruined face.

'I'll give you that. What's he doing about it all?'

'Nothing. Not a blasted thing, apart from getting drunk.'

'Sounds good to me.' Lena bent to bury her head in a cupboard under her seat, emerging with a bottle of gin, a can of tonic and two glasses. 'Sorry Tilly. It's horrible. What are you going to do? Divorce him?'

'I don't know.'

'What do you think triggered it off? Adam just isn't the type.'

'Well he obviously is and has been for years, these little boys are almost four years old.'

'Not a virgin birth then?'

'How can you make fun of this?'

'Just thinking aloud.'

'I can't blame her. She's so needy and obviously adores him.' Tilly was aware that she was mangling the braid along the front of a cushion, but did nothing to stop herself.

'Maybe she already had these boys and met Adam recently, if she's as needy as you say and just latched on to him. You know how weak he is.' Lena suggested a possibility.

'She called him her husband and their father.'

'Mmm, pretty conclusive then. Do you think he knows about you and Zander?'

Lena's words reduced Tilly to a helpless lump, the glass of

gin tipped, spilling the contents onto the ravaged cushion as she fell to her knees.

'Shit!' Lena helped her up. 'Sorry. Did I say something out of turn?'

'Oh fucking great!' Beth's voice came from the companionway.

From the deck Tilly looked up to face her.

'Just what I need. My mother and my father are both a couple of sluts!'

'That's set the sharks among the herring,' Lena muttered.

'Beth.' Tilly appealed to her daughter who was struggling to stop Daisy pushing past her. 'Please darling.'

'You're as bad as each other and you should be at the hospital with Sean and Harry.' With a snarl of rage Beth turned. She pushed past Krista and knocking Daisy on to her bottom ran away.

Tilly launched herself from her knees to the stairs in one swift movement and pushing Daisy to the deck ran after her.

Beth was fast. She flew along the promenade and was soon lost to sight. Tilly looked in the bars and cafes along the road to Alcudia, but they were too busy to find one furious girl who, was familiar with most of them and didn't want to be found. She could be anywhere. The Stay restaurant was a likely place or any one of hundreds of boats tied up in the marina, or any carful of raucous boys racing along the coast road to any one of a dozen ports, anywhere on the island. Dejected and now worrying about the boys Tilly turned back to the beach house and her obligations. Beth was the only one who had remembered the hospital appointment for Sean and Harry.

As she hurried back along the crowded promenade, Tilly's head reeled with the senselessness of it all. It was all so chaotic, not what she had planned at all. This summer she had intended to spend industriously working on new designs for the ToteTilly range of bags, she had been so elated with the order from Bewicks, on a high because finally she was making a life for herself separate from the roles of mother and wife. But now, how could she concentrate? She remembered the boys, neglected and alone in the house, abandoned after their ordeal, because she was certain Adam wouldn't have stayed to care for them, he'd be in the yacht club. She began to run, Beth would have to wait, she needed to concentrate on the boys, ring the hospital and see if she could re-schedule their appointment.

Glancing down the length of the jetty she couldn't see any sign of Beth's new friend Krista or Daisy. It was unlikely that Lena would be bothered with them, she didn't take to children. Odd how little she knew about Lena, even though they were friends here in the Bay every summer, they had never got into the habit of corresponding and were incurious about each other's lives. Despite the fact that Tilly had often detected a north of England drawl in Lena's speech, she'd never asked where she came from. Suddenly it struck her that she was very self-absorbed. Perhaps that was how she'd not noticed Adam's affair with Lonore, because surely he'd been a changed man from time to time. Buoyant and a bit more spruced up than usual when he first met her, worried when he realised she was pregnant, had they discussed abortion, were they illegally married, surely he'd been elated when the twins were born, how had she missed that. She worked back through the dates and tried to remember what she and Adam had been doing when Lonore went into labour. Well obviously they'd been here. Typical of Adam! He hadn't even been with her when she'd needed him most. He was so unreliable. Who if anyone had been with her, her mother, a friend, a friend who lived in Tynemouth? A friend who knew Adam and her too, one of their friends who they met every week in the Gibraltar Rock pub? Surely people had seen Adam and Lonore together, at school or in a restaurant, you can't hide a woman and two boisterous boys. Six years her husband had been intimate with another woman in the small, nosy, gossipy village where they all lived, someone must have seen them together, how many people had been keeping this scandal from her all these years, how many of their friends had been shaking their heads in disbelief at her, dozy Tilly so wrapped up in her children and her plans for their future that she hadn't noticed what was under her nose. It was unbelievable. If it wasn't so tragic she'd laugh. But it wasn't all her fault, she wasn't so wrapped up in herself, was she? She couldn't be blamed or ridiculed for caring for her children, making sure their lives were running smoothly, always been there for them, true she hadn't always cosseted Adam, but he was a grown man, surely he could look after himself and not be so reliant on her for every small detail of his life.

Finally she was at the house on Pine Walk and all was normal, the twins hadn't been murdered or kidnapped, nor had they burned the house down or flooded the place. Of course they hadn't, they were very sensible and responsible boys. She called to them and they came thundering down the stairs.

'We called the hospital ...' Sean.

'And they said to just go ...' Harry.

'They wondered where you were and we ...' Sean.

'I'm telling it ...' Harry.

'Whoa, calm down. I know I'm late, I had things to do, but I'll just get changed and we'll go.' As she ran upstairs she told them. 'Thanks for sorting the appointment boys. Are you feeling ok. Can I tell the doctor you're better now?'

CHAPTER SIX

LENA

Lena smiled at the beautiful black girl who was helping Daisy to her feet. 'Hello.'

'Does Tilly love my Dad?' Daisy appealed to Lena, who felt ill-equipped to handle her. Children were not her forte, give her a boat any day, a boat in a force ten gale wasn't half as scary as Daisy under full sail. 'I hope not. I think he loves Krista.'

The girl moved back up the stairs. 'I'd better go.' She gestured up and away.

Lena wished she could go with her, but pulled herself together in time to stop her leaving. Anyone, even a stranger, would do as long as Daisy wasn't left on board the *Brigantia*. 'No, please come in. It's not your fault the whole of the island has gone mad.' She stuck out a work worn hand. 'I'm Lena Kirkwood.' The girl was hesitant, for a few seconds it seemed as if she'd change her mind then she stepped forward, turning her gorgeous face towards Lena.

'Krista. I came with Beth. We've been to see Olly.'

'Welcome aboard. Sit down.' Lena busied herself with pouring juice for Daisy. 'Drink?' She gestured to the gin.

'Yes please,' said Daisy.

'Just juice,' said Krista.

Lena sank onto the upholstered bench, focusing on the torn cushion. 'Tilly, she's a bit upset.' Lena, a master at small talk was never comfortable with emotional issues, especially other people's. She could feel Daisy staring at her and turned to confront the blinding blue scrutiny. 'What?' She knew she sounded harsh, but it couldn't be helped. She was hopeless with kids.

'You won't marry my Dad will you?' Daisy asked her.

'No. That is one thing you can be absolutely certain will never happen.'

'Good.' Daisy challenged. 'Dad says you're a lesbian.'

'Well you should listen to him then, 'cos he's right.' This kid knew more than was good for her, good for anybody, jeez she had big ears.

'He's always right.' Daisy stated then lapsed into silence staring from her to Krista and back again, waiting for more ammunition.

'I don't believe you will ever find a man who is even sometimes right,' Lena countered.

'Then you don't know my Dad.'

'I've known your Dad longer tha ….' Lena tailed off. She was arguing with an eight-year-old child! 'Where is he anyhow?' she finished.

'Gone to Palma with a boat and coming back with Tony.'

'But that's not until tonight.' Lena howled, she was horrified. No way was she prepared to be responsible for this nosy kid until after midnight, and it would take them that long to get back. She looked hopefully at Krista.

'Not her fault her Dad's done a runner.'

'He hasn't, he'll be back.'

'He needs to work.' Daisy told them as she stretched her hand out for the gin bottle.

Deftly swapping it for the juice carton Lena glared at her. 'Yes we know.'

'Do you hate all kids or just this one?' Krista asked.

'I don't hate her! I'm just not used to them is all. Anyway, what were you doing with Olly?' She felt she just had to get off the subject of Daisy and men. It could turn nasty with both of them ganging up on her.

Krista repeated the story of her unfortunate encounter with the lecherous Olly. 'So now I'm looking for a berth. Do you know anybody?'

'How good are you?' Lena was immensely proud of her boat. Built in nineteen thirty-two, the *Brigantia* was a fine example of wooden boats and had even survived service as an anti submarine patrol vessel in the Second World War. John Windsor, a wily old-timer who'd bought it from the breakers and rebuilt it, had willed it to Lena after she'd sailed with him as mate for more than ten years. He'd had no family and the love they shared for the *Brigantia* had brought them close. They'd sailed all over the world and twice won the prestigious King Edward Gold Cup before he died, having willed the priceless vessel to Lena. She hadn't raced for some years preferring to spend her time bestowing lifetime memories to tourists around the shores of Mallorca, memories of blue skies and adventurous dreams. However, with the Cutty Sark Tall Ships Race starting from

Newcastle this year it had stirred up odd feelings of homesickness, which in their turn had goaded her into entering. Unfortunately she'd been let down by two of her crew who'd decided to open a hotel on Ibiza. That left her with Jazzy, Tony's two daughters Adalia and Endora, their current boy-friends and Beth. This still left Lena in need of two reliable members.

Daisy interrupted her train of thought. 'Krista's swimming on Saturday.'

Lena turned to the calm, quiet, beautiful stranger. 'In the race?'

'Beating a bunch of men? Yea!'

'I'm impressed.'

'I need to build up my stamina though, carbs.' Krista's forthright answer gave Lena an idea. Jack would be at the yacht club and after all, the old bore was the kid's grandfather and it was sure as hell Beth wasn't coming back for her. Like all the ex-pats on the island, Lena was aware of Zander's estrangement from his father, but didn't see that it was any of her business. 'We'll go to the yacht club. I'll buy you lunch and you can tell me all about yourself. I'm a hand down for the trip up to Newcastle, but I don't hire just anybody.'

'Can I have ice cream?' Daisy asked as she slipped off the ruined cushion, unravelling the braid even more, and darted up the companionway.

'You can.' Lena felt more comfortable now with a plan in place.

Over lunch she got down to business. 'What experience do you have?' she asked Krista.

'I crewed down from the Tyne to Gib with Cary Ennis.'

This sparked Lena's interest. She knew a Cary Ennis. 'On the *Genista*?'

'Yea, you know him?'

Krista didn't seem surprised, but then why would she, crews on the oceans tall ships were a tight-knit community and even if they hadn't met at least they all knew the boats. 'Would you mind if I phoned him?'

'No. He's packed it in you know.'

'I heard a rumour.'

'True, his old grandad died, just rowed away in his boat and that was that, he's put the *Gen* up for sale.'

'Bummer.' Lena was horrified to think that a man so spliced to the sea and his boat could give it all up. 'I'll give him a bell tonight. And now, talking of grandfathers.' She got up and holding tight to Daisy's hand she guided her over to the bar where Jack was in profound conversation with his cronies. 'Gentlemen.' Lena greeted them all. 'Jack.' She placed her free hand on his. 'Got to go and Zander won't be back till late. Look after Daisy.' And with that she brought their two hands together and left them.

Not looking back, she passed Krista saying, 'Let's get while the gettin's good.' And hurried her out to the clean fresh air and down the jetty to her boat where Endora, Adalia, Paulo and Juan were now aboard and getting ready to set sail. 'Great timing, let's go boys and girls.' Krista hesitated and Lena sensed the wall go up again. What was it with this kid? She was hiding something. Always very tactile Lena didn't think anything odd about stretching out a hand to touch Krista's soft, brown arm in a gesture of reassurance. 'Want to come?' She waited an age while Krista just stared at the roughened red hand against her own smooth, dark skin. Lena took her hand away. It was obvious that Krista had slipped into a world of her own and took an age to return with a lazy smile that affected Lena in a way she didn't want to think about. What was the attraction of this girl?

'Might as well.'

'Anchors aweigh then. Cast off fore.' She ordered Krista while she swung into the cabin to radio the harbour office, then took the wheel to guide the *Brigantia* away from the moorings and through the opening between the mountains.

There was no doubt the girl could sail. As they tacked back and forth in a rising swell Krista fit right in and was easy and sure with the crew. As they hoisted the heavy sail up the seventy-three foot mast she positioned herself at the back of the rope and her powerful shoulders took the strain. As the wind increased Lena called for the sailors' sail to be hoisted. This was a free flying quadrangle of canvas like a huge kite with ropes at its four corners. It would give them an extra knot and test both crew and ship to the most they could manage short of whistling up a gale. Again Krista pulled, running across the white oak deck efficiently and tying off without fouling anything. The day's sailing was smooth and instructive and as they headed back to the Bay of Pollensa Lena felt lucky to have her aboard.

Before they entered the bay Lena left the wheel to Adalia and joined Krista in the prow to enjoy a well earned cup of coffee. 'You certainly know your stuff,' she praised her.

'I said, didn't I?'

'Yes, yes, you did. And anyway I know Cary wouldn't take on anyone who wasn't competent.'

'He didn't have much choice. I swam after him once he'd cleared the bar at Tynemouth.'

Lena burst out laughing at this boastful feat. The currents at the bar between the Tyne lighthouses were not easily negotiated with a boat let alone swimming in them. 'Yea that'll be right!'

'It's easy.' Krista stated what to her was clearly the obvious.

'You're that good a swimmer?' Lena couldn't quite believe this.

'Why do I have to keep telling people? I swam the Channel.'

Lena nodded her head. 'OK, I believe you. You're a very mysterious girl, but I'm glad to have you aboard.' She extended her hand to seal the deal. Krista took it wonderingly, there it was again, this concentration over the two hands, it was as if she was comparing the different colours, as if she'd never before noticed that she was black. Odd girl.

'Where do you come from?'

Lena was surprised at the question. Although in itself innocent enough, it just seemed something more than idle curiosity. 'Tyneside.'

'Like me.'

Lena's heart dropped into her guts and churned them around. She searched for a topic of conversation to lighten this intense mood, as her past was not a place she chose to visit. 'Where will you sleep tonight?'

'Supposed to be at Beth's place, but …'

'Things are a bit confused over there.'

'What a thing to discover about your parents. Poor Beth.'

'Yea, bummer, poor Tilly too.'

'Are you and Tilly old friends?'

'No, no not really.' This was all getting too personal, but the casual question had dredged up a past Lena preferred to forget.

She had run away from North Shields when she was a young teenager and although she remembered Tilly she was certain Tilly didn't know who she was. Tilly was the prissy red-haired girl who had lived with her mother Mai the sculptor, commonly known as The Witch, who roamed the beaches and talked to mermaids. At aged fourteen and terrified of the twist her life had taken, Lena had watched the sea for days on end. It talked to her, soothed her, numbed her mind. Huge as a whale with a baby she didn't want she had confided in Mai who had practical solutions and moral support. She had also given her a small silver medallion, depicting a mermaid baby in the womb. She said that Lena would soon be leaving for a life of adventure and things that were now troubling her would not intrude into her life for many many years. At the time Lena had scoffed at this prediction. Her life and its troubles were as certain as the rising moon, but then she met a young and carefree boy called Cary Enis and he introduced her to a life at sea. Occasionally, on still night watches, Mai's prediction would resurface and Lena would wonder if this life had come about because she had tried to fulfil the prophecy or would it have happened even if she'd never heard the words. Who knows? She never dwelled too much on the subject. Life was for living not regretting. Regret was a useless obsession. She noticed that Krista was watching, she reached out a hand and lifted a silver chain from her satin skin, the trinket at the end identical to the one she wore under her shirt, a mermaid baby in the womb, made by Mai. Krista didn't move she was still waiting for an answer. Lena dropped the pendant, unremarked. 'You can stay up at the pub with us if you're really stuck.'

'Thanks I will.'

'You can ring your family if you want. Where do you come from?'

'Here and there. We moved around.'

'Does your mother know where you are?'

'Oh yes. Yes she most certainly does.'

Lena thought again that this girl definitely carried a secret she was daring everyone to discover. She'd have a lot to ask Cary when she rang him.

The Stay restaurant was owned and run by Tony and his wife Guadalupe, who also owned the supermarket. Tilly, Sean and Harry were there, the boys pronounced fit and no further treatment required, but Tilly looked as if she'd just been dumped back on Earth by aliens. Dinner was the usual boisterous affair and the party was hotting up, but Lena had promised her partner, Jazzy, that she'd head straight home. She called to Tilly and asked if she and the boys fancied going up to Pollensa Town.

'Gotta do it Mum.' Sean stated.

Lena got him in a head lock, their usual greeting, and as they tussled Tilly agreed to the trip, as Lena had known she would.

So with the boys either side of their mother in the back of the jeep and Krista, the quiet girl, beside her, Lena soon had them pulling up in front of her home in the ancient town of Pollensa, where they trooped into the busy bar and Lena gave Jazzy, her sweet sweet girl, a hearty kiss before getting to work.

Jane Wilson, known as Jazzy, was the treasurer and equal partner in their joint enterprises, but she depended on Lena to be the sociable one and Lena worked the crowd. Showing off her skills she twirled bottles and glasses, mixing the cocktails that made the bar famous all over the north of Mallorca. The boys were easily impressed and always delighted in trying to emulate the complicated moves and tonight Lena had another admirer. Krista kept on studying her. Lena hoped she didn't have a crush on her because Jazzy was Lena's one and only love, however she couldn't help feeling flattered and found herself flirting a little. Mindful of the fact that the girl was only seventeen she whizzed tomato and cranberry juice with ice in the blender and served the Orangatang to Krista and the boys. She scanned the bar. God, Tilly was miserable. Twirling the bottles again she blended peach schnapps and orange juice with crushed ice and a dash of Curacao, before pouring it into a martini glass. 'Here ye go babes, a Fuzzy Shark to bite your bum.'

'Sorry Lena, I'm so worried about Beth. Where can she be?'

'She won't be far and she can take care of herself.'

'No, no she can't Lena. She's got something worrying her.'

'Apart from you and Adam!' A sharp kick on her shin from Jazzy halted the laugh that bubbled up. 'What?' She appealed.

Jazzy shook her head. 'You don't know when to stop. Do you.'

'Me?' Lena started, but was halted by the bar phone. Shrugging her shoulders she stretched out a hand and put the phone to her ear. It was hard to make out the voice, the words were garbled, something about Beth. It took a few seconds to identify Jack, who was warbling on about Daisy.

'Sorry Jack, but I had to leave her, things to do, ye know?' Lena justified her earlier actions. He was still talking. 'What's that? Speak up.' Finally Lena realised he was saying that Beth and Daisy were at his house and would she tell someone to come and get them.

Resenting having to become further embroiled in Tilly's family problems, never-the-less Lena felt she had no choice but to drive Tilly and the twins up to Jack's house in the mountains.

To leave room for Beth on the homeward journey Krista had said she'd stay with Jazzy, volunteering to wash glasses.

The door was open so they all piled out of the jeep and went inside the big house to be welcomed by Cloris. 'Come in dears. Do you know Daisy? She's our grandaughter you know.

'Yes I do know Daisy she's a sweet little thing. Is she here, she and Beth?' Tilly asked.

'She's not really my grandaughter you know, only Jack's. Alexander is Jack's son, his and his dear departed. I never knew her of course.'

'No.' Tilly murmured motioning to the boys to sit.

Strange woman Cloris, Lena thought, not that she was all that familiar with either her or Jack. There was no sign of Beth, but on a deep sofa, almost hidden in an alcove, Harry found a sleeping Daisy.

Cloris took Lena's arm and leaning toward her confidentially whispered, 'She dropped off. She's been showing me how to cook pancakes. Jack brought her. Can't think why.' And with that she turned to climb the stairs.

'Cloris, Cloris?' Tilly called, anxiously.

Cloris turned back. 'Yes dear?' She smiled graciously, her elegant figure ramrod straight and her fine boned features smooth and untroubled.

'My daughter Beth. Is she here?'

'Have you lost her? Oh dear.' And with that she stepped elegantly up the stairs and into the gloom of a narrow landing.

Lena tried not to look at the boys, who were muffling their hysterical laughter.

Sean, as ever, the spokesman. 'God Mum she's weird. Maybe she's got Beth locked in the cellar.'

Lena hovered at the door. She'd rather be anywhere than getting involved in other people's personal problems. She had her work cut out managing her own.

Bored with sitting the boys went off exploring, skipping quietly around the silent house, then there was muffled laughter, before they returned, pushing each other out of the way to be first with their news. 'Mum, Mum we've found Beth.' Harry for once had got in first.

'Where is she?' Alarmed, Tilly moved forward although she had no idea where she was going.

Bursting with suppressed laughter Sean pulled her into the downstairs hallway. 'She's here. She's pissed.'

This was too good to miss. Lena followed them to a downstairs cloakroom where Beth was slumped against the toilet, her white face streaked with black mascara that had run with copious tears at some point in the last few hours. Her eyes were closed and she was so still that Lena feared she was dead.

'State of that!' Exclaimed Sean.

Tilly knelt in front of Beth, feeling her forehead, Beth lurched up, flailed about then fell back moaning. 'Thank God!' Tilly whispered and gathered her daughter in her arms, pressing her face onto the sad and ruined curls, lank and tangled with perspiration and vomit. 'Beth.'

Sighing with despair at the inevitability of involvement, Lena pushed her away, stretched Beth on the floor, on her side, one knee bent under her. She pushed her fingers into the girl's slack mouth to ensure there was no obstruction.

Tilly had got it together enough to soak the corner of a towel with cold water and wipe Beth's face.

The cold water and the action of being moved revived Beth. She coughed, pushing Tilly away and sitting up. 'Fuck off,' she snarled, and the boys burst out laughing as she pushed herself to her hands and knees, trying to stand. Tilly helped her, but Beth would have none of it. Pushing her mother away she staggered past. 'Geroff me. You fucking slut. Leave me alone.' In the hallway she fell to her knees.

Lena had more than once had to revive drunken youths, and people laid low with sea-sickness. She bent over Beth. 'What have you been drinking? Have you taken anything, drugs? pills?'

'She's not worth a pill.' Beth pushed her face close to Lena, her foul breath blasting out with the words. Then she lurched toward Tilly. 'I told you to get away from me. I'll find my own way home. No. No I won't, 'cos I don't have a home.' She looked around her as if surprised. Spotting Sean and Harry she fell on them, hugging them and kissing them while they, self conscious and unsure how to cope, tried to hold her up. 'Hi boys. How are you? Do you know our mother's a slut and so's our father, no not a slut, what do you call a man who sleeps around?' She asked Lena. But already seemed to have forgotten them and hurried to the door, falling onto the drive just as a car slid to a stop.

Lena watched with immense relief as the back doors opened and both Adam and Zander stepped out.

Tony, emerging from the front, was assailed by the boys.

'Hi Tony. Beth's pissed,' Sean told him

Also ignoring their father, Harry hung onto Tony's arm. 'We found her in the toilet. She's been sick.'

Tony looked to Lena for clarification.

Lena just wanted to get away, go back to the bar and leave them to sort out their own lives. She nodded. 'Glad you got here. I'll leave you to it.' She tried to escape but Tony pulled her back.

'Thees family is keeling me,' he moaned. 'And choo, choo come weeth me.'

Lena had no choice but to return to the confines of the villa.

Zander and Adam carried an unconscious Beth back inside and left her to her mother.

Lena was glad to observe.

Zander, assuring himself that Daisy was all right looked around the place. 'Where's Jack?'

'We haven't seen him, just Cloris. She went to bed.' Sean seemed to relish the situation and blurted out the information.

Zander took the stairs two at a time and soon they could all hear him shouting. 'How dare you leave those girls in such a state? Are you both completely insane!'

'We rung Lena,' Jack's voice answered, sounding puzzled by his son's anger.

'Lena! What the hell has any of this to do with Lena!'

Thank God, she thought, edging closer to the door.

In the lounge, while Tony and Tilly tried to revive Beth with cold flannels and coffee, they all listened while Jack told Zander how Lena had left him with Daisy.

Lena felt a bit guilty.

After a few minutes' silence the two men came downstairs. Jack went to the bar and poured himself a whisky. Then Adam went to help himself, but Tony stopped him.

Zander roamed back and forward, trying to make sense of the situation. He was angry. 'She's your grandaughter. Couldn't you look after her for just one afternoon?'

'I've told you not to give me that responsibility.' Jack deliberately stared out the black window, seeing only the scene in his own lounge reflected back at him.

'How do you think she feels?' Zander took a couple of deep breaths to calm himself and crossed the room to look down on his daughter. 'How do you think she feels about being ignored by her only grandfather? She'd love to get to know you.'

'It's no use Alexander. I've tried to warn you.'

'She's just a little girl.'

They were interrupted by Sean and Harry laughing in embarrassed choking gulps, punching each other to try and contain themselves.

Lena looked in the direction of their wide open eyes. Cloris was coming down the stairs. Fully made up, as always, and adorned in glittering diamonds she was every inch the movie star she had once been, but no moviegoer had ever seen her as radiant as when she now appeared to the assembled company, stark naked.

'This is nice, Jack. You didn't tell me we were having a party.'

Harry shouted, 'She's pissed.' And to end the affair Sean fell on the floor rolling with laughter.

Lena made good her escape and hurried home to the empty bar, eagerly sharing the gossip with Jazzy and Krista.

CHAPTER SEVEN

TILLY

The next few days were subdued. The tension in Puerto stretched like cling-film over the bay, shielding the friends from each other's words.

From the doorway of her daughter's room Tilly watched Beth, who lay on the cool floor, her head pillowed on a towel filled with ice cubes; the one act of caring she had allowed her mother while vowing never to get drunk again.

Today was festival day, but Tilly had chosen to stay at home while Adam took Sean and Harry to watch the Blessing of the Boats Festival. If she felt that Beth was OK she'd promised to meet them later for the swimming race. For the moment Beth was sleeping easily. Reluctantly Tilly left her to watch from the balcony where she could easily see the procession from the church. The statue of Mary In Tears was being carried through the streets to the harbour where the fishing boats, shining and bedecked with bunting, would be blessed, the men would then sail their idol around the bay before returning it to the church. Tilly had seen it many times and always enjoyed the spectacle, would she ever see it again? Would they ever return to Puerto? She doubted it. This would be goodbye.

'Bye Mum.'

'What?' Beth's voice shook her from her reverie. She hurried to the top of the stairs. Beth was dragging a large rucksack, bumping it down the stairs. 'Beth! Where are you going?'

'Board the *Brigantia*. See ya back home.'

'I forgot … you're supposed to be sailing tomorrow. Beth, please don't go. I can't let you just leave.'

'Why not? You left us last week, nicked off and we didn't know where you were and Harry and Sean needed you. They were upset and Harry cried. How do you think they'll feel when they realise you've often left us to go and have sex with Zander, who we all trusted. There's a hell of a difference in that and me going home. At least you'll all know where I am.'

Tilly felt a corner of her heart crumple. Of course she'd

known Beth was sailing up to the Tyne with Lena, but the events of the last few days had distorted time and robbed her of the ability to think coherently. 'Please stay a while, we can have lunch together and talk.'

'Not gonna work. I'm off to see Lena and I'll stay aboard, we'll sail with the early tide.' She turned and left without a goodbye.

Knowing further argument was futile Tilly returned to the balcony and watched her go, keeping to the shadows, away from the mid-day heat. She was worried about her, she was only sixteen and so naïve, and yet there was an independence in the set of her shoulders, the straight back that reminded her that this was her daughter and in turn her mother's granddaughter, strong women with uncompromising opinions. It didn't help much, but there was no denying the fact that Beth would plot her own course just as they had done. She decided to go and find Adam and somehow get through the day with him and the boys.

The sea-front was packed. Elderly tourists who'd seen it all before and had hoped for a quiet afternoon snooze on their loungers were now resigned to the festivities, but the crowd around the harbour was a good-natured melee vying for every vantage point.

Pushing through to their regular table at the restaurant Tilly spotted Harry who came and gave her a hug. Unlike Sean he was demonstrative and intuitive. Sean was more of a man's man, always looking for male approval, but Harry was the strong silent type and he sensed that she was upset even though, hopefully, he wasn't aware of the cause. She shuddered as she realised that the issue had so far not affected them. Adam would have some explaining to do when they got home.

'Come on, we've got a seat. Beth's with the girls cheering Krista and Lena's a marshal.' He pointed across the bay to the old scout hut, visible as a low white mark against the black cliffs west of Alcudia. When they reached the table Adam was eager to appease her, guiding her to a chair and signalling to a waiter for her usual pre-lunch drink of gin and tonic.

'Think the bank balance will stand it?' She heard herself say the words. She couldn't have stopped them, petty, but she wanted to hurt him.

Harry kissed her cheek, yelled a goodbye and ran off to join Sean at their private vantage point on the restaurant's roof, where they would be welcomed by Tony's family and kept safe.

'Can we just have one day?' Adam appealed to her.

'How many days have you had Adam, count them up. How many years of days and nights with another woman?' Suddenly she could stand it no longer, couldn't bear to be near him, to even look at him. She pushed away from the table, squeezing through the uncaring crowd, pushing forward, constant motion the only thing that mattered. How dare he do this! He had almost drowned her sons in Mallorca and Lonore's sons in Tynemouth, their daughter could have died from alcohol poisoning and he wanted 'just one day.' She was furious with him. And in Tynemouth Lonore was probably furious too as she studied the photos spread around the house, discovering that the father of her children was a two-timing lying cheating bastard. While he seemed totally unaware of the chaos he'd created. Damn him!

How had all her carefully nurtured plans come to this? Since she was a child she had longed for this life and she had manufactured it for them, for herself. When she met Adam she saw all she wanted. A handsome and successful man, a house in the country, heir to a thriving business, Adam beside her doing his part to support the family she intended to bear. He was her man, the one she had chosen to implement her plan, who would enable her to fulfil her destiny, to take her away from her mother's careless bohemian lifestyle of never knowing what the next day would bring. He would give her respectability and security.

She had loved him, hadn't she? Yes. Yes she had. She did. She loved being with him, talking to him, lying beside him, walking and living with him, enjoyed their life together. And now he had made a mockery of all that. He'd destroyed her plans and he had hurt her. He had left her and cancelled every year, month, week and minute of their lives together. It hurt so much. It was an actual pain in her heart. She gave way to tears and cried out her hurt and anger to the churning sea; cried at his betrayal and the utter carelessness he'd shown her for this loyalty.

She knelt in the sand, her arms twisted about her aching body. She had nothing left. There was no self-esteem, no confidence, because he'd spurned her ideas and her plans, taken away her love and tossed it aside. She was humiliated, she was less than she could be because it had all been in vain, wasted. Eighteen years pouring herself into him to be used like a balance sheet shredded to strips, reduced to rubbish.

She didn't know how long she sat on the beach until out of breath and limp she looked around her. The litter-strewn stretch of pebbles that ran parallel to the busy road between Puerto and Alcudia stretched out on either side. Ahead of her was the sea, where the swimmers were churning the water into a long line of white foam as they passed the half-way marker. The bay was packed to danger point. Hundreds of part-time and experienced sailors jostled their craft with hardly a belt's width between the boats. In the bright sunshine bunting fluttered and a thousand voices cheered on their particular favourite. How many of these people had, just this week, realised that their carefully planned lives were in turmoil. Surely she wasn't the only one. What a fool she'd been. Her mother had often told her to open her eyes, had drawn her attention to the hundreds of women who came to her door for a charm to make it better, make it different. But Tilly had been determined to rise above them, determined that her life would work out as she had planned. She had scoffed at the little phials of seawater and herbs her mother distilled and sold to needy women, had refused to acknowledge the yearning voices, distained those who couldn't sort out their lives without resorting to magic. What a stupid arrogant fool she'd been. She needed a bit of magic right now.

A warm little body plonked itself beside her. Expecting that Harry had intuited her need she turned, surprised to see Daisy. 'Hello Darling.'

Daisy shuffled up close and slipped her thin little arms around Tilly's waist. 'I came to find you.'

Tears pooled in Tilly's eyes and burned her throat. Unable to speak she hugged the motherless child, pulling her onto her knee and pressing her close to her swollen heart and they sat together in silence, for a while, content to watch the activity on the water. Finally Tilly managed to regain control of her emotions. 'Did you want me for something?'

'No. I just came to help you cry.'

Tilly could hardly swallow the lump that threatened to choke her. How many times had this little girl cried herself to sleep, how many times had she wished her life was different. She was so vulnerable, dependant on a father who, while not being cruel was, nevertheless, often absent and careless with her and she was unable to change anything, while she, Tilly, was a grown woman, able to take charge of her life. She felt ashamed of her weaknesses. 'How did you know I was here?'

'I watched you.' She stated the obvious. 'Look.' She pointed to the distinctive red launch following the swimmers. 'Dad's guarding lives.'

Zander was easily recognisable. His deceptively casual approach to steering the rescue boat was unmistakable, one handed, his shoulders slightly stooped, all his attention focused in his eyes, searching the sea. The familiar yearning failed to surface and Tilly wondered if it was because she was all emoted out. Or perhaps it was just that he'd been unplanned, the one thing she hadn't had on a list; and just as she'd always known, and Adam had proved categorically, unplanned events just didn't work.

She and Daisy climbed onto the wall that edged the beach. The course of the race had brought the swimmers almost in front of them. Soon they would make a sharp right turn for the final leg to the finish, pulling away from the deep current and into the shallower waters that bordered the long man-made beach. The front runners were tactically overtaking the others in turn; Tony and his two younger brother, Krista, Des Ryan, a brash Irishman who owned the Diving Centre, Yvonne St Jean, a big quiet Cornish woman who made jewellery and was one of the stalwarts of the ex-pats group, and local boys Carlos and Domingo, waiters from the Ille D'or Hotel. One after the other they held first place, but slowly Krista pulled in front. Tony broke away and for a while was level with her. After another twenty metres Krista was ahead again. Endora had managed to manoeuvre the *Brigantia*'s launch to the side of the markers, frantically shouting for her father while everyone else encouraged Krista. Beth was standing up shouting at Krista, exhorting her to swim faster. She was stronger with her friends around her, happier, the old Beth, unrecognisable from the girl who had tried to destroy herself over the last three days. She was becoming a woman. Tilly resolved to accept what she couldn't change. She would wait for her daughter to come to her. Perhaps it was a good thing that she was sailing home with Lena, as it would give them both space to heal.

Instead of worrying over the past Tilly resolved to concentrate on new plans for the future. She jumped onto the pavement and, holding Daisy's hand as she walked on the wall, they made their way back to Puerto. 'You're a wise little thing. I'm glad you're my friend.'

Daisy, from the extra height afforded by the wall, silently hugged Tilly around the neck.

'Who's meant to be looking out for you?'

'Guadalupa, she's cooking sausages for Harry and Sean.'

'She'll be worried about you.'

'No. I told her I was coming to find you.'

'And you found me.'

'Yes. You weren't lost you know.'

'I thought I was.'

'Well I'm here now and I'll take you home.'

'Thank you darling. I'd like that.'

At the Stay restaurant pandemonium reigned. Tony had lost! For the first time in fifteen years the little powerhouse had been beaten – and by a girl.

'Not even a woman,' he wailed amid derisive laughter, but finally he took it all in good part, hugging Krista and congratulating her.

Lena invited them to the *Brigantia* for a celebratory party which she was hosting to enable her to keep an eye on her crew and ensure they would stay sober and not wake up hung over for the start of their long journey into the Atlantic and the North Sea.

There was no sign of Adam so Tilly gathered up the boys and followed the raucous girls and all of Tony's large family down the promenade. Daisy stuck to her side, proprietarily, and Tilly felt grateful for that.

As day turned to evening and purple clouds massed over the mountains, the sun bowed out waving gold and crimson banners at the thinning crowds in Pollensa Bay. On board the *Brigantia* Tilly stood with her back to the rail, watching her family.

Lena pushed her way through and handed Tilly a beer. 'White oak this you know.' Lovingly she stroked the rail. 'And here, you see these, these little pegs?' She rubbed her finger over three-quarter inch dots of wood, differently coloured from the rail they were set into, darker. 'No metal nails in this beauty.'

Dutifully Tilly ran her hand over the smoothed round pegs where countless hands had also marvelled at the craftsmanship that held the ship together.

Lena stamped her foot on the deck. 'Mahogany planked.'

'You didn't leave the arms of the lovely Jazzy to tell me about your boat.'

'Ship, this is a ship, boats have oars – and I did as a matter of fact.'

Tilly shook her head.

'I came to tell you that next to Jazzy this little beauty holds my heart and I'd never put her in danger.'

Tilly nodded again. 'I know.'

'Do you?'

'Yes. I know Beth will be safe with you. And now she has Krista. They've become firm friends.'

'That girl sort of stirs a person up.'

'Beth doesn't need any stirring up, she can manage that all by herself.'

They stood in silence, watching. The crowd had thinned, lots of parties to attend. There was mostly just the crew left, two of them, Paulo played the accordion and Beth was sitting next to him strumming her guitar. Daisy, Harry and Sean were dancing hornpipes with the girls. Sean played the fool, his footwork not as graceful as Harry's, the skilful footballer who jogged deftly, his arms crossed easily over his chest. They were so masculine while still boyish; awkward and utterly, irreplaceably precious and she had almost lost them. 'No-one tells you how much it hurts to have children.'

'Far too much fuss made about the pesky critters if you ask me.'

'You don't have any so you can't feel it.' Tilly spoke the words gently.

'Had one once.'

At Lena's bombshell Tilly felt almost petrified, afraid to speak.

'I was just a kid.'

'A baby?'

'Raped by a gang in the park 'cos I was a little slut, trying to be something I'm not.'

Shock and horror surged through Tilly. She held Lena by her arms. Her voice low and strained, she choked out the words. 'Don't say that. I'm appalled you should even think it! No-one deserves to be raped. My God Lena how long have you carried this? What does Jazzy say?'

'She doesn't know.'

This was even worse. 'How can you keep this to yourself. Haven't you talked it over with anyone?'

'Your mother.'

'My Mother! I can't believe what you're saying.'

Lena tried to move away. 'Forget it. Don't know what's come over me.'

Tilly hustled her into the prow of the *Brigantia*, a shadowy place of quiet calm amid the noise. 'Forget it! You expect me to forget a thing like this. Lena you were not to blame. And what does my mother have to do with it all?'

'Wish I'd never mentioned it.' Lena was uncomfortable, her gaze shifting right and left, still trying to move away from Tilly.

'Well you did and I'm glad you did, but how does my mother fit in?'

'I met her on the beach one day. I was about ready to drop and she talked to me. You know how she is, full of wisdom, a real mother.'

This was too big a subject for private conversation at a party. From the corner of her eye Tilly could see Jazzy watching them, soon she would come over, worried, it was evident Lena was upset. 'Where is the child?'

Lena shrugged. 'Who knows? It was adopted as soon as it was born. I never saw it, don't even know if it was a boy or a girl.'

Now Jazzy was on her way, smooth as mercury, slipping through the crowd, a dangerous glint in her eye. 'Lena, you should talk about this, you should tell Jazzy.' Tilly felt drained, as if she'd gone ten rounds with a heavyweight boxer.

'Yea, that'd be right. That's the last I'd see of her.'

'Don't you think she might have guessed? Things happen to a woman's body when she gives birth, changes that can't be disguised. Emotions change, we become grounded.'

'Now you sound just like your mother.'

Jazzy was there, at their elbows. 'You two are very serious.'

Lena hugged her. 'Mother hen here clucking over her chick. I'm telling her Beth'll be fine with us.'

Jazzy kissed Tilly on the cheek. 'Of course. We'll get her home safe. Lena's not going to risk the *Brigantia*.'

'So she says.' Tilly tried to look normal, but huge waves of confusion were making her feel sick. She moved away, her eyes searching out her children. 'Time to get them all to bed I think.' She advised out of habit, not coherent thought.

'Yea.' Lena agreed. 'Time for them to turn in, early start tomorrow.' She slung a brawny arm around Jazzy's slim white shoulders, her stubby fingers stroking the smooth skin, laying claim. Secure in their love, they walked away.

Zander materialised from the shadow of the wheelhouse and stood beside her. 'Hi Till, haven't had a chance to talk today.'

He too kissed her cheek, soft like Jazzy, but different, his kiss was slow and warm, the description summing up this man conjured from sultry continental zephyrs.

'I hear you and Daisy went walkabout.'

Tilly smiled. 'She's a treasure.'

'Yea, but you know Till I've not done right by her, living here. She's on her own a lot, left with all and sundry just 'cos I wanted to mend fences with my Dad. I didn't see that she needed her Dad too.'

'Wasn't something you planned then?'

'God no. I've never planned a thing in my life. Not a lot of point, life'd just sneak around you and come up with a counter-plan all of its own.'

'Not if you're sure of what you want.'

'And have you always been so sure?'

'Yes.'

'Has it worked?'

'Up to now.'

He nodded. 'Yea, I've been thinking that once I get up to the Tyne I'll look for work, stop arsing about in boats and give her a stable home. I'm a marine engineer you know.' He sounded slightly surprised at this fact, as if he'd forgotten it.

Tilly was surprised too, she had always assumed him untrained in anything except what he'd learned about boats. 'That right?'

He nodded. 'Fact. I should be able to find a position.'

'I didn't know you were going north.'

'Sure, Lena's a crew member short so I've volunteered to be an honorary girl for the voyage.'

'And Daisy?'

He ducked his head, the low timbre of his voice making all the excuses. 'Guadalupa.'

'I would offer to take her up with us, but things are a bit fraught at the moment and I'm not sure she needs our problems.'

'Tilly?'

She turned to look out over the harbour where lights twinkled and halyards tinkled in a rising wind. The coming storm pressed down heavily with rumbles of thunder that menaced from behind the mountains.

'Tilly?'

She recognised the hunger in his voice, he needed her. She looked into the insubstantial light blue of his eyes and saw the end of things, but still she moved closer.

'Does Adam know about us?'

'I don't know. I've only just realised that Adam and I don't talk so I have no idea what he thinks.'

He took her fingers, holding them in his warm hand.

The thrill of his loving clutched at her, tightening her limbs with anticipation, but she resisted. It was over. She dowsed the rising heat in her body and with a last kiss, stood away from him. 'Bye Zander.'

He nodded. 'Bye Tilly.'

CHAPTER EIGHT

A - Z

Pushing his way back to their table with the drinks had been mission impossible, and not for the first time Adam wondered why Tilly couldn't drink at the bar instead of this constant insistence to sit at a table; always having to do things 'properly' and when he had finally achieved his goal the table had been commandeered by a family of footy types, wearing their team colours and dripping garish gold jewellery. Downing his whiskey and Tilly's G&T he'd wandered away from the deafening throng to lounge on the wall that separated the prom from the beach. Over a ciggy he'd watched Harry and Sean on the café roof, running about helping Guadalupa.

Tilly's mobile had rung, he'd commandeered it after she'd broken his, it had been Lonore, but she was pleased to find him on the other end. She sounded very reasonable telling him she knew about Tilly and him being married. To her credit she didn't blamed him, seemed only interested in getting the repairs done on Syon Place and praised Tilly for organising the workmen and allowing her and the little boys to a stay at Sea View. At this point the signal had begun to fade so he'd given up. Good show though, the two women getting along so well.

Getting himself another whiskey at the beach bar he'd sat on, musing about the situation with the factory. Then he'd spotted Tilly and Daisy at the far end of the prom. They were walking back his way and he couldn't be bothered to listen to her rantings again so he'd headed for the Pine Walk and spent the rest of the afternoon asleep in the hammock on the veranda.

He woke to find the evening well advanced and feeling ravenous decided to eat at the club. It was a bit pricy, but it kept the riff-raff out. The south harbour, away from the post-race parties was quieter. He felt relaxed walking down the jetty, noting that Lena's boat wasn't in its usual spot. She must have taken it round to the north moorings ready for the morning. It was easier for the bigger boats to clear the harbour from there.

He was surprised to find Jack on his boat. 'Going somewhere?' He watched the old man struggle to stow the tarp cover.

'Yes, thought I'd have a crack at the race.'

'What race?'

'Cutty Sark.'

This rendered Adam speechless for a minute or two. 'You mad? In this old tub!'

'One of only three left in the world hasn't been converted.' Jack boasted of the little Fife 8-metre.

'You don't even have an engine!' Adam was appalled.

'Well, yes we do, but I hardly ever use it, sail's better. Shows you're a sailor. Did I ever tell you about when Cloris and I came up from Mauritius ...'

Adam stopped him. 'Seriously Jack that was twenty years ago, you and this boat have seen better days. It hasn't been out of the water for years. Look at it.' Adam pointed out the cracked windows and peeling paint. 'She needs re-caulking.'

'No.' Jack was matter of fact, and clearly he thought Adam a hopeless amateur. 'The water has kept the planks swollen and I've a mate along in Alvore, the Algarve? He's going to have a look.'

'Yes, I know where Alvore is, and I'm telling you that even getting that far will be an effort.'

Jack wouldn't be dissuaded. He took Adam into every corner of the *Mirabel* and although the old tub was obviously in need of an overhaul Adam was surprised at how seaworthy it seemed. At Adam's suggestion they sauntered over to the club for dinner and discussed Jack's chances of even making the journey to the Tyne, let alone competing in the first leg of the race from there to Copenhagen. After a few more whiskeys Adam became impressed by Jack's obvious sailing knowledge, so much so that when Jack asked him to join as crew Adam saw a chance to escape Tilly's censure for a few weeks, and agreed.

He and Jack readied the boat for sail then Adam did a run to the supermarket. When he returned Jack told him Cloris was aboard, but had retired to her cabin. Finally Adam went to the beach house to pack a bag and tell Tilly what he'd planned, but she was still partying so he just collected a few essentials. He'd phone her as soon as he'd charged the mobile. Back at the *Mirabel* he found Jack eager to be away and stood at his shoulder as the little boat slipped quietly out of Puerto.

After making good headway they were now passing through

the Straights of Gibraltar where the Rock loomed massive and shadowy under grey clouds, with the moon shifting in then out of sight and a freshening wind that intermittently hurled squally rain across his vision. The sea rose up in steady swells, helping to push them along, but it had been some years since Adam had crewed anything under sail and was out of his depth. Jack didn't seem to notice, being eminently competent and easily able to handle the *Mirabel* on his own except for the heavy work. From time to time he barked an order at Adam, who complied, but the sails were stiff and it was a struggle for him. The big mainsail needed repairing and Adam was afraid it would tear right across as it frayed from the eyelet at the end of the boom. The night seemed endless.

ZANDER

In Pollensa Bay the morning had barely dawned when Zander opened his eyes to dull oppressive heat. The storm would eventually clear the air. Rolling from his bed he ambled into the shower, knowing he should hurry, he barely had time to get Daisy along to the supermarket and Guadalupa before Lena would be anxious to haul anchor. When he'd dressed and thrown some necessities in a bag he took his coffee to the beach and turned to look at the mountains behind the port and the glowering sky where heavy purple thunder clouds were massing. With a following wind they could run in front of the storm and once in the Atlantic they'd be free of it, but then the notorious bad weather in the Bay of Biscay would present a different set of problems, however he was confident it would be nothing he and Lena couldn't handle. He went back indoors and climbed up to Daisy's room in the top of the house.

As soon as he opened the door he realised she wasn't there. A bit irritated he began to search the house. 'Daisy, this isn't funny. I don't have time for games.' There was no sign of her indoors so, sighing because of the inconvenience, he headed outside. It was barely light, the coming storm sending a harrying wind to flatten the dark sea. Quickly scanning the empty beach he realised there was no sign of her there; perhaps she'd snuck out while his back was turned and gone to Tilly's. He wasn't worried. Daisy had done this before, crept along to Tilly's to sleep with Beth. They'd tried to impress on her that she must not wander about alone, but Daisy was a law unto herself. The sooner he got her settled into a normal routine back in England the better. A good school and friends her own age, that's what she needed, that was the plan.

At the supermarket, Guadalupa was just unlocking the door, ready for the bread delivery. She said she wasn't surprised Daisy had run away, that girl needed a loving mother to care for her and Zander ought to do something about it instead of wasting his time hanging around an old fart like Jack who didn't want to be a father any more than she wanted to be Queen of England.

He left her and knocked on Tilly's door. It took a while to raise the house, but Tilly's search provided no sign of Daisy. Together they roamed the port, Tilly in the narrow lanes and deserted squares while Zander ran up and down the jetties, waking people on the moored boats. Soon everyone was searching for Daisy.

On board the *Brigantia* they were set fair to go and Lena shouted for him to hurry up and get his gear stowed. 'Look lively sailor!'

Zander, by this time frantic, hurried past her dropping quickly down the stairs and shouting for Beth. In her shared cabin he woke the sleepy girl, shouting. 'Have you seen her?'

Beth took a minute to realise what the problem was before springing into action and organising a search of the *Brigantia*.

Zander left them and ran to the outermost end of the jetty where the concrete lighthouse plinth dropped sheer into deep water. From the corner of his eye he registered the empty berth where Jack's *Mirabel* usually wallowed. It had probably sunk to the bottom. His stomach dropped, he felt sick, Jack and Cloris. He'd not thought of asking them if Daisy had somehow managed to get herself to their place. He pulled out his mobile and dialled his father's number, but it was useless. The old coot never used his mobile much and it was probably abandoned. He phoned Tony up in Pollensa Town and asked him to go to Jack's villa and see if anyone was home.

The empty berth where the *Mirabel* should be nagged at him, tipped the balance of things. He peered down through the clear water to the sea bed and sand, no boat. Hundreds of craft had remained in the harbour after the race, crowding the already busy water and the celebrations had given small boats lots of work ferrying people back and forward all night, but the *Mirabel* had, seemingly, slipped away unnoticed. He dragged himself back along the jetty to where Lena was waiting. 'I can't go Lena. I think she's gone out with Jack. Can't think of anywhere else she'd be.'

Lena shook her head. 'You have to call the police.'

This was something he'd not thought of. Involving the police would make him look at the possibility that Daisy had come to harm and he couldn't do that. It was too final. 'No. She'll be ok. She's with Jack.'

'She may not be.' Lena's voice was soft, but still her words deafened him.

He stalked away. 'I'll look in the club.'

Tilly was coming, running down the jetty, maybe she'd found her.

She shook her head. 'Sorry Zander, everyone's looking, there's no sign. And …'

Ignoring her he sprinted towards the just opening doors of the Yacht Club. Perhaps she'd slipped in and hidden in a corner and when they'd locked up no-one had known she was there.

Tilly was running after him. She grabbed his arm. 'Zander. Listen to me.'

He whirled away from her restraining hand.

'Zander! Adam's gone too.'

'What! Are you insane! He's a grown man, he can look after himself. Daisy's missing and all you can think about is that drunken fool.'

'He's taken clothes and Beth got a text. He told her that he was sailing back home with Jack.'

'He doesn't mention Daisy?'

She shook her head. 'We've tried ringing him, but he's not answering. Beth's left messages.'

'I've got to find her.' He pushed her away, heading for the town, aware of her running behind him.

'You have to call the police, talk to the coastguard.'

'Let me alone.' He was angry. Angry at Jack who hadn't even thought to tell him he'd taken Daisy on a fool expedition.

'Zander, call the police. I'll go look in the club.'

Barely registering her presence he searched the beaches again, looking for any sign of Daisy's long, straight, mousy hair, whipping behind her, her lithe quickness, a bright flash of pink frills as she darted around hiding behind the loungers and beach huts. The car park was a good place to hide. He lifted Lena's binoes and searched again. Nothing. He didn't want to acknowledge that she might be on the *Mirabel* with Jack, but it gave a kernel of hope.

Above him Lena was standing at the rail. 'What's the harbour master say?'

Why hadn't he gone to the harbour master?

Lena sighed. 'I'll go and see what's happening.' She turned back to Jazzy. 'Hold the fort, pet.' And with that she stumped ashore and hurried to the harbour master's office.

Leaving her to the task Zander boarded the *Brigantia* and climbed to the middle spars on the mast. His eyes hurt with the effort of examining every vessel, but there was no sign of the *Mirabel* or Daisy. Fifteen minutes later Lena returned and he swung down through the ropes to see what she'd discovered.

'They've no register of the *Mirabel* clearing harbour so we're sailing. Going ahead as planned, but we'll take a zig-zag course and see if we can spot them on the way. You coming with us?'

He just knew it was the right thing to do. Daisy had to be on board the *Mirabel*. He nodded, eager to set sail. Tilly had followed Lena aboard and now she prepared to jump ashore, but he held on to her. 'Will you talk to the police?' He buried his face in her neck, but she pushed him away, her big clear green eyes filled with concern.

'We'll find her, Zander. We'll keep in touch.' And then she was gone and he was alone.

He busied himself getting the *Brigantia* out of harbour.

Lena tried to instil hope in him. 'Come on pet. We know that Adam's there too. He'll be a sensible voice on the radio when we make contact.'

'We can't rely on Dad. He's useless.' Beth spoke her fears aloud.

He stared at the frightened teenager. She was white-lipped, skinny, trembling, close to tears.

'It's my fault, Zander. I started all this 'cos I left her the other day. Went and got drunk and left her.'

Lena intervened. 'If it's anybody's fault it's mine. I left her with Jack. I put the idea into her head.'

He couldn't bear this. He stalked away, stood in the bow. He wasn't a violent man, he'd never hit anybody in his life, but last week he'd come close to punching Adam over the incident with the boys and now his anger at Jack was so overpowering he wanted to hit him too. Old as he was, he wanted to knock him senseless for being such an irresponsible, useless father. A father was supposed to look out for his children and Jack had never concerned himself in Zander's life, why now?

Soon they were beating a course along the south coast of Spain and out to Gibraltar.

Zander threw himself into his duties on board the *Brigantia*, relieved to be under way and doing something, but what if he was wrong? Supposing something unspeakable had happened to Daisy back in Pollensa Bay and he was abandoning her. He couldn't afford these thoughts, he turned his gaze back to the screen, his eyes aching from watching little green dots as the radar swept the area. He had to believe that she was on board the *Mirabel*.

The door opened to let in a gust of pelting rain and Krista with a sandwich and mugs of steaming coffee. He barely acknowledged her. His eyes felt tortured with grit, his head hurt and occasionally he'd miss a few seconds, then return his attention to see their course had slipped a few degrees.

'Give me the wheel.'

He staggered as Krista tried to push him aside, but he stood his ground. He had to be the one at the wheel. He tightened his grip. Once more he felt Krista push him and this time her strength was superior to his, he staggered back against the bulkhead.

'Lena sent the coffee. She doesn't want the ship to end up as a pile of lumber on the rocks.'

Zander grunted. He sipped at the steaming liquid, strong as sump oil and tasting almost as bad. 'What makes you such an expert?'

'At sailing? Practice I suppose.'

He watched her, her hands, capable, allowing the little wheel to slip through her long fingers, restoring their course to the correct heading, her eyes registering every screen simultaneously and her body swaying as if she was part of the deck. He blinked, rubbed his hand over his eyes. She got to him this girl, but he reminded himself she was just a girl. 'How old are you?'

'Old enough.'

'How long have you been alone?'

'All my life.'

'Lonely,' Zander mused, knowing he was describing his own teenage years.'

'No. I'm never lonely.'

'Do you know Lena from somewhere?'

'You could say that. Do you know Tilly's Mam?'
'A batty old thing, believes in mermaids?'
'You do know her.'
'No, just heard about her. Everyone who's ever been in the Tyne knows about Mai.'
'She's very wise, told me to make friends with the mermaids, said I was one of them.'

Zander had had enough of this childish banter. He returned his gaze to the sea. A squally rain spattered the windshield, before he could react Krista switched on the Clear-view.

'She's not in the sea.' She told him in a matter-of-fact tone 'I've been out and didn't feel anything, no disturbance.'

Sighing, Zander left the wheelhouse. He had enough to worry about without the fantasies of a kid who believed in mermaids

ADAM

On board the *Mirabel*, Adam was exhausted. The damn boat was so old it needed manual labour to keep it afloat and he was the man Jack had designated to labour. He'd managed it though, got them through a rough night. The storm hadn't come to anything – yet. He peered out of the tiny wheelhouse at the grey rain-dotted sea, then back, as a movement aboard alerted him to Jack hauling himself from the galley bringing tea and they stood companionably, sipping and warming their hands on the hot mugs.

Adam was tired. 'Think I'll turn in.' He was just about to leave when Cloris appeared on deck dressed in shorts and bikini top, seeming not to be aware that she was shivering in the freezing cold rain that now drove at them horizontally. Then Adam was more than surprised to see the quick little form of Daisy wriggle out from behind her. Both of them were hung about with jewellery that even in the dull light of the stormy day, glittered authentically. On Daisy's tiny head a diamond tiara was pinned in place and enormous pearls hung around her bony neck. Cloris sported earrings and bracelets made up from dozens of diamonds, big ones. Adam thought that if the sun broke through the dazzle would blind them all. Daisy climbed into the wheelhouse, straight away busying herself by learning the functions of all the instruments. This pleased Jack, who loved an audience.

'Would you like a Pims?' Cloris asked, over her shoulder, as she sashayed toward the galley.

'Could go a butty?' Adam asked hopefully as he followed her.

'Lots of greenery, that's the secret,' Cloris answered, concentrating on the well-stocked bar.

Adam sighed, looked like he'd have to fettle for himself on this voyage.

Worried that the storm might worsen he realised that the practical decisions were up to him, so, forgoing the longed for bacon sandwich he unearthed some ancient waterproofs from under the seats and struggled to get Daisy into the stiff garments that were far too big for her, but he cut the sleeves and legs shorter; they would do. The life jackets were hardly serviceable, but mindful of Sean and Harry's brush with death he insisted she allow him to tie her into one. Solemnly she examined herself then laughed with him and Jack at the comical sight she made as she struggled to stand, let alone move. She was a plucky little thing and ignoring the hampering, crackling folds climbed back into the wheelhouse where Jack stood her on a low stool in front of him.

Adam was kept busy tying sheets and stowing the big sail, it was a nuisance in the wayward winds. 'You'll have to use the engine.' He yelled to Jack. Above the noise of the storm, the wind whistled through the rigging and the hull groaned, its timbers creaking alarmingly. In the engine room Adam was appalled to find himself ankle deep in water and struggled to turn the pump on. The unused engine had seized up and it was an hour of wallowing around with spray cans and spanners before he finally got it stuttering to life, but the pump refused to respond to his ministrations and remained a lump of scrap metal. Back on deck they fought to keep the *Mirabel* on an even keel while Cloris trotted back and forth doing God knows what, other than getting sloshed, and never seemed to notice how the boat pitched and yawed. It was an enormous relief when they gained the safe harbour of Alvore in Portugal and headed for the mooring in a chaotic boatyard.

Aching and exhausted, Adam tied up while Jack and an ancient fisherman, who resembled the fabled old man of the sea, greeted each other warmly. Adam was introduced as the old fellow ordered his sons, who were of pensionable age themselves, to look at the boat, before ushering Jack and himself into a quayside café. So tired from the constant battering they'd taken in the storm Cloris elected to stay on board with Daisy and get some sleep.

In the café, under a smoke-filled, low-ceilinged room Adam found a plentiful supply of green wine and eagerly devoured the most delicious sardines he'd ever tasted. He didn't understand a word of the fast guttural Portuguese Jack and his old friend conversed in, but he was sure that Jack was just as boring in any language. As the night wore on and the storm growled around the sheltering islets, he slept where he sat, against the wall.

ZANDER

The *Brigantia* hardly noticed the storm. The big schooner slid through the swells and the crew coped easily, the vessel needing little guidance from Lena who, never-the-less, stalked the deck, her sharp eyes everywhere. They too were past Gibraltar, but didn't consider sheltering anywhere, least of all Alvore with its shallow water and low-tide mud-flats.

In the wheelhouse Zander stood behind Krista and kept his eyes on the sea, the boat, the radar and the computer screen. His ears on the faint sound of radio traffic from where any mention of the *Mirabel* would have him instantly alert. Despair wracked his whole body. Krista's hand on the back of his neck was like sunshine on frost. A part of him thawed, but she's a child he told himself, how can I even be considering any feelings other than caring. Even so he missed her tender warmth when she removed her ministering fingers.

'Lena could poison us all with this coffee,' she mentioned.

Over the airwaves the sound of his name concentrated his senses. '*Brigantia* here, over.' He responded to Tilly's voice requesting contact.

'I'll get right to it Zander. There's no sign of Daisy here. Over.'

'S'ok, Till, not expecting any news your end, I'm sure she's with Jack. Over.'

'She's been fascinated with him and Cloris lately, calling her Nana. Over.'

'Keep looking Till. Over.'

'The police are all over the place and Tony's organised a search party. We're all trying Zander. Over.'

He didn't know what to say. He thanked her and they said goodbye.

The cabin became quiet again. Zander was numb, steering on automatic. Despite his assurances to the contrary, hearing Tilly's voice had re-introduced the possibility of Daisy not being with Jack and he couldn't get the idea out of his head. What if he was entirely on the wrong track? He had no hard evidence that she was on board the *Mirabel*, just a feeling, or was it only hope that was driving him away from Mallorca, away from the other explanation, that perhaps someone had kidnapped her? His fingers gripped the mug so tightly he broke the handle and scalding liquid scattered across the deck. He had to get away from these pinging and whistling, useless instruments that were no help whatsoever.

He staggered to the door and let the rain beat on his face. At the rail he watched the storm rage at the sea and heard it snarl back. After some time he found his heart rate had slowed and his hands no longer gripped the rail with manic force. He saw Lena take command and Krista joined him on deck. Conversation was unnecessary and a silence settled easily between them. The crew changed watches and the ship ploughed efficiently through the waves. Zander was grateful for Krista's quiet company.

Finally, the sun, all conquering, rose at about five thirty and banished the storm. The clouds faded to grey and retreated to the Sierra Morena mountains and dry heat from the sheltered Portuguese plains wafted over them, bringing the keen scent of growing things. Lena insisted Zander rest but he was unable to leave the deck, instead he slumped in the bows, among neat coils of rope. Krista disappeared for a while and just when he thought she'd deserted him she returned showered and changed and bearing coffee and bacon butties. He could neither rest nor eat. Contenting himself with a frayed piece of rope end to mend, he stood, his hands occupied and his eyes forever on the sea.

After she'd eaten her sandwich, Krista asked 'Where's Daisy's mother?'

The question came at him from far away. It took a few minutes for Zander to return to the present. 'No idea.'

'Who is she?'

'Just a girl I met a couple a times.'

'How can you have a child with a girl you met a couple of times?'

'It only takes seconds Krista.' He focused on her face. Sometimes she was an ancient being who looked out of those dark eyes, a woman who knew the secrets of the ages and then it happened, a shift in her attitude that didn't seem deliberate more as if she just wasn't strong enough to maintain her guard and she became a child, scared of the dark. He touched her honey toned skin, soft and young, so young. He forced his thoughts away. 'We were sailing around in the Bahamas, sometimes we'd tie up, a few boats all together, we'd go ashore and party. We had sex. Nine months later I got a call from a hospital in Florida to say that I had a daughter.'

'How do you know she's yours?'

'Doesn't matter. I went to the hospital and there was a letter from the girl. She remembered far more than I did of those nights and was certain. She said she couldn't deal with a kid so it was my responsibility. What could I do? I held her in my arms and she was a skinny, puny, undernourished scrap who needed me. I looked after her in hospital for a couple of months then we came to Mallorca and here we are.'

'And it really doesn't matter?'

'No.'

'Is that how parents are made?'

'Maybe, some of them.'

'Will you ever have a test done?'

'Why would I? I'm Daisy's Dad, she's my little girl. We're a family.'

'Is that why Jack doesn't talk to you?'

'No, that has nothing to do with Daisy. I don't know why he's like that. He refuses to discuss it.'

'Is he the reason you're such a good Dad for Daisy?'

This girl was too astute for Zander's present state of mind. He felt uncomfortable under her scrutiny. Hauling himself to his feet he made for the wheelhouse, but was thwarted by Lena, who threw him a look that warned him to stay clear.

'If you won't sleep at least go and have a shower. You stink.'

He was thinking of something to say when the radio called them in. It was Olly on the *Fantasy*. He'd seen the *Mirabel* sailing out of Alvore only an hour ago. He was sorry to be so late calling in, but he'd been to Marrakech and ... Zander broke into his travel bulletin to ask if anyone had sighted Daisy on board, but Olly said no, only two men. They hadn't approached because they weren't aware of any problems.

The *Brigantia* erupted into action, Lena calling orders that turned them away from Capo de Roca, where they'd been preparing to round into the Bay of Biscay. Expertly they came about and beat back to the Algarve. Half an hour later they spotted the *Mirabel*.

ADAM

Daylight drilled holes in Adam's brain and movement was almost impossible, still his body tried to rouse itself. His head felt twice as heavy as it should and pain laughed at his futile attempts at normality. Lurching like the drunk he was it took more than just effort to drag himself upright and open his eyes. The café was empty but daylight streamed in through the open door, laughter and loud friendly voices. Why do these Mediterranean types have to shout all the time, he asked himself. Staggering outside he squinted at the harbour scene where the tourists were thronging the jetty, queuing for boat rides. The storm had left a day scoured clean and bright, too bright. Fumbling in his pockets for sunglasses he headed for the *Mirabel*. Jack was paying the old fisherman who stuffed the hefty bundle of pristine notes into his oily dungarees. They said their farewells and as Jack disappeared into the cabin the old man almost knocked Adam over with a hearty clap on the shoulder and yelled farewell in his ear.

Mumbling goodbye, Adam stepped gingerly aboard and felt his cautious way for'ad where Jack was watching him with a grin on his freshly shaved face. Rubbing his own neglected beard Adam lowered himself to the seat. 'Christ! What did I have to drink last night?'

'Vino Verdi, his own brew.'

'You mean he drinks that stuff regularly,' Adam asked in disbelief.

Jack laughed at such naivety. 'Course not, he's not stupid. He just sells it.'

It was painful, but nevertheless Adam cast his eyes about him, hardly able to believe that so much work had been done while he'd slept. New sails were tied tidily to the booms and the loose wires, which had tangled around the instrument panel, were neatly tucked away with new connecters evident. Forcing himself aft he inspected the engine room where a gleaming pump and shiny engine parts filled him with confidence. This he could handle. This was a boat he could sail. In no time they were leaving harbour, headed for Cap de Roca and the open Atlantic.

The day was perfect for sailing with a light breeze sending them, albeit a bit sluggishly, over the waves. 'Could do with a bottom scrape.' Adam opined from his prone position on the deck.

Jack nodded. 'Have to wait till we get to the Tyne.'

'Cost a bit.'

'Evidently. Prices these days are shocking. I remember when I had her scra …'

Adam was glad the appearance of Cloris and Daisy distracted Jack. This time they were both sporting silver and turquoise jewellery. He turned to Jack. 'That stuff real?'

'What?' Jack was still in full flow about the time he had the boat overhauled in Taiwan. He followed Adam's gaze. 'Oh the baubles? Yes, Cloris was the mistress of a Saudi Prince when I met her. She's very good,' he chuckled.

'Evidently,' Adam remarked, thinking that it might be Cloris he needed to talk to about investing in Finefit.

Daisy climbed onto the deck and Adam sat up to be watchful. 'Don't go to the edge,' he warned.

She scorned his advice. 'I've sailed with Dad and he always lets me hang over the bow. Watch me.' And before he could stop her she was sitting in the catch net that hung over the bowsprit. 'Just be careful.' He supposed she was safe there, but moved to sit behind her with his back to the rail. After a while he dozed and was woken by Daisy shouting.

'Look, Look!'

Ghastly images of Sean and Harry shouting at him crowded his alcohol fuzzed mind. And he leapt up not sure what was happening.

'Look, it's Lena. Look.'

He followed Daisy's pointing finger to where, about half a mile away, the *Brigantia* was heading for them at a rate of knots. He struggled to his feet and was just in time to catch Daisy who was rushing about shouting and waving. He tied her to a line and headed for the cabin. 'Is the radio working?' But as he said the words he noticed that the ancient device was turned off. It was so old and the lack of computerised communications probably made it illegal but you never know; he reached over to switch it on. 'Lena's steaming hard at us, must be an emergency.' He gestured out of the cabin and as he did so Jack grabbed his arm.

'Leave it be. We don't want any interference. Cloris. Cloris,' he yelled

Cloris appeared, beaming and offering her lips for a kiss. Impatiently he shook his head. 'Get below. Take the child,' he ordered.

Then the truth dawned on Adam. 'Zander doesn't know you've got Daisy does he?' He was appalled. 'Does he?' He demanded an answer, but Jack simply hooked a rope to the king pin to steady the wheel and surprising agile for such a doddery old codger he ripped the wires from the radio. Pushing past Adam he then bustled Cloris into the galley. As he made to get hold of Daisy Adam got in front of him and sheltered her. 'Have you gone insane? You can't just take off with someone's child.'

'She's my grandaughter and I'll thank you to mind your own business.' Jack spat the words as he made a grab for Daisy. 'Come here Daisy. You need to look after your Grandma.'

Daisy wasn't used to commands and constraints. 'I want to see Lena.' She scuttled away from both of them and hung over the taffrail waving to the *Brigantia,* which was having no trouble closing in on them, the *Mirabel* wallowing without a helmsman.

Adam watched as they turned about to come alongside. At the rail were Zander, Krista, Jazzy, Adalia and Beth all waving and shouting at once. In the clear air it didn't take long for him to understand they were asking if Daisy was alright. He waved back and then left the rail to go into the wheelhouse where Jack was spinning the wheel

'Get the mainsail up and rig the sailor,' Jack barked the orders at him.

It was obvious to Adam that Jack had lost his mind. He had to take control, so pushing Jack aside he hauled the wheel around to bring the little boat behind the wind and jumping on deck to lower the sail. He didn't see Cloris until she was swinging the big cast iron stew pan at his head.

ZANDER

For Zander the world had narrowed to only one point, Daisy. His daughter was standing at the rail of Jack's boat waving her thin arms, wiggling the tiny sticks of her fingers. Relief weakened his legs. Thank you God, he offered up a silent prayer. 'Daisy,' he yelled at the top of his voice. He waved.

Daisy was jumping up and down, shouting 'Daddy, Daddy.'

The girls were thumping his back in congratulation, everyone laughing and hugging each other. Daisy was safe. There was no sign of Jack, but he'd seen Adam jump into the deck well and now the little boat was swinging off its mad course, slowing to allow the *Brigantia* to close in. With the distance now narrowing to about thirty meters Lena was shouting orders to the girls who left him to shorten sail and heave the buffers over the side, she meant to get close and personal and so did he. Relief at finding Daisy safe gave way to anger at Jack, Zander's fists bunched at the thought of him. His own father! How could he put him through such agony and how could he take Daisy into danger in an unseaworthy boat. He waved to Daisy again and happiness flooded through him.

Krista put an affectionate arm about his waist. 'You've made her into such a fearless little adventurer.'

He shook his head. 'She has no boundaries. Not yet, but I'm going to change all that.'

'Don't change her too much. Let her grow.'

Despite his intention to clip Daisy's wings Zander was secretly pleased, proud of her independence. As the gap narrowed he could hardly wait to hold her and then he'd never let her go, but his pride gave way to horror as Daisy, loosening the gate, stood poised on the edge of the deck.

'I'm coming Daddy,' she shouted.

As one, Zander and Krista shouted, 'No!' but heedless of the danger, Daisy jumped into the sea. Zander dived in, struck out to where she thrashed about, her skinny arms beating the water. Diving under he forced his body forward. Beside him he felt someone else, but was concentrating on reaching Daisy. Surfacing for air he saw Krista in front of him, her strong shoulders leaping and glistening, seawater droplets raining down on him as she forged through the swells. Filling his lungs he dived again. When he surfaced Krista and Daisy were gone. He spun around, the water ahead of him churned and bubbled, he lurched at the disturbance, forced his body down into the clear sea. In the melee bubbles churned and fizzed; Daisy, Krista and other shapes, indistinct and weightless and his own limbs flailing. His lungs bursting he broke the surface and this time Krista was ahead of him, she held Daisy in her arms. Daisy's tiny heart-shaped face was white, her dark hair lank, like weed, and as they moved with the rhythm of the waves the two of them seemed to dissolve. Moments later they reappeared and he had reached them. He looked for the other swimmers, but they were gone. He held his daughter and searched for the *Mirabel*, surely nearer than the *Brigantia*, but she was cutting through the sea away from them, but Krista was there, on the other side of Daisy, pointing to the *Brigantia*. Together they held Daisy and swam on. Sometimes they were in a trough and it seemed that help was far, far away and then a rush of water and strong forces propelling them forward, closer and closer to safety and with his mind numb from fear Zander allowed himself to be guided by many hands.

Krista got them to safety where the girls were waiting to pull them aboard and Jazzy immediately knelt over Daisy who lay on the deck water streaming from her. Breathing into her mouth turning her little body into the recovery position and depressing her chest with a knowing hand, Jazzy was relentless. Zander tried to intervene, but the girls held him back. They were right. Jazzy was in control, she knew what she was doing. He knelt at Daisy's feet stroking her legs and calling her name until finally she moved her hands, coughed, vomited and sat up all at once and everyone cheered.

'Hi Dad. Did you see the mermaids?'

Even though everyone offered to sit beside the little girl Zander wouldn't leave her. Exhausted, she lay in her bunk, arms spread wide above her head, legs splayed and the duvet kicked aside, trusting, too trusting. She had no conception of danger. Because she had always lived in the shelter of happy people and trusted friends, had never mixed with children her own age or been subjected to the wider world she saw only good and she had wanted to be with her grandfather. Zander was filled with conflicting emotions. Absurdly grateful to the heavens above and all under them for the safe return of his daughter he raged against Jack. What had he been thinking? And why hadn't Adam done anything to help them. He must have known they were all frantically searching for Daisy. And why had he colluded with Jack to flee the scene, haring off in that leaky old tub as if the devil was on their heels, although he might well have been because Zander was still unclear just what he'd have done if he'd got his hands on them. A movement beside him didn't even turn his head, but he knew it was Krista. She placed a plate of sandwiches and a mug of coffee beside him, then sat and passed a gentle hand over Daisy's brow, smoothing the rats-tails hair, still wet from the hot shower Jazzy had insisted on. He took her hand and raised it to his lips. She tasted of the sea; salt and energy, mysterious, all healing and powerful. 'I didn't thank you.'

'No need.'

'Who else was there?'

'Just us Zander, just you and me.'

'No.' He turned to look into her dark brown eyes, again feeling that she knew things he'd never imagine. 'No, there were others, I saw them.'

A slow smile played around her full lips. 'Just your imagination. You needed help so you conjured it up.'

He shook his head and knew he was about to sound like a fool. 'Daisy said there were mermaids.'

'There are stranger things than a child's fantasies. Especially in the sea.'

She stood and walked away, swaying easily to the rhythm of the rolling ship and despite thinking that he'd never again concentrate on any thing or person other than Daisy he felt his body respond to this amazing girl who was the strangest being he'd known. And somehow, because of Krista, he believed in Daisy's mermaids.

As the days fled effortlessly past and they got closer to England he and Krista became closer, caring for Daisy and talking far into the starry nights, telling each other stories of days under sail, avoiding anything personal.

CHAPTER NINE

TILLY

After an emotional conversation with Zander, Tilly left the harbour master's office and headed back to the house on Pine Walk, where she sat at the kitchen table, sobbing for the safe rescue of Daisy and the deceit of a husband she'd thought she knew; she implored the fates to provide a safe harbour for them.

The jostling footsteps of Sean and Harry warned her of their progress down the street. They always pushed each other aside to be first through the door, funny, but they never did that at home, it was just a holiday thing, a thing they'd remember when they reminisced over a pint when they were grown, something that time would transform into a family tradition.

She had memories of her own from this magical island, memories that would inevitably soften with time and be remembered as amazing experiences, but at the moment only recollections of hot musty afternoons in Zander's bed disturbed her. She had been merely using time, selfishly indulging herself while her family disintegrated around her. Adam wasn't alone in being to blame for the mess they were in. She had known the business was failing, but had allowed it, busying herself as the model home-maker and mother. She had also known that the intimate relationship she and Adam had once enjoyed didn't exist ... and finally she admitted it. They had drifted into routine and she'd been happy to ignore it, using bed-time to say goodnight and have a cuddle.

Taking a deep breath, she chided herself for wallowing in self-pity. This had to stop. Nothing would be achieved if she allowed herself to weep and wail. One thing that would sustain her was her goal. A week ago she was a confidant woman who had closed a difficult deal to sell something she hadn't even made yet. She was still that person. She could rise above this. She would set things in motion as soon as she got home. In her wildest dreams she had imagined her bags would be hugely popular and she'd be head of a multi-million-pound business. This dream still had the potential to turn her life around. Using the hem of her skirt to dry her face, she stood up, hiding her devastation from the boys by pulling vegetables from the fridge.

'We've been under every single boat on the beach and no sign.' Sean hurled himself at her, cuddling her hard.

'She might have gone up to the fort. We were playing there the other day, we were spies and plotted a way into the place.' Harry pointed to the security tight villa on the mountain top. 'You see, if you go around the back of the seaplane hangar and up …'

Tilly interrupted. 'S'ok boys, Daisy's safe. She was with Jack. I just heard from Zander.' Harry wrapped his skinny arms about her and she folded them both to her, thanking God for the huge responsibility they were, for the privilege of having them to love. She kissed them and they all squeezed each other as hard as they could. 'You've been so worried haven't you?' She held them away to look into their eyes, two sets of the same blue as Adam's, but bright and lively. 'Oh darlings.' Almost choking with love, she hugged them again and they hugged her back, again.

Sean pulled away first. 'Where's Dad? Did they find Dad?'

This was hard. 'Yes, he's safe. He's safe with Jack and Cloris too. Lena's certain that some repairs have been done on the *Mirabel*, reckons there's definitely a new sail, at least.'

'Why didn't he let Zander know about Daisy?' Harry, ever thoughtful.

She could lie. She could make excuses about broken radios and obsolete equipment but she didn't. She shook her head. 'I don't know, pet.'

'Maybe he was drunk and fell asleep.' Sean remarked.

Not accusatory, just as a matter of fact. "From the mouths of babes," Tilly almost heard her mother's voice. She took a deep breath. 'Well there's only one thing to do.' She teased them, deliberately slow, pretending to think, with her head on one side and a finger against her chin … 'As everyone in the world is heading for the Tyne I think we'd better go home.' She expected groans of dismay and the usual delaying tactics of listing all the things they had yet to do, the people yet to see, but it didn't happen; they pushed each other out of the way challenging and daring, bragging that each of them would be packed first. Tilly picked up the house phone and dialled the number for Palma airport, reservations, Palma to Newcastle, as soon as possible.

The house in Sea View was a three-storey end of terrace with a tiny strip of sandy garden in front, none at the side. At the back of the house, bounded by high brick walls, ran a two hundred feet strip of garden with double garage and yellow painted wooden gate that everyone used instead of trailing around to the front door. When packing in Mallorca, Tilly had been unable to find the documents and keys for her car, waiting in the car park at Newcastle airport, and surmised that Adam had taken them. So they'd piled their stuff into a taxi and despite directing the taxi driver to the back entrance he pulled up on the private road in front of the house. Tired from the hectic day all Tilly wanted to do was get in and sag into the familiar. She and the boys manhandled the luggage while the driver sat impassive, staring at the sea. Tilly paid him and even gave him a tip. She would have to stop these impulses. There was no money. She had to get used to cutting corners. The sun was setting behind them and she turned her back on it to look at her favourite view in all the world.

To her left were the dunes and long sandy beach that stretched to the little village of Cullercoats, once the haunt of eighteenth century artists and before them infamous customs officers who hid their booty in deep caves beneath the sandstone cliffs; the bright orange roofs of the few original cottages were darkening to rust in the dying rays. Beyond them the tall white structure of St Mary's lighthouse at Whitley Bay shone rosy pink in a purple sea. But it was to the right that Tilly most often turned her gaze, to where high cliffs sheltered the little coves of King Edward's Bay and The Haven and above them to where the towering ruins of an ancient priory pointed to heaven. Around these ruins massive stones were all that remained of the walls and broken battlements of a Norman castle and behind these formidable structures she could picture another small bay and two massive, mile long piers that sheltered the harbour at the mouth of the surging Tyne. In front of her, two sailing ships were anchored off, in the lanes, their keels too big to negotiate the deadly Black Midden rocks near the entrance to the river at this, the low tide, but as she watched a cheeky schooner tore past them, gleeful in its momentary superiority. One bright morning, in about a week's time, she'd look out and see the *Brigantia* and maybe the *Mirabel*. She wished them both God Speed.

A voice behind her chased away her fancies.

'You're back. You should have told us.'

She turned, surprised to find her father-in-law in her front garden. The boys were already hugging their grandfather. 'Robert! How nice. But how, I didn't know …' Her voice tailed off, questioningly, because she had no idea why he was there.

'Thought I'd just do a bit of tidying.' Robert gestured to the secateurs in his calloused hands and the neatly trimmed honeysuckle around the wooden arch of the porch.

She nodded. He had a set of keys and she knew he kept an eye on the place when they were away. As they spoke, two little boys, kicking a ball on the grassy space between their private road and the busy coast road, came running up and hung about the gate, silently inquisitive. They were Lonore's twins, Adam's twins, his second set. Who knows, there might even be a third set somewhere. What a joyous thought. And speaking of thoughts how could she have forgotten that Lonore would still be here. 'She's still here?' she asked an embarrassed Robert.

'I'll just take the boys on the beach, bit of a kick-around. Four hours is a long time for a lad to sit in airports and planes.' He ushered the four boys away, down to the long stretch of sand.

Leaving the suitcases on the pavement, Tilly entered her house.

From the kitchen, heavenly aromas of slow stewing beef and herbs filled the air and through the stripped pine doorway, Lonore bustled into the hall.

'Tilly!' She exclaimed. 'How nice to see you. Why didn't you let us know you were coming? Robert could have met you.'

Tilly looked about her. This was her home, wasn't it? 'Didn't think I needed to let anyone know I would be arriving at my own house whenever I chose.' She returned to the street to pull in the first of the three huge cases.

'Well of course.' Lonore followed and grabbed the second case. Hauling it she pulled behind Tilly and into the hall. 'Just put it there.' She pointed to Tilly's burden and returned for the third piece of luggage.

Tilly thought she just might push the door shut and lock it. She even half stepped to do it, but Lonore was bumping the unwieldy and heavy case through and had her back turned. Maybe I could just stab her. Is there time to get a knife? Tilly turned towards the kitchen.

'Oh my dear, you're so confused. What you need is a nice cuppa and a piece of farmhouse fruit loaf.'

Tilly felt Lonore's hand in the small of her back, welcoming her into the kitchen.

'Here sit down.' Lonore pulled out a chair at the long refectory table, one of eight chairs that Robert, an expert carpenter, had crafted as a wedding present for her and Adam almost eighteen years ago. They were almost unrecognisable. The plain oak chairs sported gay cushions in a variety of pinks and purples and down the centre of the usually bare table a silk patchwork runner of the same colours was laden with an assortment of Tilly's treasured crystal vases, all of them sporting various grasses and flowers plucked from the dunes. Didn't look like the home-maker's conscience extended to conservation then. She watched as Lonore filled the kettle and busied herself with teabags and mugs, pouring milk and adding sugar without asking. At least she wasn't using the Monique Lhuillier china.

Keeping her back turned she spoke. 'Something's happened.'

'Only one thing?' Tilly couldn't keep the sarcasm from her tone.

'Well obviously lots of little things have happened, but the important thing is the business.'

'And who's business would this be?'

Lonore's big brown eyes stared at her. This women, whatever else she may be, was not afraid of confrontation. Had Tilly misjudged her?

'Our business Tilly, the business that has fed and clothed all of us and kept a roof over our heads for many years.'

Tilly was determined not to be browbeaten. 'You mean our business, Finefit, the business Adam inherited from his parents, my mother and father–in–law.'

'You're not helping.'

'I'm way past helping, could say I'm up to downright hindering, even obstructing.' Suddenly she didn't want anything more to do with Lonore and her children. She stood and walked to the doorway from where she paused and turned to face the woman who was attempting a *coup*. 'I'm going for a walk and when I come back to my house, understand that, *my house,* you'd better not be here. I've had it. Do you understand?'

'It's half past eight at night – where will we go?'

It was all too much for Tilly. She had no answers or compassion. 'I don't fucking well care.' And with that she stalked off, out of the door, across the grass, over the road, then slipping and sliding down the dunes until she finally came to a stop in the tall grasses that hid her from view. It was the last week of August and despite daylight saving it got dark at nine o'clock and a chill wind ruffled the North Sea.

Robert's head appeared at the top of the deep dune, now his shoulders. He waved. 'Come up here lass, I need to watch the lads.'

Sighing she pushed herself to her feet and scrambled up the side of the final shifting sand hill. She sat beside him and together they watched the four boys kicking a ball on the hard packed sand; the sea was just beginning to stir itself to return to the beach, a subtle shift, that only sea-born people notice. The moon was almost full, maybe four more nights. Mai had said that Tilly was a moon child and if she would only accept it and allow it to guide her she would be a calmer, more fulfilled woman. Tilly had always scoffed at this prediction. She was a calm person. Well, usually. 'What are you doing here, Robert?'

'That's the sixty-four-thousand dollar question.'

'Not that you're not welcome, but, I mean what are you doing here now, when you thought we'd all still be away. Why are you here ... with her?'

'Better hang on to your hat lass, there's a lot to tell.'

'Robert, I've just returned from a very tiring flight with two restless boys whose father betrayed and then abandoned us. My daughter is on the edge of a nervous breakdown, my friend's daughter has been missing for forty-eight hours in a leaky boat, in a storm, my husband has another woman and two sons, my father-in-law is obviously also betraying me with this woman and nothing can make me feel any worse than I do right now.' Tilly ended her tirade.

'OK, but don't say I didn't warn you.'

Tilly wasn't in the mood to be warned, and she began to get to her feet, but Robert pulled her back.

'Hear me out.'

A frustrated sigh gave her time to settle down, a bit. On the beach the boys were now on the very last rocks, dancing about, daring the incoming tide. She wasn't worried. They were sensible and this was a long-standing game. But this time they had two smaller versions of themselves teetering back and forward in the low wash; they were passing on a family tradition. 'We'd better walk down there.'

Robert looked and agreed. Together they slid down the dune and not until they were on the level beach did he speak. 'I'm staying in your house because I allowed my son to mortgage my home and now it's been repossessed by the same bailiffs who repossessed the factory and the house in Syon Street. Adam has been declared bankrupt.'

Tilly's anger was replaced by hopelessness. It rolled over her in a huge breath-taking wave from which she thought she would never emerge.

'What else could we do Tilly? I telephoned Adam and he thought it best for us to just sit it out until he got back.'

'And then he ran away, just like he always has. Why have we let him get away with it all these years?'

'Because we love him.'

'Loved, Robert, past tense. I don't feel anything for him any more, except frustration, anger, even hate. And when he gets back he and the fabric softener and their kids and you, can all find somewhere else to live and good luck to the lot of you.'

'We don't have the means to rent anywhere. The bailiffs have frozen our bank accounts and you can't throw us out of Adam's house.'

'Didn't you wonder why they didn't repossess Sea View?'

'I just assumed they have to leave you with a roof if there're children involved.'

'All these years and Adam has had you believing that he owns it. Well that's just Adam all over isn't it, bigging himself up. Sea View belongs to my mother. My grandmother left it to her. It's the house my mother and I were born in. Adam and I have always just rented it from her and she's been very generous about it.'

Robert stopped at the edge of the dry sand, his shaking hands outstretched in appeal to – what? Tilly felt so sorry for him. He'd lost everything and now it would appear that he'd lost his son, at least the son he'd imagined. He'd always thought Adam was clever, had engendered high hopes for him, but they'd been built on Adam's own opinion of himself.

She herself had been similarly deceived and had also ignored this deceit as long as her plan was still in place, but now there was only chaos. She watched the sea, unchanging yet in constant flux; like life she supposed. No matter how carefully we set a smooth course there were strong currents forever in motion, the cosmos in control. How pitiful to believe she could order her own and the lives of all the people she felt responsible for. The fates laughed at such puny efforts and moved the circumstances to suit their own whims. Maybe her mother had got it right with her acceptance of nature and all its mysteries.

At least with Tote-Tilly she could start again, for herself and the children. The rest was up to Adam. She hugged Robert and keeping her arm about his waist urged him forward. 'Come on, let's get the boys, all of them. We can sort things out after we've all talked, but not yet Robert. I'm too angry.'

'There's something else.'

'Oh God, don't tell me you and Jack plan on sailing the wrong way around the world and you want me as a campaign manager.' She smiled at him, but his grim expression didn't soften.

'There was a call from Michael Connelly.'

'He's cancelled the order.' This was a feasible guess after all that had happened.

'No, no, he was just checking that all was going as planned.'

'Thank goodness, at least that will be a source of income.'

Robert was a blunt-speaking man, he never hemmed and hawed; he got right to the point. 'The thing is Tilly, your new machines were delivered and I was at the factory at the time so I just accepted them and they were still in there when it was sealed up. I've tried explaining to the bailiffs, but they just won't listen.'

This was too much. Tilly couldn't take any more. 'Will you take the boys home. I need to walk.' And knowing she could trust her father-in-law to make sure the boys were safe, she turned toward the high cliffs and the towering ruins of the old priory.

CHAPTER TEN

LENA

Navigating Falmouth Harbour needed concentration of the keenest sort and Lena was a master of the art. The sea-lions barked a welcome from their homes on the outlying rocks as the *Brigantia* sailed past and into the estuary. The river Fal was busy with boats of all shapes and sizes, their owners, taking advantage of a stiff westerly breeze, skimmed the sun dappled waters. The new marina had been purpose built to cater for mega yachts and there was plenty of sea room, but only after Lena had eased her treasured craft safely into a berth did she breathe a sigh of relief. In Falmouth a tall ship is not a rare sight, but every one of them is unique and always causes a stir. After detailing Zander and Krista to stay aboard, to keep the more inquisitive at arms length, she and Jazzy headed off to meet Cary. She needed to talk to him without Krista around. The rest of the crew called goodbyes as they forged past, eager to let off steam after a gruelling run up the Bay of Biscay and across the Channel. The sun was high and a perfect day spread out around them, seagulls and trippers, fish and chips from the Harbour Lights restaurant, candy floss and a Punch and Judy; it was all so English.

'How do you feel after all these years away?' Jazzy eyed her quizzically.

'Odd, but, you know, somehow it's relaxing and there's still that sense of homecoming.'

'You aren't too keen on going up to the Tyne though.'

'One of these days you'll cut yourself you're that sharp.'

'Stop joking about it. I know you're a bit anxious.'

'Yes, well, things best forgotten tend to rise up and bite your bum when you stir up the past.'

'Specifically?'

'You know?' She shrugged the problem away. 'Anyway, what about you, how do you feel?'

'Different for me, being an army brat. We never stayed in one place long enough to call it home.'

Lena knew that Jazzy didn't really miss her parents and a

younger brother, who had all settled in New Zealand, because she kept in touch. Three years ago they'd even made the trip in the *Brigantia*. It had taken them almost eleven months easy sailing, there and back, and it had been a wonderful time they both treasured and Jazzy had flown there last year on her own to celebrate the birth of a new nephew.

'England was never home to me.'

'Where is home to you, pet? Where do you get that sense of belonging, that feeling of the familiar, the place that even with your eyes closed you feel you've arrived?'

'In my pub, in Pollensa with you. That's my place.'

Lena hugged her close. 'I love you, Jane Wilson?'

Jazzy was busy waving, but she flashed a smile and Lena's heart tingled. She wanted to get her alone, to strip her naked and make love to her, something hard to achieve on a boat with seven crew members swarming about. She followed the line of Jazzy's eager gaze and there, sitting at a table outside the tall, pink Quayside Inn with a foaming tankard in one of his fists was a big burly man with a mass of unruly black curls and a glinting ornament in his ear, The Pirate of Falmouth, Cary Innes. They hurried forward and soon the three of them were sharing enthusiastic hugs. Under his easy-going manner, the women could see a deep yearning to accept the fact of his grandfather's death.

They ordered drinks and as foaming pints were quaffed they gossiped about the sea-faring community until Lena could hide her curiosity no longer. 'Enough of these nonentities. What about yourself? I can't believe these tales of you anchoring yourself to a bothy in the hills.'

Cary looked pained. 'True enough, but not in the hills. I'm still in the cottage on the beach.'

Both women looked concerned, but it was Jazzy who reached out and stroked his weather-beaten face. 'Come on lover, tell us all about it.'

'You know. You know! Everybody knows I've turned into a landlubber.'

Never shy of coming forward Lena let him have it straight. 'It's being said.'

'You know that grandfer died?'

They nodded, waited.

'He just went out. In a storm one night, took the gig and didn't ever come back.'

'You lost the gig as well!' Lena tried to lighten the mood.

Cary knew her well, he took no offence. 'Yea, bloody inconsiderate of him, wasn't as if he needed it, they would have guided him. He only had to swim out, but he were a daft old buggerr, never did learn any sense.'

'Not that old story again.' Lena was exasperated. She picked up a menu.

'I know you don't believe sea lore, Lena, but 'ere in Cornwall, we do.'

She knew he did. He always said his own grandmother had been a kelpie and one day she would come for him just as she'd done for his grandfather and his father, also drowned when boson of a lifeboat that saved ten men and lost just the one.

'He waited didn't he? Waited and she didn't come for him.' Jazzy was enthralled with the tale. 'He was impatient and went out to find her?'

'Weeks before, and he watched the sea. Day and night, trolling back and forth in the gig or trudging across the sands, rain hail and snow, storms and sunshine, he spent every hour of every day watching. He weren't ill, just tired. He'd tell me he were sick of living, it was time to go and he waited until I was stuck in harbour up at Portsmouth and he went out there in a force nine. It just swallowed him up.'

'And you let that put you off and give the *Genista* up for sale!' Lena was nothing if not practical.

'Yep.'

'What a crock of shit!'

'Seriously, but no takers. Nobody's got any money.'

'So you've just berthed her out there all alone.' She pointed across the harbour to where Cary's brigantine, the *Genista*, lay in the Carrick Roads, her distinctive green and yellow paintwork shining in the sun and the twin masts swaying as the anchor pulled her back against the tide. 'Just shows doesn't it?' To Lena, watching eagerly for her food to appear, it was all too simple.

'Shows what?' Jazzy was scathing, her sympathies with the troubled man sitting between them.

'That the *Genista*'s Cary's. She won't be lucky for anybody else, nobody'll buy her, more than their lives're worth.'

'Thought you didn't hold with sea lore?' Jazzy reminded her.

'Plain as the nose on your face.' Lena sat up straight as a steaming bowl of Stargazy Pie was placed in front of her. She tucked a napkin into her shirt and picking up her knife and fork attacked the gastronomic delight with relish.

Jazzy turned her nose up at the fish-heads poking through the golden pastry. 'She will eat anything,' she told Cary, squeezing a drizzle of lemon over at her own dish of Sole Meunier.

Lena shrugged. 'Best Stargazy in the world here. Leaving your phobias aside ...' She pointed a fork at Cary, who was easily demolishing a platter of battered cod and sizzling golden chips. 'Tell me about Krista.'

'She's a strange little thing.'

'Not so little, she's a big lass by anybody's standards,' Lena amended.

'Have you seen her swim?' he asked them.

'She won the Bay Race.' Jazzy informed him.

'Not surprised. I've seen her swim the Channel.'

'Anyway?' Lena prompted him.

'It was up at Shields, I was wanting a couple of crew to come south and she applied. I chased her, but she wouldn't take no for an answer. Sat on the quayside for days and days, a scruffy kid, but with an independence I'd not come across in anyone so young. And she wouldn't move. I'd wake up at all hours of the night, restless, and go on deck and there'd she be, still sitting on the quay ... waiting. It were eerie. Like she had some sort of power over me.'

'It's called sex,' Jazzy mentioned, casually.

But it wasn't casual to the handsome sailor. Vehemently he denied any such thing. 'She's just a kid! I never thought of anything like that!'

Jazzy shook her head at the insensitivity of men. 'I meant her, you dolt.'

But again he shook his head, his shiny black curls bouncing like a shoal of live things disturbed from their lair. 'No. She thought I was her old man, her Dad. Can't think what put such a notion in 'er 'ead, but I've since learned she get these obsessions. She's a rum creature. She purely is.'

'I still haven't got her passport. Swears she left it on Olly's boat and he'd sailed before she remembered. I wasn't worried, knew he'd be back, but then we had Zander's emergency to deal with and I forgot.'

Cary shook his head. 'I got your e-mail, but no, I don't have it.'

'I'm hoping the harbour master here in Falmouth has it, otherwise it'll give her problems. I told her this, but it doesn't seem to be an issue with her, she treats it as if she doesn't need to abide by the same rules as the rest of us. Have you met her family?'

'No. The only one she ever mentioned is an aunt who, according to Krista, is a bit of a tart, always drunk.'

'Do you know her name, the aunt?' Lena asked as she pushed her empty dish away.

'Rita, Yvette, something like that.'

Lena felt a slight pang of panic, but hid it well, waving to the waiter for the bill. 'Wonder if that's why she hangs around Zander. Thinks he's her Dad?'

Jazzy laughed. 'You two are as bad as each other. If you can't sail it you don't notice what's under your nose. She fancies the pants off Zander.'

'She's seventeen?' Lena protested.

'Didn't you know about love when you was seventeen, my dear?' Cary parried.

This stilled Lena, she bent her head and said, almost to herself. 'Not love, no.' She was never comfortable discussing her feelings.

Cary stood and from his six foot two height he pulled the women up. 'Come on, it's too fine a day to be harking over the past. Besides it's been years since I was on the *Brigantia* and I haven't seen old Zander since we met up in Trinidad, over ten years ago.'

'He's got a little girl now.'

'Yes. We send the occasional e-mail and I've been monitoring the radio. And what's up with old Cracker-Jack?'

Laughing, Lena stretched out a hand for Jazzy. 'I haven't heard him called that for years. Anyway, let's go, we can't sit here boozing all day.'

'Why not, always used to.' Cary threw back his big head and his laugh echoed round the harbour.

Lena was aware of the passing of time, the good times and all the traumas they had endured. She realised that they were getting older far too fast. They paid the bar tab and the three of them set off, arm in arm, for the end of the quay. Cary had been Lena's friend for twenty-six years, she knew him better than anybody, and he knew her. He was only one of two people who knew the girl Lena had been. The other one was Mai, Tilly's mother.

At the *Brigantia* Cary spotted Zander and called out. 'Permission to come aboard skipper?'

'Ye old pirate! I thought you were dead. Permission granted,' Zander called and then Krista came forward and Daisy was introduced and much hand-shaking and hugging took place. Jazzy excused herself and retired to their cabin for a little sleep and Zander and Cary shared a bottle and caught up on each other's affairs since they last met in the warm Caribbean seas, where the girls were willing and Daisy was conceived

Lena left them to it and roamed the boat tugging on stays and tightening sheets. Then leaving the reunited pals she went below and woke Jazzy.

They made love in their little cabin with the soft lift and lilt of the water under them and a happy crew above and didn't emerge until Endora called all hands for dinner. After they'd eaten, Lena allowed them all ashore while she and Jazzy resumed their intimacies alone on the *Brigantia*. When a clear, half moon summer night displayed the stars above them, they sat on deck, tucked alongside the cabin wall, on the rubber mattresses used by the tourists for sunbathing on hot Mediterranean days.

'I'd better stow these now. Not many chances to sunbathe in the North Sea.'

'What made you come on this trip?' Jazzy broached the subject that had drifted like a fog between them since Lena had announced she was returning to Tyneside.

Lena shrugged.

'Come on, it's twisting you about day and night. You need to talk about it.'

'Nothing in particular, I just don't have any happy memories of the place.'

'Then why are we going? We can change course. We can go anywhere.'

'Too late now.'

'No it's not.'

'Right, we'll go to France. I love Bordeaux.'

'You're so full of it.' Jazzy shook her head. 'I despair of you. Why can't you face up to things? Whatever it is that's bugging you, you need to get hold of it.'

Lena looked into the past and saw a fat girl sitting on the edge of the school sports field, watching while the other girls played netball; a fat girl who was lookout while the girls fumbled with the rude boys, a fat girl who heard the rude things the boys shouted at her and when they got older the fat girl stole things to give as presents to the girls, and the boys still called obscene things after her. She saw the fat girl who was bullied and raped by those same boys while those same girls, watched and laughed. At home there was no welcome in the dank and empty house, her mother was touting for business in a back lane, drunk and neglectful, too wrapped up in her need for alcohol to care about Lena and a younger sister. Lena had haunted the filthy fish quay, a working quay then with the all-pervading stench of rotting fish and drunken foreign seamen. Occasionally ships like sea angels would furl their blinding white wings to enter the river and drift daintily between the smoke-blackened and rusting fishing fleet. Never stopping at Shields, they would sail up-river to Newcastle. The young Lena would hitch rides on a boat or hop illegally on the train to the city and run down to the quay where she'd sit day and night watching these tall ships, listening to the crews talking about journeys through the world's oceans. When they weighed anchor she would follow them to the mouth of the river and stand at the very end of the mile-long pier as once again their sails billowed into wings taking these magical vessels south to the sun and adventure.

After the rape and the baby, when she was no longer a fat girl, but a skinny waif slinking along the back lanes of Shields, hating herself more and more each day, she met Cary. They were both sixteen. The *Genista*, skippered by his grandfather, was one of hundreds of Tall Ships that had massed in the Tyne in preparation for the Cutty Sark Race. Lena was in heaven. She had never dreamed there were so many sailing ships in the whole wide world. Cary took her aboard the *Genista* and she never lived on land again.

'Hey, dreamy Dinah! Have you heard anything I've said?'

Jazzy brought her back to the present and the sounds of the crew returning stirred her into full wakefulness. In the middle of the singing, joyful crowd she saw Krista between Zander and Cary, another girl Cary had saved from the River Tyne. What was it about the sea that bound them all together? They were singing a song Cary had taught her years ago.

> *Most chivalrous fish of the ocean,*
> *to ladies forbearing and mild,*
> *though his record be dark*
> *is the man-eating shark*

> *who will eat neither woman nor child*
> *He dines upon seamen and skippers*
> *and tourists his hunger assuage*
> *and a fresh cabin boy*
> *will inspire him with joy*
> *if he's past the maturity age.*

They yelled the 'Rhyme of the Chivalrous Shark' in drunken harmonies; it was obvious they'd been with Cary's pals, the Falmouth Chanters. Stumbling aboard, they saluted her and Jazzy and after an admonition to be quiet, as other crews were trying to sleep, they all retired below decks to continue the camaraderie in the main cabin.

Cary was sober. He and Lena would take the first watch; even in port it was wise to keep a sharp lookout. With steaming mugs of coffee they settled in the wheelhouse and, just as she knew she'd be able to, Lena persuaded Cary to sail with them, but she detected a lingering reticence and while he went home to gather his gear she worried about him. She also worried about Krista, but so far the harbour master hadn't noticed her. That girl had the luck of the devil, or, if Cary was to be believed, the mermaids were watching out for her, shrouding her in a net of invisibility.

The morning dawned fine and clear and as they prepared to hoist the anchor and get under way, a Dorset gig came alongside, manned by the Chanters, all in good voice to sing them to sea.

Playing her part, Lena bellowed orders to her crew, sent them aloft to unfurl the sails ready to drop them when they reached the open sea. And even though modern technology would see them safely past the skimming launches and sail boards, she sent Beth and Daisy into the bow as lookouts. She still thought eyes were better than computers. And even though the anchor would wind in on the engine, the Chanters set them all working together on the chain with a rhythmic swing to the local version of 'Aweigh, Santy Ano.'

> *From Falmouth Town we're bound away,*
> *Heave aweigh, heave aweigh, Santy Ano*
> *Around the light of the Goodwin Sands*
> *For we're bound for North Shields town'o*
> *So heave her up and away we'll go*
> *Heave aweigh, heave aweigh, Santy Ano*
> *Heave her up and away we'll go*
> *For we're bound for North Shields town'o*

On each second line the crew echoed the words and pulled the sheets and the gleaming white canvas unfurled, until the men in the fast little gig fell away and their song grew fainter and fainter. Lena changed the heading to North, North West and pods of dolphins leapt and dived around them, escorting them into the English Channel.

Daisy hanging over the bow, in a life-jacket and tied to a safety line, called them to her. Her little face wreathed in smiles, she shouted to Krista. 'Hurry Krista they're calling for you.'

And, childlike, Krista too bent to peer into the glassy green waves.

Watching from the wheelhouse Cary looked worried. 'Be God that girl has a way with her.'

'They're just dolphins.' Lena was scathing.

"Use your eyes me dear, some of 'em have faces.'

'Rays.' She countered, not quite knowing why she was being so sour.

'Can you really not see the Others?'

'The mermaids.' She scoffed. She knew he wouldn't use their name, he considered it unlucky to talk about them when they were near. 'God! No wonder you're so morose, dwelling on stuff that like.'

'Lena, you've been at sea long enough to know that there are mysterious things in there.' He nodded to the water and handing her the wheel he waited, watching. 'Mind that heading, you're swinging to starboard.' Then he left the wheelhouse to join the girls in the bow.

Lena wouldn't allow his air of doom to infect her. He was just trying to get a rise out of her, and she knew his instructions were superfluous, they were dead on course. With a nod to Paulo, who stepped in to relieve her, she followed Cary on deck. By now a little knot of excited people was hanging over the side while Daisy pointed out the mermaids. Adalia and Beth professed to see them, but of course no-one else did. Lena joined in the fun, prepared to unbend and humour Daisy. She stood next to Cary. He was solemn and worried. He got like this whenever he convinced himself of the existence of mermaids, always wary of the warnings he said they brought. She felt him take her hand and heard him whisper to the air.

'Here she is at last.'

Lena almost burst containing the laugh that was about to explode, but as she peered into the water she was startled by what seemed to be a face peeping from under the biggest dolphin. She blinked and rubbed her eyes and looked again. It was a face. Someone was in the sea. Alarmed she called out. 'Man over ...' But her mouth was covered by Cary's big hand. She pushed him away, furious. 'Someone ...' She began again, but he just shook his head and laid a finger over his serious lips.

'Look again me dear, look again.'

Against her better judgment she directed her gaze back to the dolphins, still leaping and splashing, baptising them as Neptune ordered. She brushed sea water from her eyes and looked again. Sure enough it was a face and a body and a long sinuous tail lazily flicking this way and that in the stream of bubbles fizzing around the big, sleek mammals. But before she could turn to Cary, the figure disappeared and swiftly, flying and diving, the dolphins left them and the sea closed over its secrets, unfathomable once again.

Daisy's little voice called after them imploring them to come back. Then she rushed to Lena. 'They saw you, they saw you. Now you can talk to them.'

Lena walked back to the wheelhouse. She didn't believe in all this sea lore stuff, it was easily explained away, a reflection of one of the girls as she hung too far over the side, but she smiled at Daisy and told her, yes, she could now talk to mermaids.

The English Channel needs an experienced skipper so Zander, being more at home in the Mediterranean, allowed Cary to take the first watch. Frenetic shipping seemed to fill every inch of water, with ocean-going liners and weekenders all jostling for position. In summer every English man and woman swelled with the stout hearts of Nelson's sailors and the whole enterprise takes on a game of chicken. Another watch change and Lena did her trick at the helm. A pair of owls hitched a lift on the cross trees and a force four wind allowed perfect sailing at ten knots around the sandbanks of Dungeness Point. The crew showed off their skill and the two young men worked to maintain Lena's approbation and get them their First Mate's tickets. The wind zinged through the rigging as the *Brigantia* dipped and rose and all shipping, with bells and sirens, acknowledged her beauty which Lena accepted as her due.

Once past the South Goodwin, they suddenly lost the wind and a mist dimmed visibility. The sails were furled and under the engine they manoeuvred their way between giant container ships entering the River Thames. As night closed in and the owls flew off, Zander guided them around the East Goodwin buoy and at midnight the watch changed again, but Zander stayed in the wheelhouse at Paulo's shoulder, until the wind picked up again and they hoisted sail to take them speeding for the Norfolk coast.

Lena had been watching Cary. He wasn't the fearless buccaneer of reputation. He did all that was expected and when not on watch or sleeping he kept them entertained with shanties, but he eyed the sea warily and Lena noticed a hesitancy in his step that had never been there before, not even in the meanest of storms. He stood at the rail, his hands thrust deep into the chest pockets of his waterproof coat. Grabbing a couple of beers, she joined him. 'Night times are for sleeping.'

He twisted a grim smile, but it was an effort.

'We all have secrets Cary. You've always shared mine. I thought I shared yours.'

He took the offered beer, then, pulling his other hand out of his pocket, he opened his tight fist. A small tin lay almost crushed by the fierce pressure he'd exerted on it, a manifestation of his fear.

Taking the tin Lena prized it open and found inside a dried and wrinkled piece of skin. She knew what it was. 'A caul.'

'Grandfer's.'

Lena knew he believed that if a sailor is drowned without his caul about his person his soul cannot rest in peace, for the mermaids will keep it as a hostage until they drown another sailor. 'Why haven't you thrown it out before now?'

'I couldn't be sure they'd find it. I thought, as we pushed through the Channel, they'd give me a sign, but I can't be sure that the ones we've seen are friend or foe.'

This was way too much for Lena. 'I can't help you Cary.'

'I know. You've never believed in it all.'

'No and it's stopping you from facing up to the hurt you feel.'

'It's not just the hurt. I feel guilty. I should have been there to watch over him.'

'What rubbish. Don't you think it was his own selfish fault that he waited until you weren't there? Why didn't he think about how you'd feel?'

Cary's face shut down. 'I think that's why they're following me. Maybe it's my turn.'

'For Christ's sake Cary, will you stop this before you go mad. And I still don't see why you're determined to sell the *Genista*?'

'This is my last trip Lena. I wanted it to be with you. You sailed your first trip with him and we had to do a last one together for him. He loved you.'

'I know and I mourn him, but I still ...'

'I can't take the chance of ending up the same way.' He rummaged at his neck, under his waterproofs and came out with a tightly wrapped piece of canvas on a woven string. It was roughly the size and shape of a small sausage and tightly stitched in what sailors call 'tiddly fashion.' 'This is mine. If I was lost at sea how could I be sure it wouldn't get torn away? I have to stay ashore. I can't sail any more. I'm scared Lena.'

'Christ's sake Cary. Stop all this talk of dying.'

'What can I do about them?' He leaned over the rail and stared into the dark fathomless depths, where phosphorescence lit the churning waves. At sea, everything deceives.

'Don't ask me. Maybe you should talk to Mai.'

'Or Krista. She'll know.' And with that he headed for the cabins.

Alone at the rail Lena watched the lights of the oil rigs flash their warning; two short and one long, 'You are running into danger.' Never said a truer word, Lena thought and wondered at her friend's mood. She'd never seen Cary so lost.

CHAPTER ELEVEN

TILLY

The tide roared into the river, disturbing rafts of weed that surged about the rocks like mad women throwing out their arms in delirium. Tilly watched her mother who copied the action. Mai was on the treacherous Black Midden rocks where no sane person would venture, especially on a turning tide with the river and the sea fighting for supremacy. She was bent over, grappling with something under the water. She picked up a loose stone and began to bash and smash at something in the water. It would probably be some plant or other she needed for her potions, risking her life out there on the slippery stones with the water up to her knees and rising.

Tilly ran down the hill and along the concrete path where galvanised steel railings prevented her from jumping into the river and pulling her mother to safety. The rocks were only easily accessed from the little half moon beach at low tide so Mai must have been there for at least six hours. It was after eleven o' clock, dark, but lights from the fun-fair illuminated this corner of the river with bright colours, flashing in rhythm to the hysterical screams from girls being thrown round and around on the barely controlled machines. Mai could not hear Tilly shouting to her.

The path wasn't empty, a few couples were using it to get back and forth from North Shields to Tynemouth instead of trailing the long way around by the main road, but although one or two watched the mad woman in the river with curiosity no-one cared enough to wonder if she needed help. Unclipping a life-belt from its box, Tilly climbed over the railing and dropped onto the rocks. Immediately losing her footing, she fell, gasping as cold water engulfed her. Spluttering while instinctively trying to balance, she pushed herself up until she could cling to the sloping sea-wall, where she was still up to her thighs in the fast-flowing water that sucked at her legs, trying to pull her down and away. She wondered how her mother could stand so steadily. Calling out to her as she crawled and staggered forward, Tilly hung on to the lifebelt rope to steady herself and had managed to get within about four feet before Mai noticed her.

'Quick, quick, don't let them get away.' Mai called out while still kicking and bashing at something under the water.

Tilly saw a quicksilver flash of a white underbelly and one of those cartoon faces exposed by ray fish. She grabbed her mother's sleeve and overbalanced again.

Mai dropped the rock to reach out for Tilly. 'What on earth you doing out here?' she yelled.

Tilly was now hanging on to her mother with both arms around her middle while Mai still kicked and threshed about. 'Leave it,' she shouted, pointing to the sea, now rushing over the bar.

Mai ignored her pleas. 'That one's getting away,' she yelled in Tilly's face, and then screamed. 'You evil cow!'

'Mam! We have to go!' Briefly Tilly caught a glimpse of her mother looking surprised, as if noticing the incoming water for the first time.

With a final kick at the sliding mass of weed and dead flesh at her feet she turned and held Tilly up from the water. 'What were you thinking?' Mai asked as she guided them both towards the railings, gathering the lifebelt and its rope onto her strong free arm. 'Didn't you see the tide coming in? You were never much good in the water,' she admonished.

An elderly man had taken hold of the rope. He stretched down to help them up, then mumbling about irresponsible mad women, he replaced the lifebelt, before shuffling away.

Fighting for breath Tilly rounded on her mother. 'Me! What was I doing! You were on the rocks and the tide is coming in.' She flung her arm out to where the wide black sea rose, unstoppable waves surging up then sweeping down the granite walls of the river bank, consuming all in its path. 'What were you doing out there with the water rising?' She knew the answer, but to acknowledge the fact would be to buy into Mai's insane relationship with mermaids.

'Didn't you see them! No, you didn't. You don't look, that's your problem.' Mai pointed her freezing red hand to indicate the position where she'd been threshing and stamping. 'Coming right in! Brazen, evil little fiends, but I got one or two, they'll be quiet now for a while, but you know what they're waiting for, don't you?' She didn't wait for an answer, wasn't expecting one, it hadn't really been a question. 'They know the boats are on their way and they're waiting. The vicious little spawn!' She yelled a last insult at the water.

'Mam, you have to stop this insane obsession.' Tilly spoke knowing it was a waste of breath.

'You don't believe because you've never had personal experience. I've kept you safe, but just you be prepared, because one day, one day, they'll realise who you are and they'll be after you and yours, then you won't be so quick to laugh. No my girl you won't.'

Tilly couldn't be bothered with the old argument. She was barely holding her sanity together as it was. The events of the night were suddenly too much to handle and words of frustration burst from her. 'There're more important things threatening my family right now, I don't need fairy tales,' she shouted at her mother.

'Arh, I'm sorry pet. Come here.' Her mother pulled her close and smoothed her shaking shoulders with her large capable hands.

Tilly pulled away and set off along the path that lead to her long-ago home. She hadn't used this path, along by the river, for years. Tilly didn't like the river, but in the half darkness her feet remembered hidden dips and rises, she forged ahead, up the bank and inside the Brew House, where, as she could have predicted, Mai gathered towels and began to undress and dry her. 'I can do that myself.' Tilly took the towels and shivered into the bathroom.

Mai had always been a free spirit. It had never mattered to her who was in the house as she wandered from bedroom to bathroom naked, not flaunting herself, just a means to an end, getting from a to b without having to fuss about looking for a robe. But Tilly had not inherited this spirit of freedom, only Adam had ever seen her naked, oh, and Zander. It shocked her to realise she'd almost forgotten those passionate liaisons so quickly. Finding her mother's robe she slipped into it and suddenly she could feel her, smell her, relive the easy love Mai had always had in abundance, but somehow along the way Tilly had rejected it. Not completely, she did love Mai, but she was aware of her reluctance to accept her tactile affection.

'You all right pet? Need anything?'

There it was again – that mother thing, the thing that Tilly had certainly inherited, care that turned concern to interference.

Did her children also feel this compulsion to return her smothering love, just to please her, from a sense of guilt? Praying that it wasn't the case she shook the past out of her head and returned to the kitchen where her mother was warming her feet at the fire and sipping a glass of rich ruby red wine.

'There you are pet.' Mai pointed to a bottle and glass on a small round table beside the opposite chair, she had also made ham sandwiches and arranged them artfully on a plate with a few leaves of salad and chunks of cheese. All this while Tilly was in the bathroom.

Settling in the chair, Tilly realised how hungry she was and enjoyed the food and wine, allowing herself to relax.

'What are you doing wandering around the quay at this time of night?' Mai asked.

'I'm not a kid any more. I'm allowed to go out at night.'

'Yes, but you don't usually and certainly not down here.'

Tilly dipped her eyes.

'The other woman?'

It had always been impossible to fool Mai.

Tilly nodded and felt the tears ooze under her lashes.

'Arh, don't pet. He's not worth it.'

Suddenly she couldn't stop. For the first time in many, many years Tilly confided all her fears and emotions, her anger and distress to the woman she had tried to outgrow, her ever-patient mother. When the bottle was empty and all the secrets revealed Tilly was exhausted enough to allow Mai to lead her to her old bed and tuck her in, accepting the kiss and the blessing.

'God bless pet.'

The words floated down on fluffy clouds and lingered in Tilly's dreams.

Waking to a sunny, noisy morning Tilly lay still, listening to the work of the quay being shouted abroad. The fishing boats were unloading, and that meant it was early, about five or half past. The familiar enfolded her, enriching her spirit with tradition and permanence as it had never done when she was young, when she had scorned the Quay, wanting no part of Mai's bohemian existence. She allowed her eyes to wander; the room was different, redecorated and refurnished, but the bed was Tilly's teenage bed. A Slumberland she had insisted on, in favour of the futon from Ikea that her mother had wanted.

Not wanting to re-live the past, she had enough problems in

the present, she threw back the covers and dressed, noting that Mai had dried her clothes and left them ready on the chair, not ironed. Mai didn't do ironing.

The flat was empty, her mother up and out foraging for bread and other essentials, haggling for the best tasting bacon on Tyneside at English's Chandlery where Charley would sell her the goods a few pence under the asking price, but they both knew it was a game and he was still making a profit. From the window Tilly watched the quay, a few sail boats were in, - middle- sized, the bigger ones by-passing Shields for the deeper berths and bright lights of Newcastle. One or two fitness enthusiasts jogged along the river path under the high cliffs. A young lad loped down the grassy banks under Collingwood's monument attracted her attention. It was Harry. What was he doing out this early? She hadn't worried about leaving him and Sean in their own home. Robert was there and she could rely on him to care for them; it occurred to her that he would also care for his other grandchildren, Lonore's twins, Justin and Joseph, because that's what family did and however much it hurt and however much she hated to think of it she would eventually accept those two little boys who were half brothers to her own children; Lonore was a different problem altogether and would need much more charity of heart. Adam? She couldn't think about Adam.

A heavy sea fret was creeping in from a still sea. It would probably close the port down by midday. Mai was striding up the bank with a baguette under her arm. Harry saw her and shouted, waving and running madly towards her. When they met they hugged enthusiastically and continued walking, close together, bound by loving arms. Harry had always felt at ease with Mai, more so than Sean, but that was because Sean was fiercely independent and not because he loved his grandmother less than his twin did. Beth was a different matter, she wasn't close to Mai. Tilly felt an overwhelming shame as she realised that her inability to show love to her mother might be the cause of Beth's neglect. Had her reluctance to accept Mai's love deprived her daughter of a grandmother's easy support? Nothing could excuse it and it made Tilly feel less than she was.

When Harry rushed in he was telling his grandmother that he'd been talking to Beth on Facebook and they had all had such an adventure when Daisy had fallen overboard. 'Just like us she almost drowned, but the mermaids saved her, then one of them followed them 'cos Cary's on board and they're after him.'

'They're always after somebody, the bloody little upstarts,' Mai remarked. Breakfast would have been uneasy but for Harry who entertained his grandmother with all the gossip about their holiday. Then he escorted his mother home, insisting on the river path.

Visibility was poor, the mist shrouded the piers, the river was calm and still, the tide slack. Tilly couldn't understand why, sometimes, she felt mortally afraid of the sea.

The next few days were a sad time for Tilly. She tried to absorb the fact that Tote-Tilly was doomed. Without the industrial machines, she was unable to make the promised bags and what was more demoralising was that she couldn't be bothered. Lonore slipped into the role of housewife for their little disjointed family and Tilly didn't care. After the fret had rolled away with the tide, a heatwave pressed down on them, the days merging into one another, until one day watching over Harry's shoulder as he spoke to Beth on Facebook she realised the *Brigantia* would be in port the next day.

After the evening meal, Harry and Sean, following a strenuous day on the beach, were chilling out in the lounge, playing games on the X-box. Tilly envied them the carefree attitude of youth that enabled them all to form a friendly group, while she was hung up on the implications and legalities of this ménage. She couldn't imagine what they'd do when or even if Adam arrived – and Beth. Beth would find this situation intolerable. She had reacted so badly to the cruel discovery of her and Adam's infidelity, thrust so abruptly at her, that Tilly was unable to imagine how they were ever going to regain their former relationship. It was now in tatters.

The ringing doorbell stirred her from the kitchen table, which still wore the new covering, that matched the comfy cushions on the chairs. The bell rang and rang and no-one answered. Wearily Tilly pushed herself up and trailed to the door just as Lonore reached the bend in the stairs.

Two police officers nodded in friendly fashion. 'Evening. Is this the Maitland household?'

Behind her Lonore and Robert waited.

'Adam?' Tilly asked, but it was more curiosity than worry. Adam would be all right. He always was.

'Are you the keyholder of the factory on Tanners Road?' The little chubby officer consulted his notes. 'Finefit?'

'Er, no, not.' Tilly began to tell them about the repossession, but Lonore interrupted.

'That'd be me. Mrs Maitland. My husband Adam is away on business. Is there a problem?'

'I'm sorry, but there's been a break in. Can you come and check that everything's in order and make the place secure.'

'Yes. Of course. I'll get the keys. My father-in-law and I will meet you there.'

'Very well.' The officers moved away, back to their car, parked on the main road.

Tilly was amazed at the bare-faced nerve of the woman. Her indifference over the past few days fled out and away across the retreating sea as she shut the door and turned to face this usurper, this adulterer, this fabric softener. 'What the hell do you think you're doing?' She tried to pull away from Robert as he took her by the arm and pushed her along the hallway. 'Get off me!'

'Tilly, pet, calm down. It's all in hand.'

She fought the strong grip of her father-in-law and then as if recognising a liberating revelation. 'Yes! My father-in-law! Not yours,' she yelled at Lonore, who paused, halfway out the back door with her bag over her arm. The boys alerted by Tilly's raised voice came into the hall.

'What's up Mum?' Sean pushed between her and Robert, easing his grandfather's hand from her arm. 'Grandad, don't,' he appealed to him.

'Sorry son. Sorry Tilly, but it's all in hand.'

'I'm the key holder. I'm Mrs Maitland. And anyway the factory's sealed. It doesn't belong to us now.'

'Tilly. You trust me don't you?'

Robert was calm and dependable, of course she trusted him. 'I used to, before she, she …' Words failed her.

'Trust me Tilly. Please pet. Just stay here and let me deal with this. I promise we'll explain it all when we come back, but for now you have to let us go.' And with that he followed Lonore out of the door.

The boys went to bed, their heads filled with the next day's plans to teach the little ones how to surf. In the quiet house Tilly stood in the kitchen without any coherent thought in her head. What was happening? She felt subsumed by events, by Lonore.

Where was that confidant woman who had closed a difficult deal to sell something that didn't yet exist? She seemed years away.

The silence was broken by a grumbling from the boys. Harry and Sean were in Sean's room and Justin and Joseph were in Harry's, an arrangement that had been brokered by their grandfather and agreed by the boys. Their voices became louder, more angry, Harry and Sean shouting at each other. The two little boys had been asleep for hours, worn out by running on the beach all day with Robert who showed every sign of enjoying his new, larger family. Harry came barrelling down the stairs followed by Sean's bedroom door banging shut. Her arms were then filled by a sobbing, angry boy.

'Make them go Mum. Sean hates me.'

Cuddling him closer she pushed his damp hair from his eyes. 'You've made yourself ill with all this crying. Don't cry pet. Come and sit with me and we'll talk.' She guided him into the lounge and they settled into a corner of the sofa.

'Make them go Mum.' He repeated. 'Sean hates me and won't let me in his bed.

'Why do you want to go in with Sean. You have your own bed.'

'Don't know.'

She wiped his tears with her sleeve and held him close. She knew. Of course she knew, but she'd been ignoring the sullen faces of her sons. They enjoyed playing with the younger twins, but they needed their space back. They had they own rooms for a reason. They had chosen not to be together since they were small, because they had different hobbies and tended to argue if one had to impose his choice on the other, football was Harry's abiding passion and Sean wasn't interested, he plastered his bedroom walls with posters of BMX riders and sea blown surfers. They needed to be in their own world, a space to invite their own vastly different groups of friends. She felt his sobs subside as she hugged him close. This absence of care she had allowed to overtake her since the news of Adam's betrayal was destroying her family more surely than he had and she could not allow it to continue. 'Too late tonight love, but I'll talk to them tomorrow. Tell them they must leave. How about my bed for tonight, you're so tired. I'll talk to Sean too. Please don't worry.'

'Is Dad coming home?' Harry sniffed.

'I won't lie to you Harry. I don't know what he's doing, but this house will return to normal. We'll have Grandad, but he's OK in the study and Beth will be home tomorrow.'

At this news he turned his weary face up to hers. 'Can we go and meet them, just us and Grandad and Nana?'

'Yes. Yes. It'll be lovely seeing everyone again and having Beth home. Just us together like we used to. I promise Harry. I promise. How about some hot chocolate?'

He nodded.

'Come on then it's so late. Off you go and I'll be up in a minute.'

An hour later he was asleep in her bed and she was again sitting at the kitchen table. Sounds from the garage heralded the return of Robert and Lonore. It was half past three, almost dawn. She waited until Robert and Lonore came in, breathless and giggling like a couple of naughty school kids.

'Sorted pet, all sorted.' Robert hugged her. 'We've played a blinder. Talk about the left hand not knowing what the right hand is doing. The police hadn't a clue about the bailiffs. Good idea of Lonore's.'

'A very good idea to lie to the police and get us all hauled into court, for the newspapers to find out about our cosy little arrangement. We'll be splashed across the Sunday tabloids. The bankrupt man who conned the police and has two families all living together.'

'It's got nothing to do with Adam. We did it for you.'

'Did what?'

'The break in.'

'You engineered this!'

'We've got your sewing machines back. The police just left us to lock up and we took them. It was a good plan, foolproof. I got rid of the seal on the doors this morning and bent a window catch.'

'You tampered with a bailiffs seal! Are you mad!'

'Come on Tilly. We know how important it is for you to start your bag orders.'

Tilly was speechless. She looked from one to the other, but she knew who was to blame, Robert would never have thought to do such a thing without this woman who stood in front of her, a woman without morals, a thief with no regard for the law. It was too much. 'Out!' she told Lonore. 'You will leave this house as soon as your children wake up.'

'Tilly ... ' Robert appealed.

She turned on him. 'Do not speak to me. If you want to stay here, in my mother's house, then go to your room and do not interfere again.' She lifted her chin and stared him out. Mumbling an apology to Lonore he brushed past Tilly and left the two women alone.

'Please be sensible Tilly, I ca …'

'I don't care to listen to you. I think it might be a good idea for you to spend the next few hours wisely. You need to pack. You and your children will not be here when I come down for breakfast at half past seven.'

Turning on her heel Tilly left the kitchen. She had one foot on the stair when a noise at the back door halted her. She could see Lonore standing in the kitchen, so it wasn't her. She took her foot off the stair and stepped to the side, looked down the hall and through the big kitchen where the back door was clearly visible. Standing in front of it was Adam. Moving with a speed and ferocity she hadn't known she possessed and screaming like a mad woman, she ran full pelt and punched him in the face.

CHAPTER TWELVE

BETH

Up in the shrouds Beth felt free; no decisions to worry about, no boyfriend to satisfy, no father to placate, no mother to deceive, only one person to please, Lena – with Cary relaying her orders as they steered a little west of north, through the Wold's narrow stretch of turbulent water. Between the land and the gas platforms, powerful currents roared and screamed, pushing the flying vessel faster and faster, rolling over the hours. She called below that she had sighted the white and red of Whitby High Light. The journey was almost over, soon they'd be in the Tyne and then she'd have to face her problems. Throughout the voyage she'd been proud to be part of the hard-working crew, easing the labour by ribbing each other, correcting Juan's appalling English and singing shanties led by Cary. Daisy had run here, there and everywhere, endearing herself by helping at every task with her puny strength, hauling sheets, washing pots, peeling the endless vegetables and adding her piping, off-key voice to the sometimes risqué shanties that she, hopefully, didn't understand.

Five hectic hours later they turned into the Tyne and there were Harry and Sean and Nana, the boys waving and shouting, wildly running the length of the pier to keep up with the *Brigantia*. As Beth worked with her crew-mates to haul in sail, she found herself laughing. Suddenly everything seemed normal. She would get home to find her mother organising the house, her father at work and she'd go and find Mitchell and the gang, they'd all go to school together and get their exam results. The dreaded GCSE results, she'd forgotten all about them. But she wasn't worried, she was confidant she'd done well and she'd still be able to go to college. It suddenly seemed that things would work out, so what had she been so worried about? She even felt hungry. In the last few weeks she'd not had much appetite and what she had eaten had come straight back up. The seasickness pills Jazzy had given her, and stood over her while she swallowed them, hadn't made much difference, but then why would they? She was looking forward to just getting into her own room and feeling the familiar fold around her.

By the time they'd berthed, the boys and Nana had caught up. Mai was introduced to the Spanish contingent and hugged by Cary, whom she'd known for years. Beth was surprised to learn that Nana knew Lena.

'We're old mates from way back,' Mai told her as she stood with an arm around Lena's shoulders.

'Your Nana helped me make the most important decision of my life, when I was just a girl.'

Zander and Daisy were introduced, and Krista, who nodded shyly to Mai. A look passed between them that seemed to Beth to embody the mystery of Mai's magic. She shook her head to rid herself of such fancies. What a load of rubbish.

Daisy presented Mai with a bracelet of plaited and knotted string; she had been making them for all the crew.

Mai knelt in front of her and kissed her cheek. 'Symbols of friendship are very potent magic. My acceptance of this bracelet means I'll keep you safe in my heart forever and I must find something for you to keep the circle strong.' Everyone watched as Mai studied Daisy's little face and looked deeply into her lively and curious eyes, shining with pleasure at being taken so seriously by this colourful woman.

'You have magic eyes.' Daisy spoke solemnly to Mai and reached out a tiny hand to close each eyelid in turn.

'You and I are sisters,' Mai whispered to her and opening her eyes said, 'You must come to my studio tomorrow and I'll have something for you, something that will seal our pact.'

Beth felt a little bit jealous. When she was about Daisy's age she too had been part of Mai's magical world, but over the years she had lost that connection. Maybe it was because her mother scorned it so vehemently, maybe it was just herself to blame for not seeing as much of her grandmother as she could have. She stepped closer to Mai, who responded with an easy hug. 'Have you seen Mum?'

'Yes. Things are a bit fraught at your house.'

This wasn't what Beth wanted to hear. She felt the black uneasiness begin in her belly and panic tightened her lungs. 'Why isn't Mum here, or Dad?' she could only whisper.

'I don't think your Dad's back yet.'

Harry, overhearing, turned to them. 'Yea, he came home last night, he and Mum are fighting.'

Beth wanted to be at home. All this talk about things she had missed, everyone but her knowing what was happening. She couldn't stand it any longer. 'I'll just get my bag.' She turned away, ran down to the cabin and stuffing the last of her toiletries into the rucksack rejoined them on deck. 'I need a lift home.'

'I'll take you.' Mai walked her away from the friends she'd shared so much with over the last few weeks and Beth found it hard to say goodbye. She'd felt so much a part of them, the work and living in such close quarters and the camaraderie, it had all been so good so – grown up. Yes, that was it, she'd felt like a responsible adult and mocking her earlier feelings she thought that joining up with her school friends just wouldn't be enough any more. With heavy feet she followed Mai. The twins decided they'd stay. Everyone was shouting goodbye and promising to meet up that evening. Beth felt so confused.

In the car it was Mai who broke the silence. 'You feeling all right? You look a bit peaky.'

'A bit seasickness. I'll be fine once I get back home.'

'Beth.' Mai hummed and hawed. 'Beth, do you know about Lonore?'

'I don't want to talk about it.'

'Might be a bit hard not to. Things at home have changed and it's a bit, er, crowded.'

'What do you mean?'

'Well there was a flood and then ... you do know about the bankruptcy?'

'I know Dad's business is in trouble.'

'It's a bit more serious than that.'

'What?'

Mai stopped the car in the back lane. Beth could see up the garden to the house, to her bedroom window, with the strings of patterned mobiles turning slowly in a draught from the open frame. 'I don't want to talk about these things, Mum and Dad or the people they know. I just want to get in.'

'Maybe you should be ...'

But her grandmother's voice was behind her now and she was half way up the path.

'Beth!'

Beth ignored her.

In the house a woman was cooking and her father was sitting drinking coffee, his specs on the end of nose as he read the paper.

He stood up to hug her. 'Darling. So glad you're home safely.'

'I thought you would all be at the quay to see us in.' Beth stepped away from him and watched the woman who was standing smiling, waiting to be introduced, but her father ignored her. He picked up her rucksack. 'We've put you in the attic, pet.' He walked quickly away and was half way up the stairs before she caught up with him.

'Why? I don't want to be in the attic, I want my own room.'

'Well that might be a little difficult. Your Mum's having a lie down.'

'In my room?'

'Yes.'

'Why? What's wrong with your room?'

'I was in it.'

'So?'

'It's complicated.'

'If you two are still fighting I think I'll go and stay at Nana's.' The door to Beth's room was in front of her. She put her hand on the gleaming glass knob where the sun spit prisms along the ceiling and was just turning it when her father stopped her, placing his hand and his big tanned fingers over hers.

'No, really pet, just leave her for now. Be a good girl and settle down in the attic for a while. We'll sort things out later.'

'And we've loads to sort out haven't we, people want to talk to you, hang you from the yards, keel haul you and Jack,' she shouted at him.

'Sh, sh, your Mum's asleep.'

'So you said.' And grabbing the bag from him she stamped up the stairs and into the attic where she threw the heavy bag on the floor and herself onto the narrow bed. Using her mobile she phoned Mitchell. It went to voice mail. She left a message and phoned Tanya whose wild whooping almost deafened her. At least someone was pleased she was home. They arranged to meet in the park.

With a bottle of cider swinging from her hand she trudged down the path. Northumberland Park was where they all hung out to drink and have a laugh. It was a valley with a lake and a stream that disappeared underground to re-emerge in her Nana's back garden, then into the river. High trees bordered flower beds and a few wooden shelters, abandoned by the council, afforded places to hide from the cops. She knew the gang would be behind the ancient trees, high up in the corner, sheltered and hidden from the public by the ivy-covered wreckage of a summer house. She began to run.

It wasn't as she'd expected. She had thought things would be just as she'd left them, but after the initial greetings and screams of welcome the girls only wanted to know how many new boys she'd met in Mallorca and the boys just wanted the cider, then it all settled down and they resumed talking about the wild drunken time they'd had the previous evening at a party. She pretended it was cool, but it wasn't; it was boring. As she'd suspected Mitchell had lost no time or tears over her absence. Mandy Ferguson was draped all over him, giving Beth looks of triumph. Beth wanted to get Mitchell alone, but Mandy never left his side so, biding her time, she wandered over to where the boys and Tanya and a girl she didn't know were drinking. After a while she gave Karl some money to go to the offy. His brother worked there and would serve him. After he came back laden with cider and vodka, Beth's jealousy had built up to such a level she couldn't think straight and began to play up to all the boys, kissing and drinking with any of them who were up for it. Tanya was her best friend and she too was drinking as much as Beth. After a while Beth felt a bit woozy and sick. Shit, not again. This was getting beyond a joke. She threw up in the bushes.

'What's wrong with you?' Tanya wiped her mouth and pushed her upright, against the wall.

'I'm fine. It's just seasickness.'

'You're lovely and thin.' Tanya examined her flat tummy. 'God I'm so jell. I'm like a big fat pig.'

'How long has Mitchell been with that slag?'

'Oh weeks, you'd hardly got to the airport when she got her claws in.'

'Why didn't you tell me?'

Tanya shrugged. 'Dunno. Come on, it doesn't matter. Jack and Karl are well fit.'

Beth decided to make Mitchell jealous. She'd show him. She resumed drinking and someone brought out some weed and the makings, so they shared a few tokes. After a while she began to flirt with Karl, he'd always fancied her. She hung on to him as they staggered away from the gang to the spot behind the shelter where they all went to have a snog. She'd show Mitchell. Giggling and stumbling she kissed Karl; he was hot for her, he was up for it. She'd show Mitchell. Soon he'd come and butt in, take her away. She didn't actually fancy Karl.

Things got a bit confused then. Still feeling a bit woozy she didn't, at first, realise what he was doing, didn't realise until it was too late and he had pushed her on the ground and was on top of her, heavy with his knee between her legs, his hands pulling at her jeans. Mitchell would come any minute. He'd be so angry. Maybe he'd punch Karl. She giggled. She'd never had boys fighting over her before. Karl's hands were now more urgent and he was sucking at her neck. 'Stop it Karl.' But he didn't, he just went on and on, suffocating her with his body. He was big and strong and she had no strength and he was pushing at her, trying to get his fingers inside of her. She hated him. She pushed him away and called out. Where was Mitchell? She managed to call his name, but it made Karl laugh and grabbing her hand he shoved it down between them where he had his willy out. He was pressing against her. Catching him off balance she managed to twist her body away from the wall. She had more room now and dragged her hand free. Then someone else was there. Oh no, no! Now she was terrified. Surely these boys wouldn't do anything to her. They were her friends. She felt the new person pull her away from Karl and she renewed her efforts. kicking and screaming, clawing at the face hanging above her. Slowly she realised it was Krista; Krista who kicked at Karl while she dragged Beth away from him.

'You piece of shitty slime. Get off her. Get off her before I cripple you.' She kicked him again.

Beth stumbled over her own feet, clinging to Krista, who pushed her through the gang, Tanya drunk and laughing, Jack making obscene gestures as he pointed at Karl, now on his knees and clutching his genitals where Krista had kicked him, all of them watching her; and at the back, Mitchell, with Mandy still hanging on to him, Mitchell who looked at her with disgust and then turned his back and walked away. Krista shouted at them all, telling them to get away before she set about them too. Beth clung to her leaving the faces still laughing and jeering, leaving her so called friends.

Later in bed in her grandmother's house, Beth let herself cry. She cried not for what Karl had done or what she had allowed him to do, but for Mitchell, who she'd thought loved her, Mitchell, who she had allowed to do those things that Karl had wanted, because she loved him. Mitchell, the only boy she'd ever been intimate with. And now they'd all know. He'd tell Mandy and she'd laugh and scoff and tell everyone. She'd never be able to face them; she'd not be able to go to college. Her life was finished, she might as well throw herself off the pier.

The following morning she lay in bed with a mighty hangover listening to her mother and grandmother in the kitchen, talking about her unreasonable behaviour. Nana, as usual was urging caution, Mum wanted to have it out with her. Oh no, that's one thing I don't want. She buried her aching head under the duvet, refusing to move when she felt a hand tug at it.

'Come on, get dressed. You and me'll go shopping.'

It was Krista again. Beth shrugged her away. 'Let me alone.'

'Come on. I've blagged us a lift in a launch.'

Throwing aside the duvet Beth ran to the bathroom, making it just in time. After heaving up nothing but liquid she looked at her face in the mirror. She hardly recognised the zombie who stared back. Her body ached all over, bruised inside and out, but she didn't care, she deserved it, she was worthless and had asked for it.

'You didn't deserve that you know.' The serene and beautiful face of Krista appeared over her shoulder.

'So now you're a mind reader.'

'I have many talents. If you don't come with me you'll have to face your mother and man is she in a mean mood.'

'Shit.' Beth muttered, 'Shit, shit, shit.'

Knowing she'd won Krista turned away and left her to shower.

As they headed for the river Beth felt marginally better, physically, but in her mind she still felt like a slag. No matter how much Krista persuaded her that Karl was a jerk-off, she knew it wouldn't have happened if she hadn't got drunk and tried to show off in front of Mitchell, another jerk-off. Her heart ached for Mitchell. How could he have betrayed her like that, getting off with Mandy. She had asked him if he'd wanted to come with them to Mallorca for the summer, but he'd refused. At the time she believed him when he'd said he needed to find a job to pay his tuition fees. She knew his family really couldn't afford for him to go to college if he didn't contribute. But now it was obvious he'd just wanted rid of her. Shame flooded her, leaving her weak, and she couldn't meet Krista's searching eyes.

'Stop it.'

'What?'

'Stop watching me.'

'Oh for God's sake, get over yourself. You're not the only girl who ever got in a mess with a boy.'

'Boys, plural, two boys.'

'Well one of them didn't get anywhere. I pulled him off before he'd hardly got it out.'

'So?'

'So, who's the other boy?'

'Mitchell.' Beth thought she'd never tell anyone about her and Mitchell, it was too big a deal, too precious to talk about, but Krista had a way with her. She was like Nana, they made you talk. So she told Krista how much she loved Mitchell and how he'd betrayed her.

'Yea, well that's men for you. Lena's got the right idea.'

Not really concentrating, Beth agreed.

At the quayside some of crew from the *Brigantia* were waiting in a launch, shouting and laughing, hugging her and kissing her, telling her they were relying on her to show them the sights of Newcastle. They'd heard all about the Big Market and were dying to sample the delights of the 'Toon,' the boys chanting 'Sheara, Sheara, Sheara,' in imitation of the local football fanatics worshipping their hero Alan Shearer. Beth felt at home in a way she never had with her class mates, could it be that she'd outgrown her former life? Did she really want to go back and struggle through years of academic headaches, hanging out with a bunch of drunken amateurs, when she could be a part of these people, this life, for ever? And there'd be Krista, who was standing right alongside her, so close that Beth felt the earthy heat from her body. They had become so close. This girl could be a friend and sister, someone she could confide in and know her secrets would be safe. Merging easily into this happy, joyful crowd she eased an arm around Krista's waist and threw her head back feeling the rush of air as the launch sped up-river. She felt free at last, this was a new plan for her future, one she'd embrace with all her heart.

At Newcastle all was noise and madness. Tall Ships from around the world were tied up waiting for the start of the Cutty Sark Race, their crews calling compliments and insults to each other in equal measure. Groups of street entertainers gathered pockets of audiences, and those not interested meandered about, visiting the bigger ships that were floating embassies for their countries. Food stalls lined the quayside and beer tents flanked the big entertainment stages heaving with thousands and thousands of sightseers in holiday mood.

Beth was invited, with the others, on board the Italian ship, the *Amerigo Vespucci*, a huge three-masted schooner with a crew of over a hundred where all on duty were smartly turned out in navy and white uniforms. After an hour being shown around and drinking the health of the crew, they headed off to explore the bars of Newcastle City. As they travelled from one bar to another the crowd grew, it changed, people came and went, with promises to meet up again that evening. Beth felt sick just watching them drinking.

She had plenty of money. She had her debit card, that as far as she knew was still topped up by her mother, and Lena had paid them all two hundred pounds as well as the free trip to the Tyne with all board and lodging. Krista had stuck to her all day, but the arrival of Zander diverted her attention and finding herself hovering at the edge of the noisy crowd Beth slipped away and headed for the shops.

Feeling pleased with herself and much better, after a chicken salad and juice in the Cosmopolitan Café on Market Street, Beth thought she'd just have a look in Bewicks before catching the Metro home. She'd sort things out with her mother and get her bedroom back. Wandering through the busy shop where tourists, who had arrived for the race, were spending like it was going out of fashion, a bright green top in boned denim attracted her eye. She tried it on and decided she'd have it for the pre-race party. It looked wonderful, setting off her red curls and tanned skin to perfection. 'Eat your heart out Mitchell,' she muttered to herself as she looked at the price tag. Shit! Two hundred pounds, for a top! She couldn't pay that, could she? Well yes, she could, she had the money, but two hundred pounds for a top, oh what the hell. She took it to the cash desk and stood in the queue. It was slow, with loads of screaming kids pushing and whingeing while their mothers either ignored or threatened them. She felt a bit woozy, a bit sick, it was hot in the shop and the hangover was still pounding at her system. She promised herself that she'd never drink like that again. Five minutes later and she didn't feel as if she'd moved. She adjusted her bags and as she did so the bright green denim top fell into the Jane Norman bag. Without even thinking about her actions she walked away from the queue and out of the shop. But before she could feel either shame or elation, she was grabbed by two burly security guards and asked to show them what was in her bags. The top was discovered and she was marched back through the shop to the office where two police officers eventually arrived and arrested her.

CHAPTER TWELVE

TILLY

In her dream Tilly was a fat marker pen, methodically marking off the days of an infinite calendar, days in squares that fell away under a bright red tick, years and years of days; Beth graduating, Sean rowing for Oxford, Harry scoring for England, she and Adam celebrating their silver wedding anniversary; all red letter days she had planned for: days in limbo now.

The telephone saved her from madness. The police? Why did the police want her? Elizabeth? She was staying with her grandmother, she told them. No, they explained, she didn't understand, they had Elizabeth, they needed Tilly to come and get her, Elizabeth would be cautioned. Stumbling from her nap and grabbing her mother's car keys, Tilly sped up the road to Newcastle where she stood by while Beth was cautioned and released and now she was back in Mai's kitchen and Beth was behind a locked bedroom door refusing to talk.

Tilly knew how stubborn Beth could be and the siege could go on for days so she left her with Mai and wandered along the quayside thinking about the mess her family had deteriorated into. But thinking about it was never going to achieve anything. Apparently there'd been a discussion while she was in bed yesterday afternoon. Not caring what would be decided she had declined to join the committee of Adam, Robert, Lonore and the boys. Afterwards, Harry and Sean had crept in and wound themselves around her, in Beth's narrow bed, to tell her what had been decided. Day-to-day expenses would be paid for by Robert, who had enough to see them all through for a year if they stayed together. The boys had agreed as long as their father would clear out the attics and Robert would use his skills to renovate the area and provide separate bedrooms for them. The two little boys, Justin and Jonathan, would have their old rooms, Beth would stay in her own room and Grandad would stay in the study. She didn't ask them what arrangements their father had made for his harem. Now she actually gave it some thought she realised she would never sleep with Adam again.

The river was busy, she leaned on the railings and watched boats of all shapes and sizes to-ing and fro-ing, everyone with a plan, no-one getting in anyone else's way, no-one encroaching. Some people on a smart little cabin cruiser were waving. Surely it couldn't be ... but it was ... Jack and Cloris. My God! She waved back, feeling that the world was spinning out of kilter. She was like Alice down the rabbit hole, confused and lost. Alone, she wandered through the crowds massing to wonder at the tall ships, couples and families watching out for each other, sharing the sights, having a laugh, and she realised that this is how it would be in the future. Alone, she would walk through the crowds, lonely and invisible. She wouldn't be missed at home, she was surplus to requirements, even the boys were fine without her, they had their own lives of friends and sport.

She had left them helping Robert and Adam to clear out the attics and a trip had been planned to Tom Swan's building suppliers for materials to begin the conversion. They would plan the layout and help construct their own rooms. They didn't have time for Tilly. Beth, her only daughter, didn't want her and Adam didn't need her. Adam. He was her husband. She still loved him, didn't she? True it had never been a marriage of grand passion, but it was what she'd wanted. She had been happy and she missed that life. She missed Adam. She missed his arms around her and his presence in her life, she wanted to feel his love pull them together again, but it was never going to happen, it was over. She realised she could never really have known Adam. How could she have? He was a man perfectly at ease living with two wives and this was not anything Tilly had ever thought him capable of, indeed had never given any thought at all to such a possibility.

An arm hugged her close, she leaned against a steady strong body and in her daydream it was Adam and everything was back to normal, the nightmare was over. But it wasn't Adam. It was Mai.

'Hello Pet.'
'Mam.'
'I've been looking for you.'
'Why, what's happened now?'
'Nothing that wasn't already there to see.'
'I can't cope with this Mam. I'm not like you. I need things planned. I need my life to be organised.'

'Then do something about it. You're the only one who can change your own life.'

'But I don't want it changed. I want it back.'

'Do you?'

'Of course I do. What's the matter with you, are you blind! Do you really know what's happened to me?'

'Yes I know and it's horrible. You feel rejected, worthless, lost, but didn't you feel like that before you knew about Lonore?'

'No! How can you think such a thing?'

'Because it was in your mind long before you found out about Adam. You've been wanting your independence for years.'

'Not to have my children homeless and drifting, not to find out that my husband has been cheating on me for years, I haven't wanted my independence at that price, not like that. So don't try to shift the blame onto me. It's Adam's fault and he gets to go on as normal, in my house with my family.'

'If you wanted that life and that house you would have taken charge before now, but you haven't because it's not what you want.'

'I want my children!'

'For now, because you're confused and you can't sanction any mother leaving her children, but it's not a crime.'

'What! Are you mad!'

'Be honest. Don't you want a life free of responsibility?'

'No, not if it means abandoning my children.'

'There's a big difference in abandoning and stepping aside.'

'Don't! Don't do this. This is all Adam's fault and you're trying to blame me, saying that I want to leave my kids.'

'Let's leave that for a moment and concentrate on Beth.'

'All this drinking and now shop-lifting. She's out of control. I can't deal with her.'

'Only because you don't know what you're dealing with.'

'Do you?' Tilly was sick of Mai pretending to be the great Earth Mother, all knowing and all seeing. 'Just go away Mam. This isn't your problem. I'll take care of my family.'

'You can't sort everything out no matter how well-intentioned you feel. You can't change the fact that Beth's been rejected too. The man she loved has also gone off with someone else.'

'It's not the same. Beth wasn't married to him and he's just a boy, they're just kids.'

'It feels the same. It hurts the same and all that business in the park ... she was just trying to get back at him, flirting with someone else. Silly and dangerous as it turned out, but you couldn't have stopped it.'

Tilly ran her shaking hands over the tears that flooded her face and then she was being pulled close, her mother shielding her from passers-by, who were too interested in the spectacle on the water to notice her anyway. It was just what she needed, she allowed her body to relax, to absorb Mai's warmth, accept her steady arms and constant love, a love that had always been there, but she had rejected it. Had she turned away once too often? She lifted her face to her mother. 'Mam ...' Doubts assailed her mind and her voice tailed off to silence. There were so many years to bridge.

'Sh, sh, sh.' Mai shook her head, her wild hair blowing in the breeze, her eyes soft and loving, her big wide mouth smiling. 'I know. Forget it, let's just go home. Stay with me for a while until things look better, you and Beth. You need time together.'

'She's ill Mam.' Tilly allowed her mother to guide her away from the railings, show her the way home. 'I think she's anorexic.'

'No she's not.'

'She's so thin.'

'The fall before the rise.'

'Is this your magical powers talking to you?' Tilly asked smiling, trying to lighten her mood.

'No. It's my common sense.'

'And what does your common sense tell you?'

'She's not anorexic. She's pregnant.'

Suddenly Tilly could see it. Of course she was. How had she been so blind? She'd been so concerned with her own troubles, wallowing in self-pity, that she had failed Beth when she needed her most. While she was thinking only of herself and her plans lying in ruins, her daughter had been sinking lower and lower into a pit from which she couldn't climb out. Tilly turned to her mother and Mai was there, as usual. Mai knew how to deal with her child's worries and if she'd taken more notice of Beth's moods instead of being obsessed with stupid plans, then she too would have been there for her daughter. 'Does she know?' Her voice was a terrified whisper.

Mai shook her head. 'I don't know. It's something you need to talk about. It's not too late pet, it's never too late.'

Now Tilly's steps were firm and sure. She knew where to go. A man shouting and gesticulating attracted her attention. It was Zander yelling at Jack, ordering him to pull in so that he could board the shiny new boat. Jack was ignoring him, but poor old Cloris was waving and holding up the inevitable glass, inviting them all aboard for *drinky-poos*.

Zander saw Tilly and made a bee-line for her. 'Tilly! Do you see that mad man! I'll have it out with him! I will. If it takes forever I'll have the truth.'

Tilly was shocked at this side of him. He looked wild and powerful, not the usual calm and considerate Zander she knew and loved. She held out her hands to him. 'Leave it for now Zander. Wait until he comes ashore then ...' But it was too much for her. She had so many problems to deal with she just couldn't handle another.

Mai touched his shoulder and he seemed to realise the commotion he was making, he quieted and she told him. 'Come to my place Zander. You know where it is. One of my artists has upped sticks and left me, so his place is empty. Get your father to come. You can talk in private there.'

'He won't come. He's insane.' Zander stopped shouting. He now seemed more confused than angry.

Tilly couldn't make herself be interested in Zander's problems. She was eager to talk to Beth. Back at the Brew House she hurried in and up the stairs to where her mother's private flat spread out across the whole of the top floor. Beth lounged in one of Mai's big fat easy chairs, the cheerful yellow upholstery matching nothing else in the room. Mai's furniture was an eclectic mix of any piece that had taken her fancy over the years without any thought of whether or not it might harmonize with the other pieces, but it was pure Mai and the room had a charm that suited the building.

'Hello darling.' Tilly bent to kiss Beth, who turned her face away and left Tilly tangled in her wild hair, usually straightened, but since she had taken to the sea she'd just let it hang any way, occasionally tying it out of the way with bands of covered elastic. For the first time since Beth had been born, Tilly realised that she bore a striking resemblance to Mai. She stepped back, sat opposite in a wooden rocker padded with pale green leather cushions crafted by a young woman called Naomi, who rented a workshop on the second floor and fashioned decorative belts and slippers, all tassels and flowers. 'I'm not going to keep on and on about things. I just need to know you're ok.'

'I'm fine.'

Tilly took hope from the two words. At least she hadn't been ignored. 'Can I get you anything?'

'My bedroom.'

'Beth, I know this is intolerable for you, for all of us, but it's happened and we have to make the best of it. The fact of the matter is that your father has a responsibility to another family. Whether you like it or not you have two half brothers and none of this is their fault.'

'It's not mine either. Dad's a selfish dickhead. He's been shacked up with that bimbo for six years and you never noticed. What the hell's wrong with you! And I've lost all my stuff and been thrown out.'

'I'm moving in here with Nana and your room is still there just as you left it. You can go home any time you want.'

'Well I don't want.'

'I've been thinking …'

'Oh shit, not another plan.'

The remark took Tilly by surprise. She had accepted that she liked her life to be moving forward on the prescribed route, but hadn't realised her family hated it.

'Anyway, I'm sailing back to Mallorca with Lena.'

'But the house is closed up, it was never ours. You know it belongs to Jack.'

'I don't mean I'll stay there. I'm going to learn to sail, become more experienced.'

'It's the off-season.'

'If there's no work I'll get down to the Bahamas. Endora and Paulo are going and a few others. There's plenty of work. I'm not staying here, in this mess.'

Numbness threaded through Tilly's veins. She had to stay focused on Beth, be calm and reasonable. She took a deep breath. 'If that's what you want.'

'I expect you'll be glad to get rid of me.'

'No. Not at all. You know I love you Beth and I only want what's best. I thought we might both stay here at Nana's for a few weeks, talk things out.'

'Nothing to say.'

Tilly felt as if she was about to faint. She wasn't handling this very well, there was no plan. Walking to the open window she breathed in the sounds of the quay, the sights of the river, all bustle and purpose. After the race the quayside would be empty again, quiet, and so would she, they'd be gone, Beth would be gone. She had to make her face the truth. 'Are you feeling any better?' An inadequate question, but the only one occupying her mind.

'I'm fine.'

'You've had a hard few days.'

'S'ok.'

'I think you need to stay here with us and get yourself fit again. If you really want to sail with Lena I won't stop you, but I do want you to go and see a doctor, have a complete check-up. I was worried you might be anorexic.'

'I've been chucking up 'cos I'm fucking well stressed. Did that not occur to you!'

Tilly tried to ignore Beth's shouting. She took a deep breath. 'I don't suppose you might be pregnant.'

Beth turned away from her, hunched her shoulders against the truth.

Tilly reached out and laid her hands on Beth's shoulders where the bones were hard and tense and the muscles knotted. 'Beth?'

'Get off me,' Beth yelled and sprang up from the chair, pushing past Tilly as she hurtled down the stairs.

Mai, who had been about to enter, was clinging to the banister after colliding with Beth. She hauled herself into the kitchen. 'That went well.'

'Mam, it's not funny.'

'Oh come on, lighten up. That baby's not going anywhere and you're losing all sense of proportion. Let's go and get something to eat. You need a bit of company. Take your mind off things. Unless you'd rather go meet your crowd. I saw Dawn and she was pleased you were home, told me to say they'd be in the Gib as usual.'

The thought of trying to be cheerful among the crowd of friends she shared with Adam was unthinkable. They'd be asking where he was and how the holiday had been and why had they returned so soon; but then, of course, they probably knew all about Adam and Lonore and would just bait the trap for her to fall into, supply them with more gossip. Some friends! 'I'm not feeling very sociable.'

'Tough. Let's go.'

And having nothing better to do Tilly followed her mother outside and onto the long stretch of quayside where the restaurants overflowed with happy people. Mostly all the ships were in and the folk of Tyneside were making the most of it, thronging the river banks along the whole twelve-mile stretch from Newcastle to the sea and all in celebratory mood.

North Shields quayside was no longer the place where drunken foreign sailors were the norm; the days of pubs with a world-wide reputation for welcoming a host of raucous crews from the world's roughest ports had long gone. Nowadays well-ordered restaurants lined the quayside catering to the residents of the new flats that fell in tiers from the high town to the river.

The crew of the *Brigantia* called to Tilly and Mai as they passed Richie's Bistro. Tilly groaned inside. She really wasn't up to this. Beth was there, sitting beside Zander and Krista, with Daisy dodging about selling her jewellery. She rushed up to Tilly and tied a woven thread bracelet around her wrist. Tilly swallowed a lump in her throat; this child had a weird knack of knowing exactly what she needed.

Mai beckoned Daisy to her side and brought from her pocket a silver chain. Swinging daintily from it hung a silver charm, a baby mermaid in a womb. She fastened it around the entranced child's neck. 'There. Now you'll be kept safe from their evil ways.'

Tilly fingered her own silver mermaid and watched Beth, who did the same. And then from the neck of her T-shirt, Krista pulled her identical ornament; and surreptitiously fingering hers through her shirt, Lena also touched her talisman. Tilly turned to her mother. 'You've been a very busy lady, Mam.'

'Silver is good for women. It uses the moon and we all follow the moon.'

'Why did you give these to us?' Krista asked, her voice low and carrying a hint of confrontation.

'To keep you safe.'

'No, I mean why us.' She gestured to Tilly and Beth. 'You and your daughter, Tilly and her daughter, yes, but why Lena and me?'

'You're not the only women in Shields to be protected by the magic of the silver womb.'

'Does my mother have one?'

Krista's voice hardly carried to those outside of Mai's

presence. The rest of the company was too busy singing bawdy songs to hear them, but never-the-less a few did.

A man who had sat with his back to Mai turned and casually slung an arm about her shoulders, kissing her cheek. 'This lady is a blessing to all of us who sail the mighty waves. Her magic keeps us from the mermaids.' And he gestured to an ornament dangling from his left ear. It was the same as the pendant worn by the women, a mermaid baby in a womb. 'If we keep their babies hostage they can't harm us.'

Tilly gazed at him in wonder. Her heart literally missed a beat, her stomach did dizzying twists and a surge of wanton heat swelled between her thighs. Licking swollen lips she forced herself to breathe deeply and allow her damaged soul to rest on him. He was easily the biggest man in the company with muscles straining against the denim of his faded blue fisherman's tunic. His hair was black and tangled around his tanned face. Twinkling black eyes watched her and she felt so complete, as if he knew all about her and loved every bit. But this was incidental to the wildness of his being, the way he looked like he wanted to eat her and as her gaze rested on his lips, dark and red, they curved up at the edges showing dazzling white teeth, and she knew she'd let him do whatever he pleased. He moved to allow her and Mai to sit, him at her side.

Mai introduced him. 'This is Cary Innes. Cary, my daughter, Tilly.'

Before Tilly could take his proffered hand she caught sight of Beth's face. It was filled with disgust.

She jumped up from her seat shouting loudly so that everyone could hear. 'You just can't help yourself, can you mother? How many more have there been?' She turned, grimaced to the assembled company who sat silent and expectant. 'Everyone this is my mother, the slut.' And leaving Tilly more embarrassed than she'd ever felt in her life, Beth staggered from the bar to lose herself in the crowd.

Tilly wished for the ground to swallow her. The whole company was watching. Her body burned with the heat of shame. She looked to her mother for help, but it was Lena who took hold of her.

'My round I think. Come on Tilly, I can't carry them all on my own.'

'I have to go after her.' Tilly tried to get away from Lena's clam-like grip.

'No, no that's the last thing you should do, but I need a smoke.' She paid for another round then dragged Tilly outside, into the cool of the evening.

The quayside was filled with revellers, the beer tents and bars overflowing, music blasting from a stage, the fairground churning out a beat of its own and fast food vans barely keeping up with demand.

Making up a cigarette as she walked, Lena headed up a steep bank of stone steps. 'Do you remember, before they built all these posh flats, these steps were overgrown with weeds, derelict pubs and ruined houses?'

Tilly forced herself to remember where she had come from. 'Full of drunks and prossies. Mam wouldn't let me down this end of the quay on my own.'

'You were lucky.'

'Lucky! My mother the witch! Have you any idea how I felt being laughed at by all the kids at school. My mother the weirdo!'

'You were lucky.'

'I didn't feel especially lucky. Mam was always too engrossed with her lame ducks to notice me. There were always other girls hanging around, she encouraged them, women and girls off the streets, she said they needed a little comfort, somewhere to hide, to have a rest, they stayed in the studios. They weren't used then, she was busy renovating them.'

'Mai was a saint. All the girls knew how kind she was. They needed her to keep them healthy and safe.'

Tilly mumbled assent but her thoughts were closer to home. 'What am to do with Beth? She hates me so much.'

'She doesn't.'

'Does so.'

'Does not.'

'Does so.'

'Not,' Lena insisted, laughing.

'Does.' And Tilly laughed and they laughed together. 'God! It seems years since I had a good laugh.'

'Can't say I blame you. I've watched women lusting after Cary for years. He's a bit of a man.'

'I'll say.' Turning to Lena, Tilly felt burning embarrassment scorch her face again. 'Was I so obvious?'

'You and every woman in the bar. Even I know he's got it all. Handsome, virile, sexy and he's one of the good guys.'

'Not sure I want good anymore, they tend to turn out to be weak.'

'Cary's not weak. He was married once, long time ago. She died in childbirth, a boy. Cary went to sea. Sailed away on his own for over a year. Now and again I'd hear about him, but he wouldn't answer his messages and finally I just left him to it. He knew where his friends were if he needed us. And then one day he came to me in France. He was a different man, more introvert and cautious. The man who loved Louise never came back, but he was doing great. Then his grandfather drowned at sea and it knocked the stuffing out of him. The man you see now is only half alive.'

'We all have our secret lives.' Tilly mused on hers. Her affair with Zander and now this strange accepting of the situation at home, where was the real Tilly? Had there ever been one?

For a while they walked and Lena guided her to the only bar that hadn't changed in a hundred years. The Golden Lion was a low pub where people of low morals gathered to get drunk. They habitually spilled into the cobbled back lane and fought or indulged in a hungry kind of love, couples thrown together by a need greater than a craving for beer and cigarettes. In her teens Tilly had once or twice been forced this way when the late bus hadn't stopped at the top of the bank. She'd hurried past, shivering with relief when she'd arrive safely on the modernised quayside. 'Where are we going Lena?'

'We're here.'

'We're here?' Tilly echoed her.

'You've fought against your mother for years. You have no idea just how lucky you are.'

'So you keep saying.' Puzzled, Tilly stood behind her, feeling that Lena offered some protection from the seedy bar and its raucous clients.

Lena stood looking at the place, with its peeling paint and one of its five windows boarded, her face blank, no hint at what her thoughts might be. Finally she seemed to gather herself and taking a deep breath muttered. 'Come on.'

To Tilly's horror she dragged her inside the dim smoky pub. The smell of alcohol, nicotine and other rank bodily odours assailed Tilly's nostrils, and she almost gagged. She pulled Lena's sleeve. 'Lena, let's go.' But her voice was lost under the deafening noise of a karaoke song being belted out with enthusiasm by two huge fat women, whose flimsy tops, with their shoe-string straps and micro mini-skirts left nothing to the imagination. Pillows of pallid flesh spilled over the tight fastenings and as they tottered to the beat on six-inch heels and open-work stockings, their veined and swollen legs wobbling like dead fish in a net.

Lena led her to a corner where four or five older women were sitting. Between downing pints of beer and smoking they were having an argument with a group behind them. From the little Tilly understood, one of them owed the other money; won or lost, she really didn't know, but it appeared to be over the result of the darts match. One huge raddled woman in the first group, whose dress was a riot of reds and yellows and barely covered her sixty-odd-year-old wobbling body, was on her feet threatening to throw all of the other group in the river.

'She means it too,' Lena yelled in Tilly's ear. 'I've seen her do it.'

Tilly was terrified, she pulled at Lena's sleeve again. 'Please Lena,' she begged.

The huge woman shouted and crashed her way through the tables, spilling beer in waves onto the already sticky floor. Grabbing hold of one of the other women she then pulled back an arm the size of a ham and hammered her fist straight into the woman's face.

'Hoy!' yelled the barmaid, a dark-skinned young woman almost as big as the battling Amazon. 'Mother, you're barred – again. Get out!'

'Am gannin, divvin knaa wharr-a-come in here for anyhow. Aa can stop at home and be insulted.' And grabbing the woman she had punched, whose nose was streaming blood, she hauled her, stumbling and cursing past Tilly and Lena, out into the street.

Lena followed her and Tilly couldn't wait to abandon the alien bar. The two drunken women were tottering along the road in front of them, now in each other's arms, sobbing and begging forgiveness for unidentifiable sins.

'My mother and my Auntie Edna,' pronounced Lena.

'Didn't they see you …?' Tilly's voice tailed off as she saw the obvious. 'They didn't recognise you. Your own mother didn't recognise you.'

Lena's face gave nothing away. 'Result I'd say, wouldn't you? Mission well and truly accomplished.'

'And the barmaid – your sister?'

'She saw me.'

Striding in front of her, so fast that Tilly could barely keep pace, Lena had a face so blank it seemed as if she wasn't there at all and Tilly was certain that if memories of her family were desolate and if Lena was hurting deep inside, no-one would ever know. Shouldering a path through the crowds she was soon lost to sight. Tilly decided just to go back to Mai's and fall into bed. It had been an eventful day.

CHAPTER FOURTEEN

ADAM

His late mother's car was an ancient Rover, massive boot, loads of leg room and a space in the back to slide in skis; that had always been a wish of Adam's – to go on a winter holiday, but Tilly had never allowed it It didn't have much adventure in her, liked things to go according to her ordered world, not like Lonore who was much more casual. He lamented the loss of his Beema, bloody minded officials, bailiffs. Lonore, bless her heart, had gone to try and get it back on account of he needed it for business, but they would have none of it. Tilly's car, the Peugeot had gone too.

Adam seethed at the injustice of it all, to lose his business like that, how was a chap supposed to pay his debts if he couldn't work; and behind his back, while he was away trying his damndest to find an investor.

He glanced in the mirror at Justin and Joseph. They were sitting very quiet and still, not like Sean and Harry who were a nightmare to take anywhere, even when little they would take sly hits at each other, call each other names deliberately to start a fight, which would end in the 'he did it, I didn't, he did' routine which would start another row until the car had to be stopped and Beth would have to come up front while Tilly sat between the miscreants. Adam blamed Tilly, far too soft. Lonore, now she had these little boys well taught. They were no bother at all.

Things weren't panning out as planned, but all in all it might be better if Tilly stayed at her mother's. Whenever she came to Sea View it caused another row, upset everyone just when Lonore had got things running smoothly. The attics were almost finished, even though Sean and Harry hadn't been much help to their grandfather. Harry was busy with his football and Sean was forever in the water, swimming, surfing, sailing, anything but stay in and get some work done, they were hardly in the house at all. Oh well, if they couldn't be bothered to help out they would only have themselves to blame if their rooms weren't as they wanted them. He realised that he hadn't seen Beth for a while. He thought she was probably on the boat with Lena and the girls, having a great time. He didn't think she'd bothered to go to school for her exam results. On the hall table there were few letters for her that she hadn't bothered to open. Oh well he'd just have to wait until she saw fit to inform him of her plans, nothing to do with him, she was sixteen now, must be wonderful to be so free, no responsibilities.

He'd heard that Jack and Cloris were here and had bought a boat. They must have a stash somewhere, an off-shore account spilling money like a fountain and the old bugger had said he had none. If he'd only invested in Finefit they wouldn't all be in such a pickle now and he owed him, big time, what with all the business about Daisy and Cloris whacking him on the head with the pan. When he'd come round and Cloris, full of apologies, had told him about Daisy jumping in the water and the mermaids saving her, he thought he still had a concussion but no, it was just that mad old bat fantasising to cover up the fact that they'd kidnapped the little girl . He'd wanted to get away from them and had staggered to the rail hoping to catch a lift with Lena, but the *Brigantia* was far away and Jack had shifted the heading so the *Mirabel* was on course for France. Unable to do anything he'd stayed with them until they anchored in Honfleur, but how that leaking old tub had made it was a miracle. As soon as they'd tied up, the harbour master had been horrified and impounded the boat as unsafe. Jack and Cloris had booked into an hotel, but he'd been glad to leave them with their problems and caught the next flight back home, just managing to scrape the fare together by flogging his Rolex and gold chains. So, in light of Jack's new wealth, he'd been thinking he might have another word with him. He just needed a bit of capital and he'd get started.

The sky had darkened and heavy, squally rain spattered the windscreen. He pulled into the community football ground where he'd promised to watch Harry play, but no way was getting out in that to get soaked. The new season hadn't started yet but Harry's coach was a fanatic and played all year round. Adam wasn't sure how that worked. Stupid game anyway. Now a bit of rugger, that was the thing for real men, nothing like it, watching a good game in the bar with a few mates and a few bevies. It looked like the match was over, boys were streaming off the pitch, parents were helping them to pull boots off before ushering them into cars, probably off to the pub for Sunday carvery; how predictable were the plebs.

He glanced at his watch, the old Sekonda the kids had bought him for Father's Day years ago. If he hurried he'd be in time for the second round of drinks at the golf club, no point in getting there too early, let someone else get the first round in.

Harry trudged toward them. Adam leaned over and pushed the door open. 'Come on Harry, time's a wasting.' He watched as Harry struggled in, pushing bags and jackets and stuff under his legs. His footy boots on top, he sat in his stocking feet, sweat and rain dripping from him, his hair plastered to his head, his face red and his breath still gasping.

Voices shrill and piping from the back tried to be friendly.

'Harry, Harry, come and sit beside us.'

'Did you win Harry?'

'Did you score?'

'We wanted to watch you.'

'Are we too late?'

'What're they doing here?' Harry was sullen.

Adam looked at his son's miserable expression. 'Lost then did you?' He backed the car out and roared down the drive onto the main road.

'Thought it would just be us, you and me for lunch at the Queens Head, like we always do.'

'Not today Harry old man, not today. Things to do, places to go, people to see.'

'You always say that, you think it's funny.'

'Fair does, you like my jokes.'

'No I don't. We just laugh to please you.'

'Did you win Harry?'

'Did you score Harry?'

'We wanted to watch you play.'

'Will you play with us when we get home?'

'Why did they have to come?' Harry ignored the little boys.

''Cos they wanted to see you and they're your brothers.'

'No they're not. Sean's my brother. Sean and me – we're brothers. That's all the brothers we want.'

'We want to play football with you Harry.'

'We think you're like the greatest footballer in the world.'

'You know nothing about it so shut up!' Harry didn't even turn around to them.

'That's enough of that. Apologise to your brothers.'

'They're not my brothers!'

Adam was shocked at this outburst. Not like Harry at all to be shouting loudly, his voice ugly, stunning the little boys into silence. 'No need for this Harry. When we get home you'll go to your room.'

'As if I had one.'

By this time Adam was relieved to find they were home and released the door catches to let them out. Harry ran up the garden path, leaving his footy stuff in the car. 'Harry …' But he was gone. Justin and Joseph stood waiting.

'Is Harry upset 'cos his team lost?' Joseph asked.

'We'll get him an ice cream. He likes ice cream.' Justin found a solution.

Adam's head was pounding. He needed a drink. 'Go on, off you go and find your mother.' Thankfully he gunned the big car back onto the road and headed for the club, as far away from this madness as he could get, in as short a time as possible.

After a couple of whiskies in the almost empty bar of the golf club, Adam thought about his situation; really thought about it. He'd been irresponsible to have had such an intense affair with Lonore, he could admit that, but he wasn't solely to blame. Perhaps he should have insisted she be more careful about birth control, maybe even done something about it himself, but he'd relied on her, should have known not to rely on a woman, but at the time he was in a position financially to support two families so it hadn't been such a big deal.

For years he'd been a bit edgy wondering if the two women would discover each other, making excuses not to go to nursery for the babies, finding out-of-the-way restaurants, shopping when he knew Tilly was somewhere else, fictitious business appointments to get away from both families, finding some time for himself had been hard. It was a relief to have it all out in the open. Tilly could have made things pretty nasty if she'd chosen. The house in Sea View for instance, it was her mother's, who had been waiting eighteen years to tell Tilly *I told you not to marry that feckless, pathetic waste of space.* He knew this for a fact because Mai had told him so, the day he and Tilly were married. He'd thought she was joking and laughed, but in the intervening years he'd realised that she had meant it, forever giving him warning looks and making those ridiculous signs with her hands, *to ward off evil* she said, of course that didn't worry him, but he did object to her relentless disapproval; the mad old witch.

The biggest problems now were, one, they had no income and two, the shadow of a court case to establish his bankruptcy. Lonore had been on at him to get his papers in order, apparently the court needed proof that the business was unviable from an economic standpoint and he hadn't run it into the ground deliberately. Deliberately! They were all mad. He'd done everything in his power to keep things going. What did they think he'd been doing in Mallorca? Having a holiday!

He wondered if he might be able to turn his Dad's talent for woodwork into a profit making concern, perhaps send him to a few classes to acquaint him with new techniques. Dad had been a jobbing carpenter for so long he hadn't moved with the times, it took him months to make even one small table but, if they set up a production line, get Dad to show others what he wanted, mass produce the parts, stick em together and there you are, a dining set. Of course he'd need premises and he wouldn't be able to operate under his name, good job he hadn't married Lonore, they'd be able to trade under her name. The more he thought about it the more it became a reality. He hadn't felt so excited for months. This would work. No more touting for business with bloody double glazing, that had never been his choice anyway, his Mother had made him do it. But this was his idea. Furniture of a good quality, and slow the old man might be but no-one could fault the quality of his work. It would sell like hot cakes, they'd be knocking the door down to buy and Dad had a ready market up and running, small outlets admittedly, but a start, a start.

The club bar was almost empty, blue sky had replaced rain clouds and everyone was on the greens. Adam didn't play, never get anything done trailing round a golf course, a man needed a bit of solitude to think. He felt renewed as he drove home and he wanted someone to congratulate him. Lonore always understood how he felt, pampered him when he was feeling down praised him when he felt good about things. If Dad had the boys on the beach maybe she'd be amenable to a little afternoon delight, it had been a few weeks and he needed her.

Tilly would still be at her mothers' so no chance there. Perhaps she'd stay there, it would solve a lot of problems, not least, where to sleep, he had felt a bit awkward about sleeping with Lonore under the same roof as Tilly, but what was he supposed to do, take Holy Orders!

The house was quiet. He called Lonore's name, but no answer. He was just about to try her mobile when he heard movement upstairs, he'd surprise her. He crept up to their room, but it was empty, the movement was above his head, ah, maybe she was making beds for Sean and Harry. Quietly he stepped up the last flight, but it was Harry's voice he could hear. Damn it!

'I can't help it Grandad. I didn't want this to happen. no-one asked me.' Harry was almost crying.

'Can't you just try son.' His father's voice was soft.

'No!'

'We aren't really in a position to be picky. Things are bad Harry. You know the business is dead in the water.'

'No. How would I know anything? No-one talks to us, we just get shifted about.'

'How does Sean feel about it all?'

The sound of glasspaper rasping against wood reminded Adam of when he was a boy and would go out to his father's shed in the garden to talk things over. Not very often, it was usually his mother who would solve his problems, tell him how to deal with the bullies who waited at the end of the lonely lane to beat him up. Her council had stood him in good stead; just hide from them and they'll get sick of waiting, she'd told him, and he had and it worked, for a while, but it was useless when they'd surround him outside the Tucky and force their hands into his pockets to steal his money. They'd touch him too, feel his willy and balls, just for a laugh, just to humiliate him as he stood there and shrivelled. In his Dad's shed he'd listened to the rasping of the glasspaper and felt such shame as he lied to his Dad that he'd got the better of the bullies at school, that he'd been tough and punched one of them on the nose until it bled. His Dad had listened and then talked just like he was talking to Harry now, slow, reasonable, persuasive. 'They're cowards,' he'd said. 'That doesn't make them any less frightening, I know, but the trick is not to let them see your fear, 'cos like sharks they'll smell blood and gang up. A thing to do might be to get a group of friends, girls, other lads like a chap who has a girl. This had been easy for Adam, girls liked him, loved his easy smile and good looks. Even as a young teenager he'd been handsome and charming, and he liked girls, so he'd taken his Dad's advise and his circle of girls grew. They were loyal and protective and soon the boys wanted to be his friend, and although he let them think it was all forgiven, it was not it, still rankled, but he'd never forgotten his Dad's words.

He listened to them now, soft, reasonable, informing Harry about the situation.

'I don't care.' Harry was stubborn. 'This wasn't supposed to happen. Mum never said this would happen, that we'd have to share everything and she'd leave us and she and Beth and Nana would live together without me. I'm going to Nana's.'

'A bit crowded down there son.'

'Don't care. Nana won't care neither, 'cos she always says, *mi casa es su casa*, it means that her house is my house, and she won't stuff us in the attic like old toys.'

'So all my hard work is for nothing?'

'I might come to visit. It's all right for a visit, but it's not home like it was.'

'Sure I can't persuade you?'

'No. And you'll tell Sean where I am, won't you?'

During the last year Harry's twelve-year-old voice had been constantly breaking, but this break was filled with tightly held tears, filled with a bravery Adam recognised, an illusion. He stepped into the attic. Harry was stuffing clothes into a back pack. He'd showered since his footy session, but his usually well-groomed hair was a bit tousled and his eyes were rimmed red. Adam felt his scorn.

'What do you want? This is my room and I never said you could come in.'

He was always defiant in the face of uncertainty.

'I heard what you said, just now. It's something no-one could help Harry.'

'You could help it. I'm not stupid you know, I know about safe sex. It's the responsibility of both partners not just the girl.'

Despite the tense situation Adam found it difficult to conceal a smile as his son spouted government doctrine, learned at school. 'Sometimes it's not that simple old man.'

'It is. It's very simple. You had us. Why weren't we enough? Why did you need other sons?' He almost knocked Adam over as he rushed past him. 'I'm going to live with Mum.'

'Can't we talk about it old man?'

'No, and I'm not an old man. I'm just a boy and I want my Mum.'

He clattered down the stairs leaving the front door open so they could hear his ragged steps as he ran down the street.

Adam moved to the window to watch him running, running along the cliff path, the back pack bumping unevenly from one shoulder. He turned to his father, but this time there was no help from the bullies. The old man continued, in silence, to sand the shelves he was crafting so lovingly for his grandsons.

Lonore. Adam never needed her as much as he needed her now. He followed Harry, almost seeing his scorched prints in the stair carpet. He called her name, again and again. In the kitchen it was quiet and cool. A note was propped on the table beside an empty vase and a few crumbs from a loaf that was hardening on a board, it said. *Adam, I'm very busy today. Will you get tea for the boys, the little ones are on the beach with Sean.*

The house seemed alien. It crept around him, tight, gripping, suffocating him. Then the whispering started, all the voices from all the years, sounds that lingered; the births, new babies in baskets and with them a feeling of such overwhelming responsibility and awe; Christmases with carols around the old keyboard in the study and Easter when Tilly chivvied them all to church and he hid eggs in the sand dunes for finding after a lunch of steamed fish and new potatoes; certificates heralding proud accomplishments pinned to the fridge and the disappointments and worries that brought tears and hugs; phantoms that swirled about, swept him up then dropped him with dizzy abandon. His head reeled as he looked around him, he was confused, then she came, Tilly, cool and calm in the middle of chaos, Tilly who unfastened the belt of iron around his head and calmed the whirlwind, filled the kettle and began to take stuff from the fridge, soup in a bowl miraculously appeared in front of him, with bread cut and buttered. Tilly sat opposite him with the unopened post. He'd been meaning to look at it.

'You're drunk,' she told him.

'Sorry.'

'We need to talk, Adam.'

'What happened, Tilly?'

'Only you know that. You're the one who couldn't keep it zipped.'

'Stay with us Tilly. We can learn to rub along together.'

'You're not just drunk, you are completely insane. At least I didn't expect Zander and Daisy to move in with us. And I didn't make us bankrupt.'

'I made a living for all of us.'

'But not a life Adam.'

'I tried damn hard Tilly.'

'Why did you do it Adam? Weren't we enough?'

'You and Zander?' He watched the colour creep up her neck and fill her cheeks while she dipped her head, hiding her lovely smoky lavender eyes. 'Do you love him?'

'No. I never did.'

'Why then?'

'Because he wanted me and you always made me feel inadequate as if I was rubbish at sex. Sex with Zander was wonderful, beyond anything I'd ever imagined and it made me feel alive and less useless.'

This made Adam feel that he was useless and inadequate, as if he should have been the one to guide his wife in these matters, as if he had failed. 'I still loved you.'

'Do you love Lonore?'

'Yes, but no more than I love you, just differently ... like ... it's not the same with her.'

'Good.'

'Good?'

'Well I'd hate to think this was all for nothing.'

He thought he'd just agree, that would smooth things over, but he felt he needed to justify himself, after all it was clear now that Tilly had never been the passionate wife he'd hoped for, and it wasn't a failing in him because he and Lonore had no trouble being sexually adventurous and trusting. He found himself saying 'I wanted a wife who put me first and you were always busy organising the children; school and hobbies, always filling our time in, always wanting us to be out doing something, never content to spend an afternoon in bed while the kids went off and did their own thing. It was never about me was it? You just wanted a life away from your mother. A life you could plan and know it would be so. A chap couldn't relax in his own home.'

'It's not your home.'

He watched her as she sat with the pile of post, slitting open the envelopes with ruthless efficiently. Three little stacks rose before her, he knew they would be in order of importance. 'It's not my house, but it is my home. Why bring this up now.'

'Because I want the children together. Harry's in bits.'

'Tried to talk to him.'

'You don't know how.'

'Dad tried.'

'When I need advise on child care I won't go to your father.'

'He's going to help us get on our feet.'

'I don't care.'

'You don't understand. I've thought of a way out. We can get Dad to start up a business in Lonore's name, making furniture.'

'You're not listening. I don't care.' She was calm, intent on the letters. 'I want you, your father, your slutty woman and her children out of my house. My house Adam! Not yours, not theirs, not even my mother's. She has given it to me. It is mine, signed and sealed. My house! And I want you gone by the end of the week.'

'Where to?'

'Wherever the hell you like.'

Adam felt uncomfortable, things were getting out of hand. He'd never had to find a home. He'd just left his mother and moved in with Tilly and her grandmother, then the old woman had died and he sort of forgot about the house being Mai's. If she was truly intent on throwing them out what would he do? Would Lonore be able to find them somewhere, perhaps with her mother up in Edinburgh? That wouldn't be so bad, a new start, yes that might work. And with Lonore's mother to child-mind she too would be free to get a job. Tilly was still talking.

'I will not have my children torn from pillar to post and neglected any longer. They need their home, they need me to be here for them.'

This was a step too far, too soon. Adam loved his sons. He was very proud of them. 'They need me.'

'Sadly, Adam, that's not true. They've never had you, not really, and there have been times when I've felt that with you around to worry over I've had four not …'

She stopped mid sentence staring intently at the letter in her hand.

'Adam!'

He bent to look at the postmark on the envelope. It bore the logo of the boys' school, Prior's Walk. He'd seen the envelope lying on the hall table and knew what it was, but hadn't been able to admit to the problems it carried in its neatly typed lines.

'The fees Adam! The cheque bounced!' Frantically she sorted through the remainder of the post, then, stony faced, pushed her chair back and hurried to the desk. Moved from the study to make room for his father, it almost blocked the hallway.

He bent his head to finish the soup. Nice soup, he wondered who'd made it, Tilly or Lonore, he really couldn't tell. He knew what Tilly would find in the desk, hidden at the back. There were three letters dating back to the end of the Easter break, each one reminding him the fees were due and now the final one ... Tilly returned. In her hand she held the letters, all with the same logo ...

She stood over him, intimidating. '*Unable to continue their education at Priors Walk!* You knew about this. How could you not tell me! They have two weeks Adam, two weeks and they are not enrolled in any school. You moron!'

'But if Dad gets cracking and gets a few pieces done, we'll get paid before it's too late.'

'It is too late Adam! They've been refused entry for next term. Starting in two weeks!'

'We'll sort it, and the state schools are really good around here, top of all the tables. Beth's done ok at Marden.'

'How do you know? Has she told you the results of her GCSE's? No, 'cos she has lost all interest in school and hasn't even opened her letter.' She riffled through a pile of envelopes and withdrew one. 'This is it Adam. This is the letter with her future in it and she doesn't care. She has bigger problems, problems you can't even imagine and as for the boys going to any school? It's too late. How many more times do I have to say it? The places will be filled, they'll end up in some sink school in the west end of Newcastle! How could you do this to them!'

He shrank from her anger. For a moment he thought she would strike him again. That punch she'd landed on the night he'd arrived home had really hurt. 'This furniture business ...'

'You, your father and Lonore! The treacherous trio! Well I wish you luck, but it doesn't concern me.'

'Tilly ...'

She was standing in front of the patio doors, the late evening sun shining through her thin summer skirt, showing off her amazing legs, legs that could be very supple ... behind her

Lonore was struggling up the garden path with a large cardboard box, she couldn't see in front of her and was unaware of Tilly and her demands, poor Lonore, this wasn't fair. 'Surely we can talk about this, the children need me.'

'No Adam, no they don't. They need their home back, Beth's pr ...'

Then everything happened at once. Lonore, struggling, finally made it through the back door, Sean and the little twins barrelled in the front, the rain filled wind howled through the house slamming doors and rattling windows as it passed and Lonore dropped the box. It fell at Tilly's feet disgorging its contents. He watched as Tilly bent and slowly gathered up an armful of bags. She turned to him, her face white. She was trembling with fury as she thrust the bags under his nose, spilling them across the table. Her lips were white, compressed and her eyes transformed to a dark dangerous purple. Her voice was quiet and filled with menace.

'Out. Now. All of you. Get out of my house.'

And he realised why Lonore had been disappearing for hours on end lately. She had been in the garage where she and Robert had hidden Tilly's new sewing machines. She'd been making bags, taking Tote-Tilly as her own.

CHAPTER FIFTEEN

TILLY

School, school, school; her head could hardly deal with just this one word, school, school, bouncing from ear to ear inside her brain. What could she do for the boys who had been in the school they loved since they were toddlers, just three years old, so proud of their purple and gold uniforms. The uniforms that were respected throughout North Tyneside, people were even moving to North Tyneside so that their children could be educated at Prior's Walk. The boys would be devastated. Their lives revolved around the school; after school clubs for chess and maths, English and science, footy and sailing clubs, the social scene where they were popular in a large circle of like-minded friends. Was it too late to get them placed? Beth would be fine. She had never wanted the private education Prior's Walk offered and had opted for Marden High after junior school, but the boys were different, they loved their lives. Beth's future was for thinking about at a later date, for now it was more than she could cope with just concentrating on the boys.

Tilly was almost alone on the beach. She had asked Sean to come with her, but he and the little boys had thrown themselves in front of the X-Box screen and were arguing about who got first turn. He'd just looked at her and shook his head, as if the very idea was unthinkable, so she'd left him in the menagerie, blissfully ignorant of his precarious position.

A wind whipped sand along the beach, gleefully dropping it to pile up at the base of the tall cliffs under the ancient ruins of Tynemouth Priory, the monument to a violent past and the building that had given the school its name. Summer was almost over. The still, hot days would soon be gone and replaced by bracing winds and unpredictable rain. Only three more days and then the Tall Ships Race would empty the river of sail and the children would return to school and life would settle down. During the day Tynemouth would belong to the retired who were buying up the new flats being built in strategic positions along the banks of the Tyne. Mothers would return to work.

Work! She was too angry to even think about her plans for work. The children must return to school. It was of paramount importance.

She could sell the house and move in with her mother. It might be a solution? As long as they were together it would work, it'd be a tight squeeze and they'd moan a bit, but as long as she kept them together they'd be fine. The boys would have to share and when Beth's baby came along it would have to be in the same room as she and Beth, unless she put up a single bed in her mother's room for herself. Oh God no! That wouldn't do at all. Her mother liked a man to share her room from time to time. None of these relationships had ever come to anything and Tilly suspected that her mother didn't want them to, she valued her independence. Would she mind them all moving in with her?

Would Beth want to keep the baby, was she even having a baby, that was by no means sure. School, school, school, the problem interfered with her thoughts again. She needed money. The bags. Tote-Tilly bags. Not fucking well Tote Lonore! How dare she! The slut! The hussy! How dare she! Tilly screamed to the wind, but it didn't care and bounced her words off the rising waves. And Robert, her father-in-law who had always been so kind and courteous to her, he'd nailed his colours to Lonore's mast. He and the slut engineered a hoax break in at the factory so that they could steal the sewing machines. No wonder they were so keen to respond and now, the machines are in the garage! A grudging admiration for Lonore flickered, but she dowsed it.

She was at the limit of the Long Sands now and began to trudge back up the dunes. Half way up a man was lying on the grass. He stood up, towering over her, his black curls whipping about his handsome head.

'Hello again. Cary, Cary Innes.' He offered by way of introduction.

She had got a bit of a fright, suddenly coming over him like that. She took a step back and he repeated himself.

'Cary, I'm Lena's friend. I know your mother.'

She nodded. 'Yes hello. I'm sorry, things on my mind.'

'Good place to sort things out.' He gestured to the beach. 'I do my best thinking here.'

He took her hand to help her up the last steep bit. His was warm and dry, hot even, or was that her hand. They fell into step along the pavement that skirted the towering cliffs. The street lights began to glow, casting a strange orange tint over him, he seemed gilded. Tilly scoffed at her fancies. This business with Adam was beginning to addle her brain. She stole a look at Cary and their eyes met. God! He stirred urges she was in no mood to pursue, she had enough complications in her life at the moment.

'And what were you thinking about, lying in the dunes, waiting for unsuspecting women?'

'I've been offered a chance to take a boat down to the Caribbean.'

'That's a toughie, all that sun and fun.'

'It is for me, not sure I want to go sailing again, just can't seem to think of a good enough reason.'

'Wish I could sail away and leave all my problems behind.'

'They'd follow you.'

'Sounds as if you have experience with problems.'

'Some.'

They walked on, each lost in their own thoughts.

Then he asked. 'Fancy a drink?'

The Gibraltar Rock pub was just ahead of them. A public house had stood on the site since before Collingwood had sailed to do battle against the French, but it had been changed and remodelled over and over again as each new manager arrived. 'I remember this when it was a lovely old pub,' she told him. 'Always busy and they had a parrot on the back bar. Now it's a carvery that's only busy at lunch time, but there's a little bar upstairs, we might find a space there.' She followed him up the widened stairs, picturing them when they were narrow and twisted, slanted and creaking under her feet when she was a teenager, drinking illicitly.

A few of her friends were at their usual positions at the bar. They waved, she waved back, but made no effort to join them or even to introduce Cary. Luckily there was one empty table by the window where two elderly people had left the bones and crumpled napkins from their fish supper. Tilly began to pile up the debris, but Cary gently pressed her into a chair.

'I'll do it. You sit here. What do you want?'

She watched him pile plates and glasses and balance them on one big hand, he had strong tanned fingers and she imagined them in her intimate places. With an effort she stopped herself, her face flushing. 'A G&T please.' She daren't look at him.

They settled and were comfortable just talking, talking and

listening, but something was happening, something she didn't want to deal with, a live thing hovering between them, a gathering heat that drew them into its dangerous centre. After an hour she had told him about Adam and the children and how she felt that perhaps her broken marriage had been her fault and he had opened his heart about his shame at allowing the sea to become so powerful he couldn't fight it, couldn't protect his family and to Cary Innes that was important. It was his role in life. Neither of them tried to convince the other that it hadn't been anything they should feel guilty for, they both knew words like that were meaningless. They both knew the guilt was something they'd have to work through alone.

When the landlord called 'time' they walked home, forgoing the river path for the quicker route through the village, they passed the factory and she explained about the bankruptcy, she called goodnight to the statue of the long dead duke, and he understood, then down the bank under the railway bridge to her mother's house where a party was in full swing out the back, on the patio.

Tilly laughed. 'You can always count on my mother to bring you down to earth. No matter how complicated and troublesome our lives might be, she always has a time for a party. We'd better show our faces.'

'Not me. I think I'll just head back on board. Things to sort out, to think about.'

Tilly was five feet six and big boned, she'd always felt big and awkward, but next to him she felt small and delicate. He stepped closer and put a hand around her waist, pulled her to him. She was ready. Right now she wanted his kiss more than anything, well maybe not more than she wanted his body, his virile, handsome, hard and delicious body. She closed her eyes and leant toward him. And nothing happened. His hands were still in place, she could feel his need. She opened her eyes. He was watching her, his lips turned up just slightly, a smile playing around his eyes. He bent forward and kissed her lips, his were sweet and tender, filled with promise, but then with a wave of his hand he was away, swaggering down the bank with his cocky sailor's stride.

'Men are such swine.' Lena's voice came out of the darkness behind her. 'Sorry. I was just on my way back to the *Brigantia* and didn't want to interrupt.'

Smiling to herself Tilly felt the need to share. 'He's so, so ....'

'Sexy?'

'Among other things. It's not just sex, he's exciting, yet lovely, you know?'

Lena sat on the step, rolling a ciggy. 'You're frustrated, give yourself time to cool down.'

'Yes.'

' Cary's vulnerable just now. He's got a few probs to sort.'

'I know. We've talked.'

'He'll go away you know. Despite his present dilemma he's a sailor, and you're not adventurous, you want to stay here.'

Tilly sighed. 'I've so much to sort out and the latest problem is that Adam didn't pay the school fees and now the boys don't have a place in any school and they don't know it yet. And guess who'll be muggins and have to break it to them?'

'I think they're pretty level-headed young men and will deal with it.'

'Harry's stressed out.'

'He just needs his mother.'

'If only it was that simple. He had great plans for the school footy team. They're top of the league now and travelling abroad to play. How can I tell him he'll not be going?'

'Sorry. I don't see these things. I'm not a natural mother.'

'Think yourself lucky.' A strained silence swelled between them and Tilly remembered Lena's admission of having had her baby adopted. 'Sorry Lena. I forgot.'

'S'alright.'

'Have you never wanted to find your baby?'

'No. I reckon that if we met we'd know, wouldn't we?'

'Don't ask me. I used to be so sure of everything. I had it all planned. Nothing was going to upset my apple cart, and now look where I am, my family scattered, my daughter not talking to me and she's hurting so much. My husband isn't the man I thought he was and his slushy has ripped my business from under my nose ...'

'Slushy?'

'Sort of a cross between a slut and a hussy.'

'Is she?'

Tilly didn't answer for a while. She thought about Lonore, who was making the best of a difficult situation that was none of her fault. She had kept things together at Sea View, rescued the sewing machines and was getting on with the job of making the bags that had to be delivered to Bewicks before the end of

October. She had sheltered Robert when his home of almost fifty years had been taken from under him and she always coped with whoever was in the house every time she, Tilly, got in a strop and walked out, and she'd done a lot of that. True the situation could not continue, but it wasn't Lonore's fault. 'No she's rather nice really and clever.'

'Steady on kid, you'll be chucking Adam out and living with her if you keep this up.'

'It's not such a bad idea. He's the one who created all this mess.'

'Men eh?' Lena finished her ciggy and gathering her very substantial self together she stood up. 'Come on, I've got some fences to mend with Jazzy.'

'Problems?' Tilly followed her through the house and into the garden where the party was beginning to wind down.

'She's got it into her head that I'm flirting with Krista.'

'And are you?'

The answer was slow forming into words, Lena hummed and hawed a bit. 'I feel a love for her, yes, but not like that. Not sure what it is.' She laughed to disguise embarrassment over showing her feelings. 'Maybe it's my mothering instinct fighting for breath before it's too late.'

'Is it possible that she is your daughter?'

'Anything's possible.'

'Can you find out?'

'Not sure I want to.'

'Perhaps she's found out and is waiting for you to admit it.'

'I couldn't even if I wanted to. I've no idea who the father is and I don't want to go back there.'

Tilly looked across at where Beth lay on the old garden bench, her head pillowed on her grandmother's lap. She put her arms around her friend. 'If she is your daughter wouldn't it be a wonderful thing?'

'Who knows? I'll talk to Jazzy.' Tilly watched her as she walked to where her lovely, sexy Jazzy sat apart from the loose group of friends who were gathered around a leaping fire. They had problems too.

Here, behind her mother's house the ground fell steeply into a small stream that funnelled through a pipe from the park and into the river, the little valley was sheltered by tall trees in front of the blank walls of warehouses on the opposite side. The bank, sloping down from the house, caught the afternoon and evening sun and her mother had spent long years cajoling many a young man into helping her terrace it. Now it was a wonderland of winding paths and beds filled with fruit trees, flowering shrubs and sweet scented herbs. In the flickering candle-light and slight breeze the strong smell of rosemary reminded Tilly of Mallorca and Paulo was conjuring images of Spain from his guitar to add to the illusion.

As she made her way towards the relaxed group Tilly felt an alien sensation take root in her breast – jealously for the easy relationship between her mother and daughter. Right at that moment she'd sell Mai to the devil for only a few minutes in her place. It had been months, even, now that she thought about it, years since she and Beth had lounged together like that. Guilt replaced jealousy as she tried unsuccessfully to remember the last time she'd been so naturally at ease with any of her children. She realised that she always disturbed any comfortable intimacy by leaping up to make pop corn, look for a DVD they could all watch or find more cushions to re-arrange to her satisfaction and by the time she'd settled herself they'd be gone, the moment lost. She had always robbed them of a natural urge to huddle together with such easy love. Now she felt awkward about joining the group, felt like an onlooker, a stranger. If she went across she was certain Beth would get up and leave. She wandered down to where Zander and Krista were playing cards with Daisy and Harry at the scarred table that she remembered from her childhood, a table she'd spent many hours at, doing homework while her mother tried unsuccessfully to persuade her to walk on the beach and look for mermaids. Again she hesitated, if she sat in it would spoil the atmosphere, the happy bantering and calling each other cheats and laughing. If Tilly ever called anyone a cheat she meant it. As she hesitated she watched a change alter Zander's relaxed slouch; he stiffened, placed his cards in front of him face up, the game, for him, was over. His lazy blue eyes shadowed and warned anyone who knew him that he was angry. Krista knew him, she followed him as he unfurled his long limbs and walked away. Tilly followed them. Behind her she could hear Cloris chattering brightly about a new ship they'd been looking at, ridiculing its extravagant décor.

'So decadent! Did you see all that silver lame and blue silk?' Her tinkling laugh rang out.

Tilly suddenly realised that despite forever inveigling all and sundry to drink one of her concoctions Cloris never seemed to drink. Was it all an act?

Zander ploughed on, determined.

Tilly stepped forward to stop him, not here, not now, please don't spoil this relaxed interlude in the busy lives of all these transient folk. 'Please Zander.' But she felt like a ghost that he just walked straight through, ignoring her hand where it trembled on his arm. She could actually feel his barely controlled anger.

Unable to stop his momentum he almost knocked Jack over with the force of his emotion. 'You maniac! Daisy almost drowned. You should be locked up!'

To his credit Jack tried to avoid his son, he started to turn away, but Cloris obstructed his intention. Smiling, hands extended, she welcomed Zander. 'Darling. This is nice. Is Daisy here?' She looked around him, past Tilly and spotting the little girl hurried toward her.

Zander's hands were deep in the pockets of his washed out Chinos, but Tilly could see the material straining over his knuckles.

'Why do you hate me so much that you want my daughter dead!'

Tilly's hand covered her mouth. She had no words to deflect his and her heart was almost bursting at the craving in his voice. Despite his anger and need for revenge Zander couldn't disguise the yearning for attention from a father who had always ignored him.

'No!' The word burst from the old man, for he was old now. Cracker Jack was no more. He was old and spent.

If Zander could only see through his hurt he'd notice that the fight was over, Jack had surrendered.

'No. It's been so hard son, always trying to keep you safe, to keep Daisy safe.'

Zander uncurled his fists, pulled them from his pocket, flung his arms in the air. 'You're completely mad. I thought it was only Cloris, but you're both insane.'

Jack stumbled backwards, away from Zander's wrath. 'Leave it son, you don't want to disturb the past, let it lie, let's be friends.'

'I've got friends. What I need is a father.'

Jack turned away, twisted to stop himself falling into the overgrown rosemary, crushing its fragrant spears, filling the air with its tangy aroma, rosemary for remembrance, and Zander was determined to evoke all the memories. He was in no mood for a cover up. He grabbed his father's jacket to haul him back. He bent his wiry frame forward, his lips tight, white, stretched and his voice hoarse with yearning and love.

Tilly could have stepped forward persuaded him back from the brink, but realised that he needed this, the time and place notwithstanding, a confrontation between him and Jack was long overdue.

'Tell me! Tell me why. Why do you hate us!' Zander shifted to change his grip, to hold one sleeve in each hand, but Jack had turned and his back was toward his son, Zander grasped the jacket, tried again to turn the old man.

Jack stretched his haggard face over his shoulder. 'I don't hate you. I love you. I love you both.' Tears coursed down his lined and defeated face, he seemed to crumple and become lifeless, he slipped, down on one knee. 'I wasn't there, don't you understand. I wasn't there to protect you and your mother, she drowned and it was my fault, because I wasn't there. I didn't keep you safe. And I couldn't be sure that I'd always be there.'

'I tried Dad, I followed you, I begged you.'

'But I couldn't risk it.' Jack implored Zander to understand his dilemma, to see that not to try had been the only way because the alternative, to try and fail was unthinkable. 'It was to keep you safe, both of you.'

'Forty years, forty years! You could have tried.'

'I was going to, then Daisy came and it might have happened again, you've seen how Cloris is.'

'What's she got to do with any of this?'

'I had to look after you both, keep her away from you because she wanted a family, she wanted you.'

'I thought Daisy would bring us together, and she's only a little girl Dad a little girl who you tired to drown.'

As if his heart had been pierced Jack wailed like his last breath was leaving him and sank to all fours in the sloping garden. 'I didn't know she was on board.'

Cloris raised her trained voice. 'Stop shouting at your father. Honestly, the two of you need your heads clashed. I took Daisy on the boat. After all she is my grandaughter and I love her.'

Everyone in the garden was still as marble, only Daisy moved. She pushed past Tilly to reach her father. She barrelled into him and Jack knocking them into a heap. The ground slid away, bushes and people and soil sliding, tumbling, hands grabbing and failing to stop their bodies from plunging into the stream.

Everyone rushed down the terraces, people jumped into the water, it wasn't very deep, about five feet, but fast flowing and cold and the bottom was uneven with heaps of stones to impede them. Tilly held Harry and Cloris back.

Mai fled to the very end where the water ran into the pipe that gushed into the river and certain death. 'Stop them. Don't let them in!' She slid into the water, pressing herself backwards across the black hole of the pipe mouth. 'Don't let them in.'

Tilly saw her, a ship's figurehead, big breasts swelling, the material of her blouse clinging, her long white hair streaming, she was magnificent. But Tilly felt like crying. Mai wasn't blocking the exit in case anyone was pulled into the pipe. Her mother was guarding them from the mermaids who she believed would swim into her garden, the mermaids she was certain were always waiting to snatch any unsuspecting soul. She too was quite mad.

In the water many hands were reaching, voices calling. Zander surfaced with blind eyes, but soon disappeared again to return with Daisy and pushing her into Lena's hands disappeared again. Men splashed and plunged, the girls pulled Daisy to higher ground, Lena ran to help Mai block the pipe and the writhing mass of heads and limbs tumbled and splashed in the ever deepening water, getting closer and closer to the pipe, but finally they were all safe, crawling onto the grassy banks, clinging to the deeply embedded rocks. Zander and Jack were safe. Cradled like a child in his son's arms Jack lay unconscious, but alive.

Daisy's little voice rang out in the stillness of the near disaster. 'Grandpa! I didn't mean to drown him.' She tore loose from Jazzy and running to where Zander was trying to revive his father she flung herself onto them. 'Wake up Grandpa.' She shook him and shook him and shook him until Jack opened his eyes. 'I love you.' She sobbed and with her thin little arms around their necks she pulled their three heads together in a tight bond.

'Jees, you sure know how to throw a party Mai.' Lena always had a quip.

Relieved laughter skipped over the assembled and dripping crowd of friends. Most of them had grown up with this feud and it was clear they were relieved it was over. But Tilly wanted to hear more. Clearly Jack had thought that some disaster would be averted if he kept away from Zander and Daisy, but this decision had been wrong and had only caused misery for all of them. She hoped that once things settled down it would all be told and they could finally move forward as a family.

Jazzy phoned for an ambulance and people drifted away, to dry off on board the *Brigantia*. Tilly ordered Beth and Harry indoors.

Reluctant to leave in case any more exciting events occurred, Harry boasted. 'I almost had him you know, I had hold of Jack, but then Zander got him.'

'Go have a bath then get your 'jarmas on and I'll make hot chocolate.'

'Aw Mum.'

'Do it Harry. I'll be up as soon as the ambulance has gone. Everyone's ok, please, you've had enough excitement for one night.'

Beth stood to one side. Tilly saw that fear had etched lines on her young face and thought, this is what she'll look like after a few years of motherhood. She looked for her own mother who, still soaking wet was sitting on the bank watching the water pour into the pipe. She kissed Beth. 'Take him up please, Beth. I'll bring Nana.'

Beth nodded and they did as they'd been asked. Zander, Jack, Cloris and Daisy huddled together. It was a start. She left them and walked down to her mother.

'It's my fault. Why on earth haven't I had a wire put across there? I should have known they'd come looking. They're more and more daring.'

'Come on Mam, let's go indoors. Everyone's all right now.'

'But they almost got in and if I don't watch they might come back and spawn. The stream will be full of them.' Mai turned her face up to Tilly. A fierce determination still burned in her eyes, she was as strong for her cause as ever.

Tilly's heart was breaking. Her strong, idiosyncratic and eccentric mother, the white witch, the earth mother, Mai the indomitable, friend and confidant of prostitutes was getting old and losing her wits. She swallowed the tears that threatened to chock her. 'Tomorrow Mam. We'll get it done tomorrow. We'll have a grill made, but now we need to go in and get dried off.'

'No! I have to watch out for them.'

The events of the day pressed in on Tilly. A tight band of pressure wrapped around her brow. 'I'm not feeling to great Mam, perhaps if you said a spell to make the water safe, just for tonight, then tomorrow when it's light we'll be able to see how things are.'

Her wet clothes clinging and muddy Mai stood up, concern for her daughter the only thing that could deflect her. She felt Tilly's forehead. 'Mmm, a bit hot. We'll get something for that.' And with a last glance at the stream she pushed Tilly up the bank.

The ambulance had just arrived and Lena and Jazzy had everything under control..

Mai was easily negotiating the steep bank, one hand behind her, reaching out to help her daughter, Tilly. 'Cloris is a bit batty isn't she?'

'I think she has Alzheimer's. It's going to cause a problem for them.' Tilly knew she'd have to address Mai's similar problem. The years were speeding up.

Inside the flat Harry and Beth were tucked into the same bed, mugs of hot chocolate in their hands. Tilly kissed them goodnight. 'Sweet dreams.'

'Can we talk Mum?' Beth asked.

The tears that had been threatening since Tilly had realised everyone was safe spilled over, out of her control and she hugged Beth. 'Yes pet, we will. Tomorrow after we've all had a good sleep.' She went to the window to pull the curtains and looking down saw Lena and Jazzy obviously arguing, then Jazzy walked away leaving Lena in a pool of lamplight, head down shoulders sagging, alone in the night.

CHAPTER SIXTEEN

LENA

Waking in a dirty grey dawn, Lena sat up, stretching, then swinging her legs off the narrow cabin sofa she stood up. Last night Jazzy had accused her of making a fool of them both with her obvious crush on Krista. Neither argument nor pleas had persuaded her that she was wrong, because the stark truth was Krista did hold an attraction for Lena, who had chosen not to analyse it because if she opened that particular Pandora's Box it might be empty of hope. What if Krista was her daughter; but that was impossible, wasn't it? No, it wasn't. Krista had a familiar way of disappearing as you watched her, her eyes becoming bland, a trick to shut you out, the same trick Lena's sister, Yvonne, used to employ to dispel the taunts of the bullies. Yvonne always did rise above them, walk away, aloof as they shouted their insults to the two little girls from the quayside who's mother was a drunken whore. Two little girls who wore dirty second-hand clothes and wellies, even in summer.

And Krista could swim.

Lena could swim, hadn't bothered for years, but at one time she too had swum Pollensa Bay. The facts were stacking up but Lena felt as if she was losing the game. Jazzy had locked their cabin door against her so she'd settled in the salon and finished the dregs in a bottle of vodka before realising that this was no answer. She'd tried sleeping, but that too had been an unsuccessful venture.

Dragging her leaden feet on deck she gasped in the freezing wind that blew off the sea, sending clouds of fret up the river. Jeez, she'd almost forgotten how this northern weather could turn and bite your bum with its bared teeth, but it woke her up and bracing herself she made a tour of her beloved ship.

Beneath her feet she could feel movement and muffled sounds as the crew stirred themselves, ready for whatever the day might bring. She stopped above their cabin 'midships, picturing Jazzy as she woke in their double bunk; she would rise fluidly, bent lightly from the middle like a willow bough in a breeze, lithe and supple, her long blond hair spreading across her shoulders in silken skeins. Lena wanted nothing more than to go to her, lie down and wrap that deliciously warm body in her arms, spoon her shape, cup her tiny breasts, gently fingering the dark nipples until, aroused, Jazzy would turn and they'd make love; easy, tender, passionate and caring, satisfying because that's how much they loved each other.

Sighing she realised she had no choice. She had to return to the place where she'd been at her lowest ebb, to a blackness in her heart that Cary had replaced with sunshine. A place that had, both physically and emotionally, almost buried her. She had to go home. First, she'd go see Mai. She fingered the little silver mermaid pendant that hung between her breasts. Mai would know where her family were living now, they wouldn't have moved far from their familiar habitat.

Briefly she toyed with the idea of going to see Jazzy, but the thought was fleeting, she had made it clear that she would not accept any more infidelities. Lena felt contrite. In the past there had been occasions when lust had triumphed over love and she hated herself for the heartache she'd caused her lover, her sweet, sweet lover.

'Thinking won't make it so. You need to go talk my dear, tell her who you are. It's not fair to expect her to love half a person.'

She turned at the sound of Cary's soft words. 'Clever bugger. Mind-reader now are you? And anyway you've no room to talk.'

'I know.'

'When you gonna fight your demons?'

'Soon.'

For a while they walked the ship, easy with each other as they tested lines and sheets, stamped on suspect planks, peered over the side, both of them dismissive of the wet wind, then satisfied that all was well they stopped in the lee of the massive main mast, solid oak, planed from one individual trunk, eight feet in circumference. Lena turned her back on the river and forced herself to look inland. North Shields was almost unrecognisable from the town she'd grown up in. In front of her, smart flats hung on the bank in graded tiers, faced with mock sandstone and planted around with shrubs and sapling trees. The whole enterprise looked nice, tasteful and she knew that all the way up the twelve-mile stretch of the River Tyne to Newcastle the same metamorphose was happening. The noisy dirty shipyards that had given work to millions of men and food to their families were gone forever, except for a few yards that still struggled along, building gas platforms or manufacturing precast concrete tunnels and plastic piping, but the residents of the regenerated Tyneside complained about them, when not so long ago they'd complained about the lack of them. Lena sighed. 'I hate this place.

'It's not the place you hate, it's the past.'

'Yes and why do I want to stir it all up again? We were happy in Mallorca and now everything's a mess. Jazzy isn't talking to me. I can't help you with your problems. Tilly's life is in ruins and Zander's entire family has almost drowned. Why the hell did we come?'

Cary leaned on the rail watching the waves as the sea won its battle again, pushing the river back to its source just as it did twice a day. 'Some things are inevitable. You can't sail into the sunset if you can't navigate the storm.'

'I'll have to go see them. I have a feeling that Krista might be my daughter.'

'She tell you that?'

'No, just hints and she keeps looking at me as if she's waiting for me to tell her something.'

'She's a rhum girl.'

'I can't figure it out, but I know I need to go and have it out with them. I'll call in at Mai's first, see if there's any news.'

'News?'

'Oh, you weren't there last night, God what a night.' She brought him up to date on the evening's drama.

'Seems like it hadn't happened a bit too soon, they've let it fester for years, maybe now we'll all find out why Cracker Jack's such a maither. As my old Nan used to say, there's al'ays trouble for some.'

Reluctant to move Lena stood beside him, welcoming his reassuring presence, but he was apart from the moment, mulling over his own problems. 'What am I to do Lena? If Jack's OK and made it up with Zander then I'm out of a job, only natural he'll want Zander to skipper the new boat down to the islands and with Krista on board too that'll be enough, the boat's not big enough to need me.'

'Stop arsing about Cary. You've got a ship. I'll give you a lift back to Falmouth and you can outfit the *Genista*, we'll both pick up crew and fuck off out of all this. It'll be right, always plenty of charters around Barbados.'

Cary didn't answer. He stepped aside, head back, narrowed eyes searching the sky, assessing the fret. 'This'll clear by noon, go out with the tide.'

Lena didn't argue, nobody she knew could read weather like him. 'You have a good night out with Tilly?'

He mumbled an accent.

'You're hopeless, but the two of you together just might make a good-un.'

'I've things to think on. Taking Mai's old crabber out for an hour or two, study the situation.'

'Tossing the caul?'

'Mebee.' He flashed his smile, designed to dazzle.

Lena barked a laugh. 'You can't fool Tilly. She's one clued up lady. Play your cards right and you might just have a chance of a life together.'

'Well, it's sort of my plan. What's yours?'

'Buggered if I know, sail off into the sunset?'

Yea, well, like I said, you need to blow a hole through the storm.'

'Oh wise one I can see now how your own life is so soddin' perfect.'

'You and Jazzy are solid, but you have to work on it. For once in your life be honest.'

She pulled her shoulders back and pointed up the bank. 'Onward and upward. Off I go.'

'Good luck.'

Lena nodded and leaving him standing at the rail she stepped ashore and hurried up the quayside, her head high her stride purposeful. Not a big women, about five four, a bit too much weight around the middle, hair prematurely white and always cut short to frame her happy round face, the skin smooth and clear with piercing blue eyes that demanded truth; a contained intensity in her bearing. Lena was a force of nature.

She exchanged greetings as she walked down the quay and up to the Brew House where everyone was up and about. Machines in Naomi's studio were whirring and Noel could be heard cursing as he literally flayed his canvas with paint soaked whips. Lena walked up the familiar stairs. Tilly was there, sitting by the window, looking sad. Lena didn't have room for anybody else's misery so she didn't ask.

'Hi. I'm looking for Mai.'

'She's gone to see Jack and Daisy. Her and Harry.'

'You heard anything?'

'Zander called. They're out of hospital and fine with no after effects from swallowing the water in the burn. Apparently we could bottle it.'

'I thought Mia did.'

'Yes, yes of course she does, doesn't she? Funny but I never thought that was the magic ingredient in her potions.'

'See, she's not as daft as she seems.'

'Speaking of which, I'm really worried. You saw her last night. I think she's going insane.'

'Mai? Never! You have to be sane first. She's not changed Till. She's always been fanatical about saving us all from the evil mermaids.'

'Exactly.'

'Can you prove she's wrong?'

'Oh come on, surely you don't believe that cods-wallop.'

'If you believe in good and evil then you've got to admit to a battle over our souls. Are mermaids any less believable than angels and demons, God or the Devil?'

'No, I suppose not.' Tilly looked up, her face haggard with worry. 'She's my mother.'

'Give her a break will you. We can't all match up to your standards.'

'Excuse me?'

Lena didn't have time for tact. 'Had to be said. You are a bit of a martyr to perfection.' She watched her friend sag in her chair, but couldn't bring herself to offer comfort, she was all comforted out. 'Oh well I'll leave you to it. Got to go.'

In the street she passed Cary.

'Mai's not in. She's round at Jack's new boat seeing how they are.'

'Need the keys for the crabber, they'll be upstairs.'

'Tilly's up there.' Lena grinned, daring him. 'Go get 'em boy.'

He hesitated.

'Faint heart, faint heart,' Lena taunted as she left him, hesitating on the step.

On Jack's boat all was happiness. Jack and Zander were in the wheelhouse discussing the various attributes of the new boat. Mai was drinking coffee with Cloris and Krista and Harry and Daisy were at the fancy chrome rail, talking to the crew of an Irish sloop moored alongside.

'Permission to come aboard skipper?' Lena called to Jack.

'Come aboard, come aboard.' Jack looked up and down the quay. 'Just you?'

''Fraid so. Looking for Mai.'

'Hello pet, here I am, come and have a coffee. Cloris has a fancy machine that makes any kind you want.'

After she delighted Cloris by ordering a Macchiato she sat up close to Mai and asked where her mother and sister were now living.

'Sure you need to know?'

Lena turned around to make sure that Krista couldn't overhear, the girl was watching, but was too far away to listen in, never-the-less Lena bent even closer and whispered. 'Is Krista my daughter?'

'Do you think she is?'

'I don't know what to think.'

'And you think that talking to those two will help? You should put your faith in the mermaids. They know the truth.'

'Please Mai, not now. This is important.'

'Course it is, that's what I'm telling you. The past is a destructive place, are you sure you want to go back there?'

'I feel something for her, but not as a girlfriend, know what I mean, more like there's some bond there, something … I can't explain it. That's why I have to go and talk to them. Krista knows something.'

'Then talk to her, talk to Jazzy, tell them both everything and leave it at that, you don't need to be related to feel like a mother, look at Zander, it doesn't matter to him if he's not Daisy's father, he doesn't ever think about it.'

Shaking her head Lena asked again for the address and before Cloris had returned with the coffee she was back on the quayside and heading up to the last surviving row of terraced houses overlooking the river. As she walked through the fancy named Squares, Cul-de-sacs and Chambers of new houses she could remember how it had been, the places she had run through, dodging piles of stinking fish offal that overflowed from skips and hurrying past furtive men looking for a woman, their physical need paramount. Her mother had been one of those women gathering under the street lamps with her cronies, selling themselves for the price of a beer. Lena and Yvonne at home, hungry and cold, would run out to find her and beg a few pence for chips. Sometimes Social Services would visit the filthy flat, they'd have meetings to discuss placing the girls in care, but her mother would appear dressed decently in borrowed clothes, clean and relatively sober and talk them around with promises of reform. These were empty promises, but the middle class social workers fell for it and went home confidant in their ability to solve the world's problems, never imagining that the same evening she'd be back out, back in the lane, on the game. Another year would pass and Lena eventually saw how easy it would be to slip down the lane one night and make money to keep her and Yvonne from starving, but something always held her back, even then she knew that she could never let a man have intimate knowledge of her, neither her body nor her mind. The rape had confirmed to her that she was different from these women who crudely flaunted their feminine sexuality for the gratification of men. And Mai had saved her. Lena wouldn't stay in the Brew House, not with smarmy smarty Tilly there, so she lived on the old crabber, sometimes earning her keep by taking it out to harvest the pots. It had been Mai who'd educated her about lesbians and Mai who'd helped her believe in herself, not as different from all the other girls she knew, just the same, all with their own way to find. It had been Mai who'd helped her through the pregnancy and the traumatic birth, Mai who'd taken the baby and sent it away, smoothed her life out and given her the space to heal and grow. And then she'd seen the one abiding love of her life. The Tall Ships had entered the river and Lena's passion was born, gone was the confusion over a child she'd never even seen, here was a love she could understand. These majestic vessels with their sleek clean lines, free and fancy and beautiful had captivated her. She immersed herself in them, in the lore, the facts, the business and the magic. Skipping from deck to deck she became a messenger, a go-for, a cleaner, a cook; she'd do anything just to feel the decks moving under her feet, but as race day loomed her whole being had become a tightly wound ball of misery. She'd begged skipper after skipper to give her a chance, but they just laughed at the scruffy, inexperienced and under aged urchin girl. They gave her a few pence to go post a letter or buy a pound of sausages for the cook. The night before the race she'd accepted an invitation from Mai to attend a party and there she'd met Cary and was saved. He and his grandfather had agreed to let her sail with them to the islands, she had always suspected that Mai had a hand in this offer and was grateful because she never again returned to her life of misery in North Shields, until now.

Prospect Terrace overlooked the river from a high vantage point along the top of the bank. It had escaped demolition and the terraced housed had been renewed and restored, new UPVC windows and doors bragged of modern times, all but one. At number ten the front door had peeling paint, no bell or knocker and a hole for a letter box, it didn't matter because the door was so swollen and warped it didn't close. The smell assailed her as she climbed the uncarpeted stairs, but she took a deep breath and pushed open the door to the living room. It was dim, the ragged curtains askew on sagging rails. Overflowing ash trays seemed welded to chair arms where the cushions sat flat and greasy. The two bedroom doors were shut and where a makeshift kitchen hung on the tiny back landing was a mess of take-away trays and dirty mugs on top of a wooden bench encrusted with mould and God alone knew what filth oozed and festered under it where a pile of dirty clothes waited for a rare trip to the launderette. Lena stood still and stared into her sister's surprised brown eyes, eyes that were closed to answers.

'Friggin hell, if it isn't the prodigal.' Yvonne swept a hand in front of her. 'Take a pew.'

Lena would rather stand. 'Mam in?'

'Bed.'

'I need to talk to you.'

'And you don't want that old hoore butting in.'

'Something like that.'

'Well how are you Vonnie, how're ye been for sixteen years, had enough money, been well?' Her sister mocked Lena's lack of greeting. 'Well spit it out, don't suppose you just popped in for a cup of tea.'

'Do you know a girl called Krista?'

'Once knew a girl called Christine. Ungrateful little git, just up and left one day, no idea what happened to her.'

'Is this her?' Lena held out a rare photo of Krista. She had found only two among the hundreds she had filled her camera with on the voyage from the Mediterranean.

Yvonne lit another cigarette from the stub of the old one before grinding it into the already full ashtray. She took a casual look, but made no attempt to take the photo from Lena. 'Yes, that's her. She run away to tell Aunty Lena about her miserable old Mammy, did she?'

'So she's your daughter?' Lena wasn't sure if relief or disappointment was the greater emotion she felt.

'Who else's could she be, have you looked at her, looked at me? But she didn't take after me, oh no, it was you she favoured, swimming, running around the boats, turning her nose up at the home I struggled to keep for her, and then like you she ran away. You both ran away leaving me here to deal with that old cow.'

'You could have left too.'

'And who would look after her then, eh? She'd be dead by now.'

'You're not responsible for her Yvonne. She made her own life long before we could influence her.'

'Easy for you to say, but then you never cared for us.'

'I had to go or become like her.'

'Like I did? Well now you can look down your nose at both of us.'

'I don't. And I didn't come here to talk about our mother. I came to find out about Krista. I'm living in Mallorca and she came to me, but she never said who she was, never said she was related, I gave her a job 'cos she was good and I needed a crew.'

Yvonne gave a short laugh. 'So, now you're a big shot with a boat an' all.'

'I've worked hard.'

'But you never sent money home. Didn't even think about us struggling with a baby to care for.'

'I didn't know you had a baby and anyway I didn't have any money for years and the ship was ...' Lena stopped, took a deep breath. She hadn't come here to make excuses for her behaviour. 'You are telling me the truth aren't you? She is definitely your daughter ... not mine.' She finished lamely.

Yvonne burst out laughing. 'And why would you think that? Haven't you noticed she's black!'

'I know but I really don't remember much about the night ...' Lena faltered, struggling to discuss the rape. 'I don't know who it was, he could have been black.'

'She's mine, mine. You weren't here. You weren't here to help me. You left me to manage on my own, I was only fourteen when I went with that filthy old bitch to the back lane, fourteen and you had left me. What was I supposed to do, starve!'

Yvonne's words shouted at her, dredged up the guilt she had forced away all these years. 'I'm sorry, but ...'

'You're sorry. Not as sorry as I was when I fell pregnant. I had to stay. I had to bring up a baby, care for it in between pulling my knickers down, hardly worth pulling them up most nights. They all wanted the fifteen-year-old black kid and she stood there and took the money.'

Lena felt as if she'd been whipped. 'I had no idea.'

'I was all by myself Lena. You left me to give my kid a life, my kid Lena not yours, you pathetic old dyke.'

Lena hung onto the back of a chair to steady herself, the years she had missed flashing before her, years of Yvonne struggling and being manipulated by their own mother. She stretched out a hand and began to speak but the door behind suddenly flew open almost knocking her over and Krista burst into the room.

'No! No! I will not let you say that about me. I am not your daughter. I can't be.' She faced Yvonne, who had rebuilt her brash exterior.

Yvonne laughed and lighting another cigarette she shuffled into the kitchen to fill the kettle with water, busying herself with a mug and teabag. 'Not good enough for you eh? Well you can't fake the truth kiddo. I'm your mother, your dear darling mother and there's not a damn think you can do about it.'

'I'll have DNA tests done. I'll prove who I am and she's my mother.' She pointed to Lena.

Standing dumb at the sight of the naked fear on Krista's usually inscrutable face, Lena looked away, looked at her sister, waited.

Yvonne left her tea making and crossed to a cupboard by the chimney breast. Rummaging around she finally unearthed, from the shelves of clutter, a shoe box. She sat down with it on her knee. Searching the contents she brought out a birth certificate, a pink baby card from the hospital and a photo, she passed them to Krista who smacked them aside and stormed out with all the fury she'd entered still intact. Lena bent and picked the pieces of paper from the ash covered carpet. The birth certificate listed the names, Mother Yvonne Turnbull. Baby Christine Patricia Turnbull, daughter. On the bent and twisted baby card the names again with date and time of birth, and on the bottom of the card, one word – caesarean. 'Caesarean?'

'Yea and full hysterectomy, good thing too given my line of work.'

'I'm sorry Yvonne.' Sympathy clouding her judgment she thought of a solution. 'You can come with us. It's not too late.'

Yvonne almost choked laughing. 'It's been too late since I was born Lena. It was always too late. But you can take her.

Look after her.' With that she left, shutting the bedroom door and Lena heard the bolt slide into place, their one defence from childhood, the bolt that would keep them safe. Placing the pathetic proof of Krista's birth on the arm of the chair she left, following Krista and in the street she looked over the railing to the quay. Krista was running along, feet and arms working, running as fast as she could to get back to Zander.

Lena went back to Jazzy.

CHAPTER SEVENTEEN

TILLY

Tilly had hardly had time to give any thought to Lena's brutal revelations before Cary came thudding up the stairs, calling her name. Lena must have told him to come up and here she was in her bath robe. She pulled it together over a short nightie, legs on show. They needed shaving, oh well, can't be helped.

He settled on the wide window sill with his back to her view of the twin piers and the North Sea and said. 'I'm taking Mai's boat out. She said I've to check the lobster pots. Come with me.' It wasn't a question.

She sat back to look up at him, too worried about Beth to pay serious attention to the invitation. 'I've things to do. Beth and I need to spend time together, she wants to talk.' As if conjured by her name the opposite door opened and Beth entered the long kitchen, her startled eyes, so like her grandmother's, took in the scene and before Tilly could explain the situation Beth's lips curled in disgust.

'Unbelievable. Unbe-fucking-lievable.' She spat at them, adding one and one and making adultery, then she marched off down the stairs and was gone.

Tilly shot up, made to follow her, called her name, but Cary caught her, turned her to him. 'Let her go, we'll talk to her later.'

'But we were going to talk. Sort out her problems.' Tilly realised she sounded like a petulant child.

'Maybe later. A short sea trip will clear your mind of this muddle. When we come back you'll feel better and she's not going anywhere.' He nodded his head toward the stairs, his jet black curls springing, his dark sea blue eyes concerned. 'Come with me Tilly.' He said again and pulled her close to his broad chest. She felt delicate next to his strength and sighed under his hand as it smoothed her tangled hair and again he said. 'Come with me.' He seemed so convinced that they should and a strange feeling of certainly blotted Beth's problems from her mind. She leaned into his hands, her senses reeling, nerve ends leaping and she didn't think about her problems any more, didn't wonder if it was the right thing to do because she knew it was. On some deep uncomprehending level she felt that it was right to follow him.

Now they were at sea in a small, very unseaworthy boat, hauling in lobster pots. The first out of six had given nothing but crabs, but this one was heavy with three huge dark brown and black lobsters, males. Tilly, helped to open the cage and tear away the interfering weed, then with one hand over each pair of pincers he pulled three big fat daddies from the string of the iron bound cage holding them for her to slip rubber bands over their pincers. 'Wow, Mam'll be overjoyed at these, they bring a good price, but she hardly gets any money herself, she usually leaves this to anybody willing to come and get them, she doesn't really like being out here, on the open sea.'

'What? And her an expert on all things mer.'

Tilly laughed as she swung into the tiny wheelhouse to gun the motor and move on to the next and final pot. 'Yea, strange isn't it. I think it all started when Dad was drowned in a storm. I was only months old. Apparently it was just about here. They were fishing, coming in actually, trying to beat a storm, but it closed down quickly and a freak wave swamped the boat, just three men aboard and the two who survived said he'd saved them, hanging on to them over a buoyancy aid when they were unconscious. Ted Miller always maintains he went under, sinking fast in his heavy sea boots and waterproof then a mermaid brought him up, but she took Dad in exchange. They never found his body and Mam recons they're waiting for her too, cos it was her boat they wrecked and there're still mad that she wasn't aboard. That's why she never goes to sea.'

'I know how she feels.'

Tilly cut the engine and he threw out a sea anchor. They were quiet while they pulled up the last pot and emptied it of two lobsters then he baited the pot and tossed it back.

'Time for a bit of lunch I think.' Pulling a thermos box from under the stern bench he invited her to sit beside him on a rug. Side by side they made sandwiches from the ham, cheese and crusty bread he'd bought, there was also beer and grapes.

On the lee side the little bay of Cullercoats shone in the sunshine, the beach beginning to fill up as people from the west end of Newcastle and locals streamed down the steep ramps from the Metro station. Cullercoats was very popular with its safe bathing for children and a Blue Flag award.

'Lena says you're worried.' Tilly thought she'd take the bull by the horns.

'Not so much now. I've come to an understanding with myself.'

'Tell me.' She was hungry to know him.

'It seems silly when I actually say it, but I've grown up in Cornwall where sea lore is taken very seriously, especially by us sailing types.' Smiling at her she knew he was trying to make light of it.

He wasn't to know she wouldn't scoff at his beliefs, not now. A few weeks ago she might have, but her life had changed in so many ways, she was no longer certain of anything. She gazed out to sea, giving him time to gather his thoughts.

He continued, in his slow Devonshire lilt. 'Grandfer always maintained that his mother was a Kelpie, that's a woman who could live on land or sea, and when she was about eighty or thereabouts, she just walked into the sea and never returned. His father, missing her, followed suit; so when it was time for him to go, the old bugger waited until I was away and did the same thing. Trouble is he was born with a caul, a membrane over his face.' He looked at her for understanding.

She nodded. She knew that seamen believed that cauls were strong magic and some would pay serious money to own one.

'A sailor should carry his caul with him at all times, that way if he's lost overboard the mermaids can't steal his soul, but Grandfer left his behind and now I've got it.' He pulled out a battered tin and opened it. Inside was a wrinkled piece of dried skin, brown with a delicate webby texture. He waited.

Drinking her beer Tilly felt that all the forces she'd denied during her life, her carefully planned life, were more powerful now, next to this big man, than she'd ever felt them when she'd been with Mai. Had that been her fault? Had she built such strong defences that the natural order couldn't get through, was that why her life was such a mess, because she'd fought the very elements that could help her? She felt such a fool. She took hold of his hand. 'I know that your beliefs are as real to you as any religion. And that's a good thing, isn't it? Because it's exactly how Mam feels and as Lena's just told me in no uncertain terms, I'm a fool to mock her. But what makes you so certain that your grandfather didn't leave it behind deliberately, either because he didn't believe any more or as a keepsake for you, his sacrifice to keep you safe.'

'I've thought of that, course I have, but I've got my own caul and I've been waiting for a sign from the mermaids.'

'Mam would tell you that you can't trust the deceitful little bastards. She says there are no good mermaids.'

'Maybe for her there's not, but for me there are, always have been.'

Her heart was bursting with love and tenderness and admiration for this huge strong virile man, now so uncertain about the fate of his dead grandfather's soul and she wanted so much to hold him, to make it better. Dusting crumbs from her hands she prepared to stand up. 'Do we have a ceremony, a chant or prayer that needs to be said, a deity to invoke?'

He looked at her to see if she was mocking him, she looked back, solemnly, knowing that he could feel her honesty, her love, yes love. She knew it was. The years with Adam fell away as if they were a story about someone else because she knew their life together was over and she wasn't even that bothered, the stolen sex with Zander became a weak passive thing and faded in the fierce passion Cary induced.

'No.' He said. 'No ceremony or chant and I said all I needed to say to Grandfer when he was alive.'

'Are you going to do it then?'

'Yes. Because this is the time and the place I've been waiting for and I'm certain that you're the reason I've been waiting.'

She leant forward to take another look at the subject causing such concern. 'It's not much is it, just a piece of old leather to hold the fate of a soul. It must have been quite a burden to him all of his life, worrying about his soul, it's not something we tend to dwell on. When we die it goes, and it's not up to us what happens to it.'

'Mebee.' He knelt and lifting the caul from the battered old tin he held it out, on the palm of his hand, bent his hand to the water and a soft wave took away his burden.

They watched it sink into the darkness, waited a few minutes more. 'Were you expecting something to happen?' Tilly turned and smiled at him, putting her arms about him.

He sat on the bench gently pulling her with him. 'Do you think I'm mad?

'No. I think you're wonderful'

His lips were strong, tasting of the sea, of unknown places and it seemed the most natural thing in the world to kiss them and let her body absorb him through that kiss, she felt him, eager, but contained, as his mouth coveted her cheeks, then stronger on her neck, gasping as he licked the skin just under her ear, whispered breathless promises then returned to suck her shoulders then down her neck again, then back to her waiting mouth. She helped him to loosen her blouse and remove her bra. She lay back on the bench while he used his tongue to trace patterns on her bare arms, her breasts. He told her they were secret pirate patterns to keep them bound together forever and that he loved her and she knew she loved him too and as the sun rose higher they stripped each other of their clothes and she knew that this was right. That this man had been hers forever, she'd just needed to find him.

Later as the sun began to fall across the land and the eastern horizon was bringing up the big guns, masses of black clouds, they chugged into the river. Feeling tired and a bit sore, the bottom of a boat was not the ideal place to make love, Tilly casually rested her hands on the wheel, behind her with his hands on her waist, Cary nuzzled her neck. 'We'll be the talk of the place, as soon as I step off this boat it'll be obvious to all that I've just had the most amazing experience of my life.' She found herself light-headed and giggling like a schoolgirl.

'Don't be silly, have you smelled yourself?' Cary snuffled his nose about her skin.

'Oh God, we stink.'

'Nobody's coming close enough to notice anything other than the size of our lobsters.'

But it couldn't last. It seemed that a deluge of freezing water obliterated everything that had happened to her during the long, wonderfully long, afternoon. Beth. What had she been thinking? She hadn't been thinking at all. The future loomed over them and she knew that Cary had felt the change in her.

He stepped back and nudging her aside took over the wheel, smartly bringing the little craft into safe harbour.

But there would no safety for Tilly; not until she faced Beth and helped her with whatever it needed for her to accept her situation. Not to mention Harry and Sean. They too needed her to make a safe place in the very real storm that threatened all of them. She turned to Cary, and shaking her head looked into his soft, trusting eyes. 'I have to go. I can't see you anymore.' Her heart hurt, her limbs were bruised, her senses bereft, her hands trembled over his arms, strong arms that had enfolded her in passionate strength and for a precious few seconds more she clung to this man who was ready to give her a love that she had never imagined. She felt his pain and silently held him close, feeling the beat of his heart solid and strong. 'I have to go Cary. My life's a mess.'

'Don't give up on us. I'm not going anywhere. I'll wait for as long as it takes.'

Tilly felt only sorrow. Close to tears she left him. Climbing out of the boat she hurried up to the Brew House.

The storm broke as soon as Tilly stepped in the door. Beth was sitting at the table eating stew, Mai was famous for her fish stew, it being the only thing she could cook that was remotely tasty.

'Lena's going to take me with her.'

Tilly sank to a chair. 'Have you deliberately chosen to ignore the fact that you might be pregnant?'

Beth ignored her. She stood up and dropped her bowl into the dishwasher, the spoon clattering into the workings under the tray. 'Right, I'm off.'

Tilly took hold of her shoulder and forced her face up, looked into her pain filled eyes. 'You know don't you? You've known from the start. Why didn't you talk to me?'

'What was the point? You can't sort out your own life never mind mine.' And with that she fled downstairs and away down the quay.

Tilly let her go. What else could she do? The flat was quiet now, soft voices and the whiff of nicotine from Mai and Naomi as they relaxed on the terrace below her, discussing their output for the day and the dubious merits of agents who took money for doing nothing as Mai was always telling her. The day was almost gone, its last blinding rays turning the rooftops red, old and new buildings indistinguishable in glory. Tilly showered and changed all the while getting more and more angry with her headstrong, maddening daughter. She rang Sea View to speak to Sean. Adam answered. Sean was surfing. Harry was there too, playing kick-about on the green with the two little boys. Did they need anything? No, he said, they were fine, he'd promised them they could camp out in the dunes, he and Robert would sleep with them. She thanked him and hung up. There was only Beth to deal with.

She hurried down the bank to the quayside where the frenzy was building. The fun fare was awash with teenagers, the beer and music tents were doing their usual extortionate business and the pavement café's overflowed with happy people. She heard Beth before she saw her. A loud raucous laugh, forced and shrill. She was at an outside table with Endora, Paulo and others from the *Brigantia*. She was pouring a shot glass of some colourless liquid into her mouth, head back, legs on the table, her short skirt hiked up so far Tilly could see her underwear, a black G-string with diamantes glistening at the crotch.

Banging the empty glass on the table Beth picked another from a row in front of her, and lifting it to swallow she spied Tilly. She stood up and threw a hand in her direction. 'Look everyone. It's my mother. Hello mother mine. This is my mother everyone. My fucking mother. Not that she's a fucking mother, well she is really, what I mean is she fucks, yea, that's it. My fucking mother fucks. Any man she fancies. My mother! She'll fuck you. Just ask her.'

Tilly was furious. She pushed her way to stand in front of Beth. 'You're drunk.' Her voice low, controlled

'Yes. Yes I am. I'm a drunk and you're a fucker.'

'Stop this Beth. It's demeaning.'

'Ooo, demeaning. Do I demean you mother?'

'You demean yourself. And you insult our friends.' She turned to face them. 'Not very good friends as it turns out. You all know she's only sixteen. Yet you allow her to pour this poison down her throat.' Turning back to Beth she swept a hand across the table sending the drinks shattering to the floor. 'Come with me Beth. I want you to come home.' She ignored the crowd who had scattered, most of them on their feet, wiping alcohol from their legs. But no-one complained; in fact they looked a bit sheepish, embarrassed to witness the scene.

'I don't think so. You see I've left home.'

'Do you think Lena will take you with her if I say I don't want you to go?'

Beth staggered to her feet. She pointed a finger, almost jabbing at Tilly's face. 'You wouldn't.'

'Yes I would and I will if you don't come with me now.'

A hand on her shoulder gently pushed her aside. She turned to confront Adalia.

'I'll take her on board Tilly. You can trust me.'

Tilly ignored her. She refocused her attention on Beth. 'Now Beth.'

Beth sat down again, she looked a bit green, and was sweating. 'Fuck off Mam. You're not wanted here.'

'I wonder if your friends would be so keen to pour alcohol into you if they knew you were pregnant.' She held her breath, stunned by her own audacity. It had just come out. She was so angry she hadn't been thinking straight. She heard, as if from far away, a gasp that came from the ring of people who had gathered to watch the commotion. Beth looked shocked.

Adalia spoke. 'Beth?'

'Get lost.' Beth was trying to get to her feet, swaying and retching.

Endora tried to help but Beth pushed her away. She looked at the crowd. 'Seen enough? Well you can go 'cos it's over now.'

Tilly walked away, through the crowd. Striding up the bank she forced herself to control her breathing, her heart was hammering in her chest. Had she done the right thing? Would Beth ever forgive her? Somehow forgiveness didn't seem important, she'd sacrifice it to have Beth safely under a doctor's care. She could hear Beth wallowing behind her. She heard her being sick in the gutter, she waited, but didn't turn, didn't offer help. She wanted to, but didn't trust herself not to slap some sense into her daughter. She'd never lifted a hand to her children, but she knew she was perilously close. She hurried up the stairs and into the bedroom Beth had been using.

She sat on the bed and waited, listening to Beth throwing up in the bathroom. Finally she came in, sheepish, ill, white as chalk, staggering and crying. She fell on the bed. Tilly turned her on her side and sat with her. Sat on and on while the day receded, while Mai put her head around the door, disappeared then returned with milky coffee and a kiss for Tilly. Sat on until a bright dawn woke the birds, the fishermen, the travellers and Beth. She helped her to shower and almost cried at the sight of her emaciated body, but said nothing. Beth returned to bed and Tilly made an appointment with the doctor for that afternoon. Then she numbed her senses by cleaning and washing, ironing and cooking. Finally it was time to go. Mai drove them and waited in the car until they returned.

Backing out of the car park she gave Tilly a questioning look.

'Yes.' Tilly told her.

'I knew you know.' Beth spoke to them for the first time in twenty-four hours.

'When?' Tilly asked.

'About seven weeks ago. I did the test before we went away.'

'Then why, in heaven's name, have you been trying to kill yourself?' Tilly shrieked.

Mai rested a hand on Tilly's leg, gave a slight shake of her head

Tilly couldn't believe it. 'You're so irresponsible. I'm sick of it Beth. I've had enough! Enough of your continual drinking and swearing and disrespectful opinion of me, about something you know nothing, by the way. And I can't believe how you've deliberately kept this from me, worrying us until I thought I'd go mad!'

'Tilly, you need to calm down, I'm trying to drive here. Leave it till we get home.'

Tilly looked around at Beth, but she was staring resolutely through the window, all her plans spoiled, her life in ruins and worryingly ill. Tilly began to cry.

CHAPTER EIGHTEEN

TILLY

An unproductive afternoon at the Education Office had left Tilly defeated.

'We'll see what can be done Mrs Maitland, but you've left it so,o,o,o late.' A portly young man with an unhealthy bonhomie pronounced as he embraced her.

Yea, I know, Tilly resisted the urge to tell him. She felt the need to wonder what he was on and could she get some. She'd left with a fist of leaflets giving advice on home schooling and a list of tutors, as that was the line he'd thought she might investigate. She'd wondered how many lines he'd investigated lately as she looked into his pin-point pupils that missed their focus completely, staring into the middle distance somewhere over her shoulder.

Sitting on the top of the dunes she looked at the list. Home Schooling? She could do it but didn't want to deprive her children of the company of their peers. A Mr Norris in Blackburn Lancashire would do maths. Lancashire, how many miles from there to here Mr Norris? A Mademoiselle Bussy in Paris would gauge their French language. That would be interesting. Sean did tend to shout a lot, but she doubted he'd be heard in France.

Below her in the car park half a dozen sea gulls wheeled, fighting and screeching over a dropped packet of crisps. Scrabbling for food? God willing, they wouldn't get to that predicament. Sighing, she stood and leaving the dunes behind she headed for her home in Sea View. The boys were in, all four of them, doing maths at the kitchen table. Tilly's eyebrows, raised at Lonore, were answered by a beckoning of her head toward the garden. Tilly bent to kiss Sean and Harry.

'We're doing Key Stage 2 with the babies,' Harry explained.

'We're not babies and I'm good at sums,' Joseph told him, his stubborn expression mirroring Sean's.

''Cos, Mum,' Harry took up the story. 'They're hopeless.'

Sean knuckled Joseph's head. 'Little numbskulls, not having them show us up at school.'

Her eldest son by ten minutes, Sean, when had this rough and tumble, live for the moment boy become so gentle Tilly wondered and marvelled at their ability to explain away two illegitimate brothers as long as they were up to scratch academically. She couldn't cry. She just had to hold it together. They were so looking forward to returning to school. She followed Lonore who was disappearing through the garden and into the garage.

Tilly followed her inside and took a step back in amazement. Gone was the accrued rubbish of years. Gardening tools hung clean and sharpened on the back wall above stacked plastic boxes, obviously filled with tools, toys and other odds and sods essential to a busy household. The main body of the floor was a workroom with a long table against the newly painted walls on one side, and sewing machines down the middle. Shelves above the table held bolts of cloth and plastic drawers stacked with packs of accessories. Three transparent skips held bags in the process of being assembled.

'The finished ones and the packing are in the dining room. I haven't packed any because obviously you need to put the Tote-Tilly seal of approval on them.' Lonore stood waiting for Tilly's opinion.

Tilly nodded, too overcome to speak. While she'd been stressing about Beth and their situation and feeling sorry for herself, the boys had accepted things, although they didn't yet know about school. And this woman, who she'd tried to despise, had taken care of them and got on with the practicalities of earning money for them all. She examined a small green sail cloth back pack with fringing and beading in leatherwork she recognised as Naomi's, another in bright blue with silver buckles and clasps in the shape of mermaids, her Mother's creations.

'I'm sorry Tilly, don't you like them? I didn't want to follow your ideas because, well, they're yours.' Lonore's words faded away.

Tilly fiddled with some cut pieces that were in the process of being tacked together. She could hardly see her through the tears.

'I'll get us some coffee,' Lonore offered and left Tilly to sort out her priorities and her emotions. It took some time before she was able to think straight, but when she did she realised immediately that a great deal of thought was unnecessary. Full marks to Lonore, who was clearly a very enterprising woman.

She stood up and dashed the tears away with the back of her hand, taking a deep breath before walking back through the long garden. The bald lawn still upheld the ancient goal posts that had been used for years for the boys and their friends to play footy, and the neglected borders with honeysuckle and roses rioting over the walls and fences surrounding the old swing which was Beth's domain, where she and her friends had grown from little girls to young women, the same girls who had let her down so badly when she needed them most. Right now Beth was as far away from the unfettered ambition of these girls to remain students as it was possible to get. She walked indoors, through the kitchen, where a cup of fragrant coffee was handed before she followed Lonore to the dining room where her bags lay on the table.

'I've had some samples of packaging and business cards and leaflets and stuff, but haven't ordered any. I wanted you to decide.'

Tilly examined the samples. 'This is amazing. You've coped better than I have.'

'I do know how you feel. It was just as much of a shock to me. I wasn't aware of any of this, of all of you, not until I came here and saw the photos then I admit I went through your private papers, I had to find out the truth and it almost destroyed me.' She spread her hands to encompass the house and its occupants. 'I'd met Robert a few times too and he hadn't said anything. I'm more than angry with Adam, more than furious, more than hurt. I almost ran away to my Mum's in Edinburgh, but I just couldn't. I'd taken him on and as far I'm concerned it's for better or worse. I don't think it can get any worse than this, so we've got to move forward. I want to kill him Tilly, for what this has the potential to do to the children. They are the most vulnerable. I want to hurt him back but I love him.'

'I don't.' Tilly admitted. 'I haven't loved him, as a lover, for many years. I just jogged along, busy with planning our lives.'

'Then you don't mind?' Lonore didn't look at her, intent on examining the rounded handles on a tangerine and white linen bag.

'No. No. You go right ahead. I'll divorce him and I won't cause any more heartache for any of us, especially the children.

The boys don't know it yet, but they can't go back to Prior's Walk school, there just isn't the money and Beth has enough problems just now.'

'She's lovely Tilly, so like your mother. A daughter is a special gift.'

'My mother wouldn't agree with you. I haven't been an easy burden for her to bear.'

Thinking that gifts like Beth she could do without right now Tilly busied herself packing tissue paper into bags. It was delicate, green with silver mermaids swimming all over. 'This is lovely. Just what I would have chosen.'

'Mai helped me. I had to decide, Tilly.' Lonore looked straight at her, large violet eyes, open and honest, wanting to do right. 'We had to crack on, for the order at Bewicks.'

'It's fine, really. I'm glad someone has done some planning. I've been a wimp.'

Adam stuck his head around the door. 'Out!' ordered Tilly.

'No,' Lonore countermanded. 'Bring all the finished bags from the garage please and wear the white cotton gloves for handling, there's a love.' She beamed at him and he left.

To Tilly she shook her head. 'He's hopeless without instruction.'

For a few minutes Tilly wondered if it might work ... living together. She liked Lonore. The boys got on well, Robert was invaluable as general handyman and Beth needed her own bed. If she moved into the guest room above the kitchen extension and Sean and Harry in the attics, Robert could stay in the study, the little twins in the biggest back bedroom together, Beth could have her own room back in the front and that just left the master suit for Lonore and Adam, but could she live with that ? And then of course there was Cary, Cary and his love. At long last she had a true all-enveloping all-consuming love; with a man who lived in Devon or sailed the world, free and easy with no plans to hinder him, it was still a mess.

The boys burst in, interrupting what was a futile train of thought. Sean pushing the little ones in front. 'Look our old pirate costumes fit them!'

'Yea.' Harry backed him up. 'They can wear them to the party.'

Justin and Joseph looked so sweet in the old pirate costumes she had made for Sean and Harry at their age and they looked so like them too, there was no doubt they were brothers, why had it taken so long for her to accept this fact. Mai always threw an end of summer party and this year they would all go together. 'Oh boys I'm sorry. I haven't made your costumes yet. You've grown so much last year's won't fit.' Tilly was appalled that she was losing touch with her old life.

'S'ok. We've got ours sorted.' Sean was easy, cool.

'You have?' Tilly was pleasantly surprised.

'We're wearing our wet suits.'

'You're not going swimming so late in the day with the tide on the turn.'

'Spoilsport.' Sean, rebellious.

'He's winding you up Mum. There're just for costumes.' Harry, laughing.

'What're you going as?' Tilly, mystified.

'Er, doh!' Sean, scathing and dangerously near a ticking off.

'Divers,' Harry supplied.

Thank God for Harry, who never tried to dissimilate.

Now they were all laughing, but Tilly realised that Lonore was hesitant, embarrassed? Of course, she knew nothing about the party. Without hesitation Tilly invited her. 'Mam has this shindig every year to celebrate Neptune's triumph. She believes he's the only one of the ancient gods to have survived when they were superseded by the new order and he's the only ally she has against the mermaids.'

'Mermaids?'

'Don't ask, but please come to the party. Fancy dress is loosely based on a sea theme.'

'Mum always goes as Sylvia Morningstar, Dad's Captain Hook and Nana's Sylvia Nightstar.'

'Well I'll have to have a think and see what I can find in my sea chest.' Lonore joined the fun.

'Can we have swords?' Joseph took up the cry, attacking Justin with his pointed finger.

'Arh, you bet your piraty ass.' Sean started sword fencing with his hand.

Tilly said no and Lonore said maybe and the boys all whooped yes and went to find the wooden weapons made years ago by Robert.

'It's the twins' birthdays, twenty ninth of August.' Lonore said. 'They'll be six. I won't have a big party, things being so confused.' She looked defeated.

For the first time since that fateful night they'd met Tilly saw a true vulnerability, but reminded herself that it was what our children do to us, expose the weaknesses. 'They'll have the biggest and best party they've ever had, we'll combine the two occasions, they can invite all their friends and it'll be fancy dress and they'll never forget it.'

Lonore stepped forward and hugged her. 'Maybe we've made progress, amazing how kids can pull you together.'

Adam arrived with the bags. 'These are pretty good ye know?'

'Oh, and you're an expert on women's accessories?' Tilly couldn't keep the sarcasm out of her voice.

'I can sell these.'

'Like you sold Fine-fit – down the river.'

'Tilly I'm getting a bit sick of you constantly blaming me for the way the business failed.'

'Who else is to blame? You were the managing director!'

'And the salesman and the accountant and the dog's body when I had to pay staff off and do all the work myself, and I tried Tilly. I tried!'

'Not hard enough.'

'You think it was easy? I walked my feet off trying to drum up business. I trailed the country from top to bottom. I begged and promised, cut prices until there was no more margin.'

His voice rose and his face took on a look of determination she hadn't seen for years. Lonore fled the battle.

'You think it was easy, dogging our friends, never able to relax 'cos the whole time I had to be hustling them for money. Do you know what it feels like when good friends turn their backs on you because they're tired of hearing you bleat on and on about how you need their money. Can you even imagine what it feels like to beg!'

She couldn't.

'I admit I should have realised sooner that we were going under and for that I do blame myself, but I won't take the blame for the economic downturn the whole world is suffering. That's not down to me alone.'

'So you just hid behind a woman, used precious time that should have been for the business to lounge around fucking anything in a skirt.

'No! No Tilly it wasn't like that. I was lonely.'

'Lonely? You had me.'

'I didn't Till. You were off at some parents meeting that you hadn't told me about, or a sports day to organise where I was obviously superfluous, offering your services as cook, treasurer, secretary, organiser, driver or planner! Do you even know how many times I offered to help with the kids and was refused? No, you don't. You didn't need me, you had it all organised, all planned, right down to the last name tag. There was nothing for me to do Tilly. No place for me in your grand scheme!' He turned to face the window, hands bunched into fists at his hips, shoulders tense and heaving with the effort of telling all the years of truth.

With blinding clarity she realised that he was right. Looking back down the years she saw that she had shut him out. 'I thought I was relieving you of a burden, you had enough to worry about with the business.'

He turned back, calmer, his eyes soft and liquid, his mouth relaxing into its familiar softness, a softness she'd always mistaken for weakness. Had she ever known him? Had she ever even looked at him? His hands relaxed, slid from his hips, but trembling still with his unaccustomed outburst. He took hold of her fingers and looked at her.

'It's too late for us Tilly. I'm sorry. I know I play the fool, but I've been so worried lately. If it hadn't been for Lonore I think I'd have run away.'

'Why didn't you tell me how hard it's been for you?'

'I shouldn't have needed to.'

'You told Lonore.' Sadly she watched his face, in defeat she saw the vulnerability that had been part of the young man she'd fallen in love with, the gift of compassion that had been ousted in favour of flippancy while he'd tried to live up to expectations, other peoples, his mother and then his organised wife, she, Tilly. Leaning forward she reached up and kissed his cheek. 'I'm sorry Adam. I've been a cow. And I'm happy that you and Lonore are together. I think you're right for each other.' She leaned her face against his chest and couldn't remember the last time they'd been so close. 'We'll get through this won't we?' she asked.

'Somehow, if we all pull together.' He held her away with one last stroke of tenderness over her face and then all business he turned and picked up a bag. 'These are good and I can sell them. People might not want double glazing right now, but women will always want a new bag.' His smile was back, disarming, charming ... if any man could charm a woman into buying a bag it was Adam.

Lonore poked her head around the door. 'Safe to come back?' She grinned.

They both waved her in.

'Do you remember Josephina Swan who has that boutique over in the Metro Centre, you did her windows two summers ago?' Lonore asked.

Adam nodded. 'Yes and the Hobarts! Chain of stores in Scotland, they have that mansion up at Rothbury, we met him at that wedding, your cousin or something?'

Tilly listened while the two of them compiled a list of potential customers. They were enthusiastic.

'We can do this Tilly,' Adam told her.

'Yes, but only if you'll knuckle down,' Lonore warned.

They all laughed when he promised he would. They were right for each other Lonore and Adam, in ways she and Adam had never been. Gentle smiles, occasional brushing of hands; love in their eyes, so obvious. Living here with them was out of the question. 'Can I leave this delivery to you?' she asked them.

'Absolutely.' Lonore was definite. 'Adam will take them up to Bewicks first thing in the morning.'

Tilly knew where she had to go and, saying goodnight to the boys, she hurried back to the quay, and Cary. Nearing the river she was suddenly engulfed in a heavy sea fret. Wet and clinging it obscured the view, only a few feet in front were visible, but she wasn't lost, she could find her way around this river bank in the densest of fogs. She was almost there when a figure materialised from the mist. It was Jazzy, inappropriately dressed in a flimsy caftan, her long hair plastered to her head, chiffon clinging to her slight form. 'Good God Jazzy, what do you think you're doing? You'll get pneumonia.'

'Tilly ... it's you.'

'Come upstairs. We'll get you dried off.' Putting an arm around her friend she wondered what had turned this confidant, happy woman into such a wreck. 'Is it Lena?'

'Sort of.'

'I told her to talk to you, tell you.'

'She did.' The forlorn little voice was filled with despair.

'There's really nothing between them; you know who Krista is don't you?'

'She's her niece. Trouble is Krista won't accept that, she's there constantly, day and night, demanding a different truth. I can't cope with her.'

They climbed the stairs and Tilly ushered Jazzy into the kitchen, noticing she was barefoot. 'Heavens Jazzy where're your shoes?'

Jazzy hesitated on the threshold, looking down, surprised at her oversight. 'I'm a mess aren't I?' Tears filled her eyes.

Mai, at the oven, turned and seeing Jazzy's distress bustled forward taking the young woman into her generous embrace. 'Come with me darling.' She ushered her into her bedroom.

Cary rose from the table where he'd been enjoying a beer and a sandwich. Opposite him Beth was gluing sparkling stones to her costume for the party. 'Arh, my lovely, come and eat. Cary took charge, kissing her mouth and sitting her next to him. He cut bread and cheese for her and poured a beer. 'Beth and I were just about to send up a flare for you.'

He had charmed Beth!

Mai and Jazzy returned, Jazzy wearing one of Mai's voluminous jumpers and harem pants, a pair of oversized, Homer Simpson slippers on her tiny feet and her hair wrapped in a fluffy towel. She looked warmer at least, but her cool grey eyes were troubled and a frown linked them in pain. She sat on the long wooden form and Mai sat sideways her legs and arms wrapped around Jazzy, protecting, healing. Tilly recognised the gesture, felt those arms and the cushioning breasts, the spread legs pressing, her mother sheltering the weak and vulnerable, always there when she was needed.

And Cary? Easy, casual, showing his love for Tilly, making them laugh with seafaring stories, concerning himself with these women, comfortable in their intimate circle; pouring drinks and replenishing their plates and always so tactile. A squeeze on the shoulder with his big hands promising strength, shutting the window against the intruding harr, retrieving Beth's costume from her careless fingers; yes, he was saying, you're safe, I'm here. I love you.

Tilly told them how efficient Lonore was and also clever, describing her flair with the bag designs and construction, how she felt comfortable about the situation.

Beth met her eyes. 'I'm OK with it Mum and I know I've been an arse lately, but I'm fine now. Nana talked to me.'

Another task she should have tackled herself. 'You sure?'

'Not sure about anything.'

Finally Jazzy spoke. 'What am I to do about Krista? Lena ignores her and Krista goes on and on about there's been a mistake and it's Lena who's her mother and not Yvonne, then Lena leaves the room and Krista starts on at me, asking me to persuade Lena to have a DNA test. She's so forceful.'

'She is that. She was once convinced I was her father and swam behind the Genista until we were over the bar and half a mile out. I had to bring her aboard and she just stubbornly refused to leave. It took me all the way to Devon to convince her that it just wasn't possible. I'd never even met her mother.'

'But, you did know Lena.' Beth threw the cat among the pigeons.

'Yes, but I'm not black.'

'No.' Mai interjected. 'But Lena's sister is.'

'Mai,' Cary warned. 'Don ye make things all up-a-nut-shot.'

'I'll get bettermost of ye anyday.'

'Do you to think you two could talk in English?' Beth was still bent to her sewing, but raised a questioning face over this outburst of Cornish dialect.

'Arh, I forgot we're in Geordieland. We're just joshing each other, sorry Beth.' Cary laughed and the table shook. 'That there girl is a might confused.'

'She's dangerous,' Jazzy told them.

'It's the mermaids,' Mai pronounced.

'Mam, can we not have one serious conversation without you weaving magic spells and trying to baffle us all with folklore.'

Her mother lifted her glass to the mist-filled window, examining the colour. 'Magic? Don't be silly. That's for the tourists. But, I know what I know and it's in the mermaids for all of you to see. I marked you on the day you were born. They tell all the secrets, if you care to look.'

They all laughed, but Tilly was worried. Cary looked quizzical, perhaps he too had noticed that Mai seemed more and more immersed in her other world. He fingered the little ornament that swung from his ear.

Mai gave Jazzy a comforting squeeze then, disentangling herself, began to clear the table. Tilly helped, there was much to do in preparation for the party night.

CHAPTER NINETEEN

BETH

During the last few weeks, Beth had left home many times. In her mind she had turned away, sailed toward new horizons with all they promised; endless blue skies, boundless water, mates who were uncompromising and non judgemental, but finally she had faced her reality and it had nothing to do with freedom; it was all about responsibility.

The house she'd grown up in felt strange. Stepping into the kitchen wasn't the same. Things were out of order, not so tidy; but prettier; wild flowers and shells decorated the usually bare and gleaming tops, sand crunched underfoot, then, the unmistakable thunder of Sean and Harry pushing and shoving each other to be first down the stairs smoothed the distortion, it became just as it should now be.

Why did Sean and Harry push and shove each other to be victorious? They never used to. It was a thing they only did on holiday. Perhaps on holiday they felt free of convention, more able to allow themselves to grow. Mallorca had been her finishing school. If they'd never left Tynemouth she would have hung out with the gang in the park. She and Mitchell would have stayed together but not married, just claimed social and been single parents. Now she knew that she had options. She could have her baby and still follow some kind of life plan. Being able to holiday in Mallorca and all the experiences she had enjoyed, thanks to Lena, had given her a maturity her contemporaries hadn't as yet achieved.

'Bethy! You're back.' Sean, the winner, came barrelling into her.

She welcomed his arms around her waist – so strong; when had that happened? Then Harry, sweet sweet Harry.

'I've missed you.' Harry's kiss on her cheek was urgent. 'Have you come home?'

'Not yet, but I have something very important to tell you. Is Dad in?'

Sean pulled her by the hand. 'In the office.'

'Office?' They had a study that she knew was now Grandad's bedroom, but they'd never had an office. Harry noticed her confusion.'

'We're a business now.'

Sean couldn't let his twin take centre stage. 'We work in the dining room, that's the office and the garage is the factory. We all work. We get paid if we do the clearing away, recycling boxes and stuff and making sure the place is always clean and risk free.'

Harry nodded. 'Health and safety.'

Beth struggled to conceal her amusement. Harry looked every inch like their late grandmother in her prime.

'And the babies sort the offcuts into colours.' Sean added.

'Babies?'

'Well, they're not babies. Justin and Joseph are six on Saturday. They're our brothers.'

In the dining room Beth laughed at her father studying a computer screen, where bands of nonsense were scrolling down with dizzying momentum. She leaned forward and corrected it. 'Still IT illiterate Dad?'

He jumped up. 'Beth, sweetheart, oh Bethy, you're here.'

'I've only been at Nana's, you could have come,' she accused him.

He looked insulted, just like Dad to turn it around so that he's the injured party.

'I didn't want to come where I'm not welcome. Your Nana's a beast of a woman.'

'You deserve whatever she does to you.' She waved her hands about in a parody of a person casting a magic spell. 'Anyway ...' She forestalled his excuses. I've come to talk to you. Is *she* here.'

'Lonore, her name's Lonore. Please be kind to her.'

'Is Lonore here?' She stressed the name, couldn't stop herself from being a bit sarky.

'No. She and the boys are out, gone to the Brew House actually to see Naomi about bits and bobs for the bags. Doing well you know, my business sense has pulled it into shape.'

'Yea, like you did at Fine-Fit. ... anyway!' Regretting her gibe she took a deep breath and tried again. 'Can we sit down?' She settled at the table, the boys hanging around her, Sean on the table with his arm about her shoulders and Harry on the chair closest to her. Three pairs of eyes waited.

'I think the boys are old enough to know the truth, there's been too much secrecy lately. Dad?'

He nodded his agreement.

She took a deep breath. 'Erm, now don't go all shitty on me. I want you to think before you say anything, erm.' She breathed again. They were waiting. She wished the wind would blow her away. 'I'm going to have a baby.'

'Everybody has babies,' Sean told them. 'I'll have some, so will Harry.'

'Shut up Sean.' Harry told him and pushed himself up from the chair. He threaded an arm under Sean's and cuddled her around the shoulders. 'Mam said you weren't very well. Are you OK now?'

Beth returned his embrace, welcoming the comfort of his thin arms about her, his hand idly playing with her hair ... normal. She looked at her father. 'Dad?'

'Bit of a body-swerver that one!'

'You have to tell me Dad. I need to know how you feel.' She waited while he shook his head, his eyes downcast, rubbing at his designer stubble; two years out of date. His hand was shaking but finally he looked at her. She'd always loved his eyes, hazy green with a soft expression always present. He never lost his temper, always dodged the issue. He didn't disappoint her. 'Too late I suppose?'

She knew he meant abortion, an act that had never been a solution, it just wasn't in her to do that. She nodded. 'Fourteenth February.'

'Valentine.'

'Good a name as any.' She tried to lighten the situation.

'Bloody hell Dad, you should lock her up.' Sean offered.

This time he didn't get away with it. 'No X-Box tonight Sean, this sloppy language has to stop. Now go, both of you. Make us a sandwich, cup of tea.'

They left, as always in competition, topping each other with a range of fillings for the bread, everything a race, Harry ever optimistic.

They sat in silence for half a minute, a minute? It felt interminable. She couldn't stand it. 'Dad?'

'Why didn't you come to me, tell me?'

She shrugged.

'Does your mother know?'

She shook her head, this was so confusing. 'Just the other day. She thought I was anorexic.'

'She said you were ill. I thought you were drunk. Beth ... you could have killed yourself.'

'I wanted to kill it.' She was defiant and then defensive of her attitude. Angry with herself for crying she brushed tears from her cheeks with the cuff of her shirt. 'I didn't want to do anything about it.'

'She said you were ill.'

'I was so mixed up and afraid. I knew it, but I didn't want it to be true.'

'Who's the father?'

She shrugged, head down, unable to meet the pain in his eyes, pain she'd caused.

'You don't know?' His voice was hard, contained, trying to be rational.

A new voice from the doorway interrupted. 'In his own ham-fisted way your father's trying to be the responsible adult.'

Her mother.

'I know. And I do know who it is. It's ... I'm not a slag.'

'Beth! Beth darling, I never meant that. I never said you ...' Her father left his chair and came to kneel on the floor in front of her, his arms around her body, his hands pressing her into his chest. 'Bethy, I never meant that.'

Her mother sat in Harry's vacated chair then her father sat beside her; both of her parents united in adversity.

He continued. 'I didn't mean that. I just wondered, you know ... these days ... young people.' He left twenty-first century morals to be imagined. 'We'll help you through this. We'll support you in every way, however you want to bring up your child. If you don't want the father then that's fine.'

She shook her head. Shit no. No! She certainly didn't want him. The episode in the park darkened her mind for an instant. She compared her school friends with Juan and Paulo and all the other young men she'd met since becoming a sailor and it confirmed, beyond doubt, that no matter what the future held Mitchell and all the immature losers she'd once regarded as friends would have no part in her life. It would be stepping backward from the future and for this baby she was determined on one thing at least, this baby would always look ahead. 'I don't know what'll happen, but I don't have to tell him, ever.'

Her mother looked down at her fingers, twisting her wedding ring round and around. 'He has to be told.'

'No! I said I don't want him to know.'

'Darling, please listen. We have to be practical. The child needs to know. You can't keep it secret. Look at the trouble secrets have caused. Look at Krista. She's torn apart. She's a wreck. She's been searching for her father all her life and because she can't find him she's denying her mother. We can manage without this baby's father, you have a family who cares, but he has to know.'

Sean and Harry returned, carrying trays. The back door opened and voices called out. She looked at her parents. This was a mess.

A woman entered, calling, 'Adam, are you there?' She halted in the doorway, her hands on the heads of two little boys.

Her father stood up. 'Lonore this is my daughter Beth, Beth this is Lonore and Justin and Joseph.' The little boys were like quicksilver, gone, giggling and sparring with each other, daring one another to be first up the stairs, just like Sean and Harry.

Lonore stepped forward her hand outstretched. 'It's so good to finally meet.'

Beth felt uncomfortable shaking her hand. She felt like a traitor to her mother who had suffered so much because of this woman. She nodded and took her hand away, then she met Lonore's wide eyes, violet, with a softness in them, like Nana's. She watched her take in the cosy scene, the sandwiches and cups for five.

'I'll just get on then.' Lonore backed out and shut the door, leaving the family alone again.

Beth felt hungry, she peered uncertainly at the sandwiches. 'Nice sanners boys. What's in them?'

Sean pointed to one unevenly cut pile. 'Ham.'

'Cheese.' Harry pointed to the other. 'Good for babies, calcium.' Solemnly he nodded his fair and wise head.

Laughing, they all began to eat. Her mother, sipping at her tea, stopped and sat up straight. 'While I've got you boys here, you know the new school being built at Monkseaton?'

Mouths full they nodded. Shit, this was a day of revelations.

'Tilly?' her Dad enquired mildly.

Beth had been apprised of the situation and knew it was because he didn't want to be around when they discovered they weren't going back to Prior's Walk. Her mother ignored him.

Sean nodded. 'It's awesome.'

'They've got a megga IT department. Bill Gates paid for it.' Harry sounded animated.

'I didn't know you were keen on IT,' Beth told him, her brother, the footie fanatic.

'Got to do something out of season.'

They all laughed. It seemed normal.

'Well,' her mother continued. 'If I can swing it how'd you like to go there?'

Beth watched the silent boys; she thought she'd stop breathing, even the air was quiet.

'Cool.' Sean nodded. 'A few kids from our year're going.'

'Their parents can't afford the fees at Prior's,' Harry supplied.

'We may have left it too late,' their father mentioned, trying to diminish the importance of the matter.

The boys shrugged.

'Can we go surfing now?' Sean asked, already standing and edging toward the door, boredom written in the slope of his bony shoulders.

Her father, defeated by the momentous revelations, nodded.

And then, realising it was the solution to her problems, Beth said. 'Yea, me too. I want to go to Monkseaton High.'

'You sure?' Her mother looked surprised. 'You want to go back to school?'

'Yes. Yes I am. They've got a sixth form and I don't want to stay at Marden.'

'I'll see what I can do, but it's not a promise,' her mother reminded them.

The boys were out the door, shouting from the hall for her to join them, and suddenly light-hearted she called that she was coming. She would go surfing.

Half an hour later she was zipped into her old wet suit, on the long slog out and paddling for all she was worth with the gang of surfers from all over North Tyneside who habitually converged on Tynemouth Long Sands for the exhilaration of riding back on a wave. Afterwards they sat outside the café, freezing, shivering, uncaring, talking and telling stories of waves that were just out of reach, and some that weren't. After an hour she left the boys with friends and climbed up to the dunes were the sand retained the sun's warmth. She lay down behind a large clump of marram grass and closed her eyes. The surfing had helped her put stuff far enough away to see it clearly. The facts were ... she was pregnant ... and all her dreams of sailing away with Lena were dead in the water. Her decision to return to school seemed the best way forward. She could cope with exams and pregnancy and with the help of the family she could, perhaps, even go to uni if she managed to be accepted by Newcastle, so that she could live at home. Where was home? Living with Lonore was a big fat no-no and Mum thought living with Nana wasn't a good idea. What was Mum going to do and would there be a place for her with the baby. A deep sigh deflated her, so many problems caused by such a little thing. She laced her fingers over her belly, soon she'd start to show and look grotesque. Mitchell might notice and guess it was his, or maybe he'd just think she was a slapper and diss her. She realised that she didn't care what he thought. She had moved on.

Heavy black clouds that had been glowering over the Cheviots all day were now overhead, rumblings of thunder echoed from the hills and it was so hot and sticky she could hardly breathe. Time to go home, but again, the word home confused her. As she climbed up to the pavement a voice called down. It was Krista, her familiar silhouette against a sudden break in the clouds was outlined by the sun as it momentarily flashed through. She stood tall and big, with her powerful swimmer's shoulders exposed under a white vest top and her long legs set off in a pair of skimpy green shorts, she was gloriously beautiful and would never be daft enough to get pregnant. 'Hi.' Beth called back. 'Haven't seen you for ages, what you been doing?' Beth tried not to judge her friend by the distressing comments made by Cary and Jazzy.

'Just hanging with Zander and that lot.'

'You and him solid?'

'Nar, just wondered, for a while, if he might be my Dad?'

Beth looked up, stared at her. Krista's face expressed no hint of a wind up. A long livid scar was scratched into her right cheek. 'Ow, that looks nasty. What did you do?'

Krista ran a be-ringed forefinger down the wound. 'Caught it on a hook.'

'It looks infected. You should get Nana to take care of it.'

'Nar, it'll be good.' She rubbed it and smeared blood across her face, staring at her stained hand before licking it clean.

Beth shuddered at the studied satisfaction of the act. This girl was definitely mental

'Where you been?' Krista seemed unaware of the weirdness in her behaviour.

Beth looked down at her wet suit partly unzipped and hanging around her hips. She gestured to it. 'Duh!'

'Never fancied it myself. I like to be under the water.'

'You mean in it.'

'Under's much more interesting.'

Crossing the busy road they made for Sea View where Krista followed Beth upstairs and into her old room. While Beth showered they talked of inconsequential things. Mai's party, Jack's boat.

'You still sailing with Lena?' Krista asked.

'No. Change of plan.'

'Why's that then?'

'I'm going back to school. What's your plan?'

'Oh, I'm def going with Mum.'

A towel around her body, Beth hovered in the doorway, unable to hide her amazement. 'Your Mum? Where's she going then?'

'Don't know yet. We can go anywhere now, no-one to stop us.'

'What about Zander?'

'Changed my mind about him.'

'You can't just use people then dump them. What about Daisy?'

'I'll still see them. I'll be living in Mallorca and they live there.'

'This is a bit confusing in'it? Lena and your Mum haven't spoken for decades. Are they friends again?'

'You're a bit slow you, talking about Yvonne, my Mum's Lena.'

'She says she's not and Jazzy hates you 'cos she thinks you fancy Lena.'

'Jazzy's not a problem anymore.'

'How's that?'

'Gone back to Mallorca. They're finished.'

Beth was stunned. 'Not Jazzy. I don't believe it!'

'Just 'cos you don't believe a thing doesn't make it any less true.'

'But Jazzy and Lena have been together for years, they're mad about each other.'

'Not any more.'

'Did you do something to make her go?'

Krista faced her down, stubborn. 'Me? Lena didn't need me to show her how Jazzy's not good for her, it's obvious, but she'll be alright 'cos I'll look after her.' She turned and stared from the window at the encroaching clouds. 'Me and my Mum, we'll be fine.'

Beth thought it best not to continue this discussion concerning Krista's bizarre predictions. She busied herself with dressing. She wanted to stretch out on her bed and sleep, she was tired. It had been weeks since she'd surfed and it had been harder than she'd expected, must be the baby. 'I've something to tell you.' She thought she'd tell her about her baby, everyone would know soon enough. 'I haven't told anybody else, just my family.'

'Ooh, secrets. I love secrets.'

'Mum says they cause more trouble than enough.'

'Some secrets are worth it though. Take me and Lena. All these years the bond between Lena and me was a secret, but I knew all along that she was my Mum, some secrets are best out there. Say it loud and proud, that's our motto, us lesbians.'

Beth decided not to tell Krista her secret, she really didn't know her, and it was plain that she was unhinged.

Beth had thought about staying the night at Sea View, but couldn't persuade Krista to leave; she just hung around, waiting. They had dinner with Dad, the boys and Lonore, who had prepared a lovely honeyed ham with green salad, baked potatoes, home-made relish and crusty bread, but Beth was so tired, she could hardly stay awake. She said to Krista that she needed to go to bed. Krista still didn't get it so Beth harried her from the house and the two of them trooped off to the Brew House. The quayside was heaving, bodies everywhere, noise and smells and chaos. Only two more days and then the quay would be empty of all but the locals and a few pensioners enjoying fish and chips. They were almost at Mai's door when Lena came rushing up the bank, puffing for breath.

'You two seen anything of Jazzy?'

Beth was shocked at the normally unflappable Lena who looked strained and worried. She opened her mouth to repeat what Krista had told her earlier, but Krista's look of complete blankness stopped her from speaking. She waited.

Krista smiled sweetly, causing the livid red weal down her cheek to crack open and blood to trickle down her neck.

Ignoring it she stepped forward and put her arms around Lena. She looked at Beth and with a slight shake of her head signalled that she not say anything. She was taller and bigger than Lena and she shushed her as a mother would a child. 'She'll not be far, come on we'll go and look for her.' And turning away, with Lena still in her embrace, she called goodbye to Beth, who stood and watched with a sense of disbelief shuddering through her body.

In the kitchen she widened her eyes to her mother and grandmother. 'Whoa, how weird is that?'

'What?' Mae was adding Pernot to a fish stew, the other ingredients spread out on a board.

'Well, I've just been with Krista and we met Lena who's totally distressed 'cause she can't find Jazzy and Krista said she'd gone back to Mallorca, but now she's telling Lena they'll go and look …'

CHAPTER TWENTY

TILLY

Thunder crashed overhead and lightning etched the black waves with silver. A full moon loaded the water with mercury, heavy and ethereal.

Tilly had told Adam that she wouldn't be staying at Sea View and his relief had been shocking. To be rid of her that easily, he'd hardly believed his luck.

In Lonore's office, that used to be her dining room, she picked at a few samples, admired the designs, recognised Naomi's artistry in the appliqué and fringes; colours that weren't in any rainbow she'd ever seen dazzled her with their subtlety. Only a couple of her original bags were in evidence, presumably the bulk was packed and ready to go to Bewicks as Adam had promised. Were Adam's promises different now? Were the words substantial enough to bare any weight, stronger than the ephemeral puffs of broken letters they used to be? She watched him for a moment, but found nothing to interest her, so picking up the tray she carried it into the kitchen.

Lonore was busy at the stove. 'Hi Tilly. Nice when it's quiet isn't it. Do you want coffee?'

'No thanks.' She emptied crockery into the dishwasher.

'I'm making lamb with salad and potatoes from the garden.'

Tilly looked out at her vegetable plot. 'You garden too?'

'No, too busy, it's your stuff, just using them up. We've talked about building a new office out there, a much better use of space now that the business is up and running.'

'My business Lonore.'

'Well strictly speaking, no it's not. You had applied for the loan in both your's and Adam's names but that's a no-no because he's banned from conducting business at this time.' She turned her head from the wall and looked at Tilly. Straight at her.

And there it was, clear as sky on a Spring morning. Tilly thought about the chain of events. From the moment she'd spoken into Adam's phone Lonore had known who she was.

When she'd invited Lonore and the boys into her home she had been caught, reeled in and gutted like a Craster kipper. She clapped her hands slowly and bowed her head slightly to Lonore's cunning then she left Sea View.

She was surprised at how unconcerned she felt about leaving her boys with Adam and Lonore. The old Tilly would never have abandoned her children. That was not part of her plan, oh no, not she, not Matilda Maitland, a woman who would have denigrated any mother she'd heard about who'd abandoned her children. But had that woman ever really existed? She'd forced herself into the role by her own stupid code. This new Tilly was expanding, breaking the constraints of convention and it seemed right.

It was obvious the boys were easy with the new situation, even Harry had settled back into the familiar. They were secure in the knowledge that they were loved, loved even more now, now they had two mothers. To them Lonore seemed less rigid than their mother, but they too would soon discover that her line was baited with honey. They'd always been comfortable running between Mai's and their own house, the two being interchangeable as homes so that was a plus. Like Beth they were close to Mai, more casual about her lifestyle than Tilly had ever been. Her own feelings for Mai had changed too. The events of the last few weeks had deepened her feelings for her mother and it felt right. Her love for Mai had grown, she had developed an urge to cuddle, to hold and to learn; how could that be? She pushed her shoulders back and looked up at the lightening streaked sky and felt as if a bright shaft of opportunity had opened her dark clouds and relief poured like rain, washing away the old Tilly to expose a new woman, a woman who wanted new ideas, new horizons, a woman who didn't need a plan.

Fat raindrops spattered the dust as she passed under the overhanging trees in front of Lord Percy's statue, muttering, 'Evening m'Lord.'

'Evening my dear.' A deep voice replied as Cary pulled her into his arms, pressing her against the soft stone wall, hot from weeks of sunshine, disturbing the buddleia bush. Butterflies fanned the air around them, settled in his tightly sprung curls, flew off again and the world was not still. It reeled and danced as hot as his lips as they covered hers, burning and sizzling, exciting as his tongue as it slid around her mouth, transforming flesh to silk. They ran, his hands guiding her through the sluicing water that flooded down Tanners Bank, where it parted temporarily at the Brew House only to merge again and speed away to its element, to the sea. Laughing and eager to be alone Tilly led Cary to Noel's empty studio, the key handy under the lintel. They fell in, clutching one another, pulling at clothes that clung to wet bodies, frantic and needy, hungry for the passion that overwhelmed them with joy and wonder, until finally exhausted they lay together, touching and still throbbing yet utterly spent. Tilly lay still, stiller than she'd ever known.

Cary caressed her body, his sure fingers drawing whorls on her skin as he whispered enchantments to make the magic powerful. 'The mermaids will never get you now, you're a Celtic queen, a woman of strength, and soon they'll know that you and yours are not for them. Mai has never realised that, she thought we had to fight them, but we just need them to realise that we're not a threat.'

Turning on her back she gazed into his far away eyes, deep and restless as a high tide, promising as horizons. 'You do talk a load of rubbish.' But despite herself she revelled in his kisses as they lay seals on the invisible runes. And she allowed him to look at her the way none had ever done before. He examined every facet of her being, every part of her body and soul, smiling his sunshine smile as he absorbed her, and she allowed it because through his eyes she saw herself as she'd never been, the little girl timid and confused, the stroppy teenager, the woman yearning for rules knowing nothing of runes and finally the woman she would become, the woman he would cause to evolve. She allowed him to whisper love, to fill the space between reality and fantasy, to bring out the new Tilly and empower her through his love and then, without planning it, they loved again, oblivious to all the hustle and bustle employed by Mai and her band of helpers.

Much later in the clear air of a storm they'd not noticed, a fluffy pink cloud launched a rainbow into the high blue sky. Rose pink borders framed the lighthouse and the top of the ruined priory and castle. The statue of Lord Nelson sported a red wig adorned with a pink gull. The river was buzzing with activity. Tomorrow was the start of the Tall Ships Race, tomorrow over one hundred boats would edge out of the river. They would spread their sails and skimming the waves would employ every tactic of seamanship to win the next leg of the race to Delfzilk in the northern Netherlands.

The littlest boats would lead the parade and most of them had moved to this edge of shelter just inside the piers. Known locally as The Fish Quay Sands, it was a tiny crescent of sand and rocks, not in any way useful as a beach for the water quality was poor. Twice a day this little backwater filled with rubbish that came down river and blew in on the tide. Gathering in rafts it washed back and forth until the water authority dredged it up. People mostly used the area to walk their dogs, but tonight it was transformed.

Mai's annual party was just beginning, tables were laid out along the front of the car park, a BBQ was tended jealously by two retired seamen who sat and criticised the young men who now ploughed the sea, they were wimps, no strength, all done by computers – apparently. They lobbed jibes and fielded those returned from another couple of salts tending the bonfire and warning young lads of dire consequences for any of them foolish enough to try and light it before the appointed hour. A team of men, lead by Adam and Cary were ferrying crates of alcohol and the women were in charge of food, sexist, but hey, it was traditional. The little boats were decked overall with bunting and lights and most of them had already begun their own parties. Jack and Cloris were anchored a bit further out, their boat being in the second class of size and therefore would leave after the first wave had cleared the piers.

From her place at the window of Mai's flat Tilly watched all of them, her friends and relatives and her loves. Sean and Harry, in their wet suits had been appointed DJ's and were linking I-Pods to speakers and arguing about the play list. Robert was putting finishing touches to a boarded area in front that would bounce to whatever rhythm the boys saw fit to devise. She had no need to search for Beth, her heart could find her children in any crowd; there she was, with the crew of the *Brigantia*, laughing and drinking from a bottle of water. It was with a sense of wonder that Tilly realised her daughter was suddenly Mrs Sensible and taking the pregnancy, and consequently her own health, seriously. Organising the positioning of food, Lonore, dressed in one of Tilly's old Sylvia Morningstar costumes, with added extras of feather and sequins, was marshalling Adam and the little twins; she was a general directing her battle line, each plate and bowl was positioned in its appointed place on the trestles with a huge birthday cake in the shape of a pirate ship with twelve cannons holding their candles. Adam was kept to heel although it was clear to Tilly he was itching to join the men at the bar.

'Come on lover. It's party time.' She cajoled Cary from his bed and he left for the *Brigantia*, with a promise to meet on the beach. She was in Mai's flat, adjusting her wispy bits of rags and left over samples that comprised her costume of Sylvia Lumpfish, but she waited a while longer enjoying the stillness of the Brew House. It was never still, as far back as she could remember it was busy, people, projects, food and drink, laughter and work, and love, love that had seeped into the walls over the years and finally Tilly was glad Mai was her mother. A sound disturbed her, she smiled, that was better, no use for the old house to be quiet, it didn't suit it; sounded like a door banging, softly, a dull thud, repeating with long intervals, sounded like it was coming from Naomi's apartment, she'd get Cary to check it, she'd begun to rely on him.

On the beach she found Zander and Daisy, who was a blue lurid mermaid, complete with tail and silver hair, pleading to be allowed to join the twins in the DJ tent.

'You can't weld her to you,' Tilly advised.

'I know, but with all that's happened I'm struggling to let her out of my sight. Don't know what she's going to get up to next.'

'I'm sensible now Daddy. And Sean and Harry are older, prac'illy adults.'

He sighed and sent a slow questioning look at Tilly.

She sighed. 'Not sure I'm the one to give advice, but I think that if you specifically ask them to keep an eye on her they will, and Robert won't leave the tent, not with all that equipment in there.'

'Please?' Daisy was irresistible.

'OK, but you stay there! You don't go anywhere else at all, no matter who asks you.'

She ran, whooping like a wild creature, her mermaid's tail hiked up above her shorts.

'How are things with Jack?' Tilly asked.

'Oh God! He's determined to join the race, entered his name and everything's shipshape and Bristol fashion, means I'll have to go with him, but with Cloris so doo-lally I don't think it's a good idea. I want him to stay here and get her to a doctor.'

'Does it matter? Even if she sees a doctor, it's not going to halt the Alzheimer's.'

'S'pose not.'

'You seem a lot more accepting of them. Have you and Jack made it up?'

'He told me. Why he's kept his distance all these years, so stupid, not a viable reason at all. He reckons it was when I was about two years old. He was away doing his James Bond stuff and my mother drowned, far as anyone could tell she just fell out of the rowboat and I was rescued just before it hurtled over the wear. From then on he blamed himself, couldn't trust himself to care for me so nannies were hired then later I was packed off to boarding school. He thought I'd be better off without him and when Daisy arrived it all happened again, the feelings of uselessness and guilt. He just couldn't handle it.'

'That's the saddest story I ever heard. All these years! You must have been such a lonely little boy.' She fastened her arms around him and they stayed like that, locked together in friendly love.

Zander moved first, kissing the top of her head and wincing. 'Your shells are slicing bits off me.'

'Vicious creatures us kelpies.' She relaxed her arms and slid away, just as Cary arrived.

'Caught you. Get off my woman.'

'Er, excuse me, I'm my own woman.'

Cary sighed. 'Kelpies – what can you do?'

They laughed, but Tilly had spied Lena on her own, just behind the DJ tent, mooching in the shadows. She looked about for Krista.

Cary had noticed her interest. 'The crazy girl's at the beer tent.'

'I saw her earlier, coming out of the Brew House, the empty flat.' Zander knew he meant Krista.

'That must have been the noise I heard.'

'She's talking to Mai now.' Cary gave a slight nod in the direction of the brightly lit tent, where most people were congregating.

'I'm going to talk to Lena. If Krista gets away from Mam waylay her. I want Lena alone.' She slipped swiftly into the shadows, around the back of Lena, who was still fumbling with rolling her cigarette. 'Hi Lena, haven't seen you for a while, sorry, been a bit caught up with things at home.' She tried to appear casual.

Lena nodded then to Tilly's shock and surprise she burst into tears. 'Jazzy's gone.'

Tilly had never seen Lena lose control of her iron will. It was unnerving. She guided her deeper into the shadows, took the half packed cigarette from her trembling fingers and finished rolling it. Then lit it and passed it Lena, who took it without a word and used it to control her ragged breathing, drawing deeply on the loosely packed tube.

'You're shit at rollies,' she stuttered.

'It's been a while.'

'Still no excuse for this mess.' Lena was still sobbing, great heaving breaths from the depths of her belly, hardly getting the words out.

'What did Jazzy say?'

A shake of the head was all Lena could manage.

'Why don't you let Cary take the *Brigantia* back and you fly out now, tonight, get it sorted?'

'Can't leave Krista.'

'Why the hell not? You're not her keeper.'

'She's my daughter.'

Tilly was shocked. 'No. No Lena, you know she's not. Lena! Right, we're going to get this sorted. Now!' Dragging Lena, limp and heavy, she pushed her way to where Mai was talking to Krista, although Mai seemed a bit distracted and kept looking at the river. That blasted river! Not now mother, not now!

'She'll be cold. She never cares about how she is. She'll be cold.'

'What?' Tilly turned to listen to Lena.

'Jazzy. She didn't take anything. She'll be cold.'

'She must have taken something. You can't fly to Mallorca with nothing at all.'

Lena shook her head. 'She left her bag, her money, everything.'

'Then she can't have gone home, not without a passport. Lena, did you look in her bag?'

They were joined by Cary, concerned. 'What's this?'

'Lena says Jazzy left suddenly and didn't take anything with her.'

Cary took charge, an arm around Lena's shoulders, absorbing her into his strength. 'Did you look in her bag?'

Lena shook her head. 'Can't find it. She's gone where I can't find her. She hates me so much.'

Behind her Tilly heard Krista saying she had to go.

Instead of trying to detain her Mai agreed. 'Yes, look I've got something to do. Tilly!' Her mother called to her. 'Talk to Krista and get your mermaids on all of you, running about like headless chickens and it's in the silver, the answer's plain if you'll only use your eyes.' She jumped onto the beach her Peggy Lumpfish rags floating after her.

'Mother!' Tilly was annoyed. Leaving Lena to Cary she turned to go after her, but was stopped by Krista trying to get to Lena. They collided and Tilly noticed the livid cut streaking across Krista's face. 'What happened to you?'

'Nothing.' Krista pushed past and tried to get between Cary and Lena.

Suddenly Tilly knew what had happened, she knew what the noise in the Brew House had been, she stared at Krista and gasped. 'You locked her in! She scratched you.'

Cary grabbed hold of Krista's arm.

The girl was strong. She easily pushed past his enormous strength, shrugged him off as if he was a puny boy. 'Jazzy's against me, won't accept that I'm with Lena now and she's not needed any more.' Her voice was without emotion, her dark eyes blank in the lightning flash that cleaved the sky.

'You lunatic!' Tilly yelled as she fled the nightmare that was only a teenage girl. Off the beach and up the bank, praying she was wrong and then hoping she was right. no-one would have imagined that Krista would have been so crazy as to lock Jazzy in an empty building and just dismiss her as if she'd never existed. At the Brew house she couldn't find the key. It wasn't on its hook under the eaves. Cary caught up with her and behind him Zander. Lena had become aware of the situation and was trying to pull away from Krista who was desperately hanging on to her. Cary kicked at the door and Lena, taking her chance, pushed Krista away. The girl stumbled on the wet cobbles, the rain now relentless and streaming down the banks, rushing headlong into the river. Tilly caught hold of Lena who had fallen to her knees and looked bewildered. 'Jazzy's here! Krista locked her in the empty apartment. She didn't leave you. Help us Lena, help Cary to break the door.'

Galvanised by the thought of Jazzy in danger Lena hurled herself at the solid wood. It wouldn't shift.

'Keys upstairs. I'll get the spare.' Tilly ran upstairs and fumbled at the key hooks. Finding the one she needed she dropped it and scrambled about in the dark before forcing herself to think clearly and switching on the light. The key lay under the table. She bent to retrieve it and felt a paralyzing blow on her spine, knocking her flat. Dizzy with pain she wrapped her hand around the cold steel as Krista punched her again, this time on the side of her neck. This was almost unendurable. Tilly fought to stay conscious, fought to push Krista away from her, but with her swimmer's muscles she was too strong. She prised open Tilly's wet fingers, her knee pressing into her neck. Choking and losing her hold on the situation, Tilly still fought and managed to stab her fingers into Krista's eyes. Howling with pain and growling obscenities, Krista banged Tilly's head on the floorboards. This was more than Tilly could bare, and she felt her arms lose their strength and the key slip from her hand. She could do nothing to stop Krista.

It was quiet when Tilly regained her senses, groaning from the pain in her hand, dizzy with the bashing her head had received she staggered to her knees and pulled on the table for support as she dragged herself up. Footsteps pounded on the uncarpeted stairs, she shook her head trying to focus and was powerless to even scream at her attacker; she buried her head in her hands.

'Mum, Mum, it's me Harry.'

'Harry? Oh! Blessed child.' She clung to her son. 'Go and get Cary, tell him Krista's got the key.

'No, no she hasn't.' There were more footsteps on the stairs. Tilly grabbed Harry's arms, pushed him towards the bedrooms. 'Run and hide, don't let Krista catch you.'

'Dad's got her. You should have seen him Mum, a smashing rugga tackle, brought her down and sat on her while Sean got the key and we've got ...'

His words were lost in the rush of activity as Cary, Lena, Jazzy, Zander and Sean filled the space around her, everyone talking at once.

Jazzy was filthy and shivering, white with cold and with black shadows ringing her eyes, she held on to Lena's hands. Lena gently lowered her into the opposite chair, kneeling and holding her.

Beth appeared and taking in the situation she ran to the bathroom, returning with towels; everyone was wet. 'I can't stay.

Gran's gone mad. She's on the Middens, yelling and bashing about and the tide's coming in and the lifeboat men are trying to get to her, but she's wading deeper and deeper, she's going to drown.' Tilly struggled to her feet, Cary helped her. Adam appeared in the doorway and Cary turned him about, Harry and Beth followed. Tilly looked back at her friends huddled together by the fire, Lena holding Jazzy tight and Jazzy sunk against her, tears running down her face. They'd be fine. Still feeling a bit groggy Tilly stumbled down the stairs and stepped out into a blinding storm with lightning cracking across the sky showing a fierce sea breaking into the harbour and pounding up river, pushing hundreds of tons of flotsam before it.

. . . .

Tilly was too late for Death. It slipped in behind the storm and left just as furtively; disappearing, dissolving into the water, taking Mai's soul with it.

The beach was hushed, as people watched the weary lifeboatmen trudging along the path, climbing the breakwater to talk to Tilly. Afterwards it was the silence she remembered most. no-one speaking, the noise from the quayside subdued, the shrieks from the funfare, so macabre, seemed part of the silence. The police arrived and cleared the sands and car park and then there was only the family, fractured though they were they came together to touch and whisper, to console with loving caresses. Cary took Tilly and Beth to the Brew House and soon everyone else followed.

Apart from Mai, whose presence haunted the building, the only person missing was Krista. Some said they'd seen her trying to pull Mai from the sea, others that she was trying to pull her in. Cloris said she'd come on board Jack's boat, but that could have been a scene from the past, replaying in her addled brain, or even some snatch of the future; with Cloris it was hard to tell.

As dawn flooded the land with brightness and the sky expanded high and blue as an angel's eyes Mai's body was recovered by the dredger clearing debris from the river to give a bright clear passage for the parade of boats, and now it lay in the mortuary at North Tyneside Hospital, a place, in life, she had never visited.

Tilly stood at the window of the Brew House and watched

the police combing the sands. The tattered remains of the party littered the beach, the bonfire was flattened and the DJ tent collapsed and Robert followed the police, trying to collect anything still serviceable. The police had spoken to the lifeboat men and were satisfied that Mai's death was a tragic accident. They were sorry, they said, and Tilly knew it to be true, everyone knew, had known, Mai's eccentric hatred of the mermaids and her overwhelming desire to avenge her husband. So Peggy Lumpfish had triumphed and the mermaids didn't get any of the family.

CHAPTER TWENTY

TILLY

The Tall Ships had gone. One hundred and fifty-three craft left the Tyne in triumph, their crews smartly at attention in the yards or working the ropes and chains, the vessels were dressed over-all in coloured bunting and message flags their brightwork gleaming as they floated through the piers and across the North Sea, cheered on by thousands of well wishers and raced by a few ambitious yachtsmen. Overnight the fair disappeared, the beer tents, the massive music marquee with its tons of scaffolding, lights and speakers had been shunted off in the back of huge trucks. The quay settled into its accustomed role of fishing and fledgling tourism.

No-one in the Brew House had taken any notice. Beth mooched around, lonely, all her friends at college, the crew Lena had assembled to sail the *Brigantia* to the Caribbean had flown back to Mallorca, because Lena and Jazzy were trying to patch up their differences and wanted to stay put. Tilly thought it had more to do with Yvonne and Krista than anything else. Lena still seemed lost and was unable to make a decision about anything. She sympathised. She, who had been the most organised of women, had fallen apart when her plans lay in disarray. She too had been unable to make any decisions, but slowly she had begun to rise above these ruins, the new relationship with Cary had been a turning point, once again she had felt like a woman who meant something to the world, but since Mai's tragic accident she had slumped. What did anything matter? All the years of keeping one step away from her mother's love had been the real tragedy. And just when they were feeling a new closeness Mai had been taken away. Tilly's guilt over the lost years weighed heavily on her mind, but it was too late.

Lonore and both sets of twins had settled in at Sea View. Sean and Harry revelling in the wonders of the new high tech Monkseaton High School didn't seem bothered that their mother was sitting about in the Brew House and not contributing anything towards their lives.

Cary, having been incredibly supportive after Mai's death, had inexplicably gone to Cornwall, saying he had urgent business. She ached with loneliness and longed for his loving body to smother hers and help her forget for a few precious moments that her heart was breaking. Jack's boat was grounded in the Haven next to the yacht club where Zander and Daisy lodged while he went job and house hunting, determined on settling on Tyneside. Cloris was in real distress with her Alzheimer's and was having treatment at the local day care centre.

The sadness when Tilly thought about never seeing her mother ever again was overwhelming, but she had to sort out a life for herself and Beth. Mai's Will had been read and there were no surprises. Tilly now owned the Brew House a few lock ups and a boat; at least she and Beth now had somewhere to live and an income from the studio rents and whatever lobsters young Bob Turnbull brought in. Beth hadn't been as lucky as the twins and still wasn't in school. And she was beginning to show. This didn't bother Tilly, she was only concerned with Beth's welfare and had broken through her misery long enough to accompany her listless daughter to the anti natal clinic where the miracle of birth lightened their moods as they had clasped each other in wonder when the scan revealed the tiny wriggling form of the baby. Beth had stuck the photo on the fridge and called it Squirm.

Tilly walked along the quay with no particular destination in mind, maybe she'd go aboard the *Brigantia*, see what Lena and Jazzy were up to, but progress was slow. Everyone wanted to sympathise with her loss. Hushed tones and hugs and kisses threatened to smother her and she was on the verge of turning back when an empty bench tucked in behind the ice factory beckoned. She sat and gazed unseeing across the slack water at the houses on the south bank. A vaguely familiar voice brought her back to the present.

'It's Tilly isn't it?'

She turned, shielding her eyes from the ever lowering sun, it was Yvonne. 'You're Lena's sister, Yvonne?'

The woman stood on the cobblestones, steady as a rock in six-inch heels and inward slanting platform soles. They reminded Tilly of pictures she'd seen of Chinese women's bound feet. The shoes were red patent leather and clashed with a short orange skirt that flaunted Yvonne's long shapely legs. She was wearing more make-up on her beautiful dark skinned face than Tilly would use in a month.

She nodded and sat down, pressing her voluptuous body close, like a spy in a film. 'Everyone thinks she's dead, ye know, but they don't know her. She can swim can our Krista and she's still out there somewhere.' She nodded towards the sea.

'I know she can swim, I've seen her, but it's been five weeks! It's freezing out there.'

'She's got problems.'

'Yes.' Tilly didn't want to get into a discussion about Krista's problems, she had enough of her own.

'You know I'm her mother.'

Not another theory about Krista's mother. She'd had enough. 'I'm not getting into this.'

'It's all your Mother's fault. No offence.' Yvonne added hastily.

'What's my Mother got to do with it?'

'Everything. It was her idea. The people she'd arranged to have Krista weren't able, I forget why … don't think I ever knew to be honest.'

This was making no sense to Tilly. 'People? What people?'

'Lena had her baby and Mai arranged for a young couple in Scotland to take her, but they couldn't, so she gave her to me.'

Madness must run in the family Tilly thought as she walked away and left Yvonne to her ranting.

'No, no don't go. It's true.' Yvonne was following her, holding on to her arm.

Tilly remembered how strong Krista had been as she tried to stop them rescuing Jazzy. She panicked and pulled away, running towards home.

But Yvonne, despite the improbable shoes, kept up the pace. 'Mai was always very good to girls who needed help.'

'She was good to lots of girls. She gave them a place to stay when their parents threw them on the streets for making a mistake.'

'Krista is Lena's daughter.'

'Please don't start all this again Yvonne. It's too late anyway. Krista's gone. You have to accept it.'

Yvonne shook her head. 'I got pregnant too. About the same time Lena left, but I had a miscarriage and the baby died. I left her at the hospital and came home and then Mai came looking for me. Lena had gone off on her adventures, and I was in bits after the baby died and I was ill, a caesarean, so when Mai brought Lena's baby it was just what we needed, her and me.'

Tilly stopped running. 'Does Lena know this?'

'I wrote a few times. She never answered.'

'Right, we'll end this once and for all.' Suddenly she was striding across to the *Brigantia*.

Lena heard them coming. She popped her head around the doorway at the bottom of the companionway. 'Hi, thought it was …'

Her words dwindled as she noticed Yvonne on deck, hesitating, unsure.

'Heels,' Lena warned.

'We've more important things to discuss than your precious deck.' Tilly was angry. She pushed past Lena and stood in the middle of the salon. 'Yvonne!' She called. 'Get down here.'

'My shoes.' Yvonne was struggling to loosen the many buckles on the one item of clothing Lena never allowed on board the *Brigantia*.

'Can we forget about the bloody shoes! Get down here.'

'Excuse me.' Lena interrupted. 'I'll be the judge of what happens on this ship.'

'You think the world begins and ends on this bloody ship. Do you ever look around you and wonder what else is happening. Did you ever wonder what happened to the baby you gave birth to and abandoned? Have you ever wondered if my mother was completely sane!' Tilly was beyond polite conversation.

Yvonne was standing, hanging for grim death onto the companion rail. Jazzy stepped forward and helped her to sit down.

'Jazzy, can you give us some space?' Lena asked.

Jazzy shook her head. 'No. Whatever's going on here I need to know.'

Tilly was vaguely aware that Beth had appeared from the aft passageway and was sitting in a corner, quietly listening, hoping no-one would notice her.

They were all waiting.

Lena lit a cigarette, blew out a long stream of smoke and began to pour drinks. She swallowed a slug of gin and poured another. 'I was fourteen, no money, on the streets, raped and pregnant; Mai was the only person who helped me. She was a friend when I needed one. I had the baby and I didn't want it. I can't describe to you how I felt over the whole fucking mess.

Dealing with the rape was bad enough; boys using me, laughing and pushing inside till I was bleeding, punching and kicking me 'cos I tried to get away. And that wasn't all. Even then I knew the thing between men and women wasn't for me. I'm sure it's bad for any woman to cope with rape, but for a lesbian it's indescribable. Then the whole motherhood thing, pregnancy, it was abhorrent, I wanted to kill myself.

'Why didn't you have an abortion?' Yvonne thrust her face at Lena, the words harsh and demanding.

'Too late.' Lena shook her head as if to dislodge the unbearable memories. 'I was a mess, mad with the horror of it all. I went to see Mai, all the girls went to see Mai.'

'What do you mean, all the girls?' Tilly asked.

Lena turned on Tilly, snarling. 'You, you with your satchel and white socks, you had no idea what she was doing. Mai ran an adoption agency, made the money to pay for all your books and fancy uniforms. You stupid cow!'

Tilly was stunned. She sank to the seat behind her.

Lena wasn't finished. 'The birth itself was the worst experience of my life. I never even looked at the thing that survived the trauma. I only knew that Mai took it away and saved me. I think I went a bit mad, but Mai nursed me and I eventually survived. The baby had gone and I was glad. I put it from my mind and got on with my life.'

Jazzy stirred, asked the question they were all thinking. 'When you met Krista in Mallorca did you know she was yours?'

Lena was shocked. 'No. No! Why would I even suspect such a thing? I've had dozens of girls crewing for me; she was just the latest.'

'But it was there, between you. I knew you loved her.'

'Yes there was an attraction, but I didn't realise it was anything maternal.'

'You're unbelievable. Disgusting, randy, horny Lena who says she loves me, but you have a strange and selfish way of showing it. I thought there was hope for us, but there's not. I can't do this anymore Lena. Your questionable morals almost had you having sex with your own daughter. She is her daughter, isn't she?' Jazzy implored Yvonne for the truth, but before Yvonne nodded her head, Jazzy had left the cabin.

Lena made to follow her but Tilly stepped forward. 'I need more Lena. Were you the only girl Mam helped in this way?'

'No!' Lena screamed at her. 'No! Why the hell do you think I went to her for help in the first place? All the girls who worked the quay knew they could go to Mai for an abortion or an adoption, it was all the same to her.' And with that parting shot she pulled herself up the stairs and could be heard pounding down the deck after Jazzy.

Tilly sat on, the silence ringing in her ears.

Yvonne spoke. 'She's never even asked me how I feel. Krista's my little girl and she's missing and Lena doesn't care, she never did. Help me, please help me to find Krista.' Her beautiful face, so like Krista's was contorted in pain.

Tilly's heart was breaking for the sad plight of this distraught mother mourning her only child, but she had nothing left to give. 'I can't even help myself.' She couldn't stay in the cabin any longer. The pain and suffering her mother had engendered filled the place like the emanation of an evil spell. Tilly left Yvonne slumped across the table and climbed off the *Brigantia*.

Back in the Brew House all was quiet. Tilly pulled the ladder down from the loft and spent the rest of the evening and best part of the night searching through boxes of miscellaneous papers. Nothing. All the reams of withered brown paper uncovered nothing about babies. She fell asleep at the table in front of the cold fireplace.

When she woke up it was instantly on her mind. There had to be some records, surely. A search of Mai's bedroom yielded nothing. Next she delved into the garden shed, but the enormity of the task overwhelmed her, there was too much junk to sort through and it all looked like bits of sculptures and tools and what paperwork there was seemed to be invoices and bills for materials for Mai's work. Tilly had not eaten nor slept properly for days and it was sunset again, she felt drained of all energy and ideas, she needed to sleep. Wearily she climbed the path through the bushes, their broken branches the only evidence of Jack's near brush with death. Above her, through the open kitchen window, she heard Beth's voice.

'Mum, Mum, you here? Doesn't look like it.'

Then Cary's soft drawl. 'No matter my dear. She'll not be far. Just hope she's not on the quay. Don't want to spoil the surprise.'

Tilly pulled herself up the stairs and into the kitchen. 'I'm here.' And then Cary's arms were about her, his mouth kissing her with promises of love. It was more than she could bear. His love and kindness brought on a fit of sobbing.

Safe in his arms and with Beth listening in Tilly related the whole sorry story. 'I have to sort it out, but I can't find any proof. I've searched everywhere, the loft, her bedroom.'

'Mum, that's not everywhere, there's the lock-ups, the rest of this house, the garden, the boat, you might never find any proof.'

'Even if any exists,' Cary added. 'Mai was always a bit canny.'

'She was insane!' Tilly blurted out her worst fears. 'I need to find those babies and let them know who they really are.'

Beth obviously didn't think much of this as a solution. 'Please don't. Without proof where would you start?'

'Those poor little mites, they need to know who they really are.'

'They're not little mites any more, they're grown up, adults most of them. And maybe they already know and won't thank you for wrecking their lives.' Beth was Mrs Practical again.

'But I'd be putting things right, giving them a choice so they can plan their lives.'

'Will you stop this with the bloody plans!' Beth implored.

Tilly was too tired to argue. She excused herself and went to bed, but sleep drifted away from her troubled mind leaving her to toss and turn until dawn cracked a sliver of sky and poured in a bright new day, a day not yet used, a day filled with opportunities.

The kitchen was empty, but breakfast was prepared, the table set prettily with Mai's mismatched china and a small jar of sea pinks, sweet smelling fresh bread in a cloth covered basket and scrambled egg and salmon waiting in front of the settling fire. Cary, it could only be him, no-one else would be so thoughtful. He must have gone out early, but when she glanced at the clock it was after nine and she realised she was ravenous.

After she'd eaten and tidied the kitchen she wandered around the flat until Cary returned and suggested they look through Mai's workshop. There was so much stuff, the implements of her craft that Mai had gathered over her working life and everywhere they looked the mermaids stared back.

'What can it be about these blessed things that Mai had wanted us to see?'

Cary shrugged. 'Who knows? This is useless and it's driving you mad. Come outside for a walk. I've got a surprise.'

'I've had enough surprises.'

'I'll see you later then, come when you need me.' And with a casual kiss he left the studio and swung down the stairs.

'Come where?' But he had gone. She focused on the job in hand. The shelves were crammed with books on sea lore and recipes for a multitude of medicines that could be extracted from seaweed and the plants that grew in abundance on the surrounding cliffs. This talent of Mai's had been a real thing, tangible. She herself had often used Mai's remedies for her family, and not been surprised that they were effective; seaweed was, after all, a natural antibiotic. She studied the mermaids. 'She said the secret is in the mermaids, look at the mermaids, they have the answers.' With a growing sense of purpose Tilly began to examine them. The little ones she dismissed. If anything was hidden it would be in the big pieces. She ran her hands over the curves and hollows of the biggest one, the one Mai had been working on, but it yielded no hidden compartment or anything that could be a switch. She tried the next one and the next. Nothing.

She was interrupted by an extremely excited Beth who burst in and pulled at her hand. 'Leave that Mum, come on!'

Tilly pulled away from Beth's grabbing hand. 'No, I can't. Help me Beth. You see the answer's in the mermaids. Come on …' But she stopped at the stricken look on her daughter's face. It shocked her. 'Darling, what is it? What's happened?'

Beth shook her head tears fell onto her cheeks. 'Don't Mum, d … don't.'

'What? What is it?'

'Don't you know?'

Tilly tried to sit Beth on the stool Mai used when she sculpted, but she resisted, backed away.

'You're just like Nana; mad, rambling on about bloody mermaids.'

'No darling. No, don't you see, Nana used to say the answer was in the mermaids. It's got to be inside one of them. Help me to find it. People are depending on me. It's for their lives Beth.'

'No Mum. No. It's not. It's for you. You're going to spoil everything again.'

'Wha … I don't understand? What are you talking about?'

'Cary is waiting for you.' Beth took her hand. 'Forget this Mum. Think about us.'

'But you know who you are. These people don't. I can help them.'

Beth stepped away, then farther and farther, backing down the stairs. 'Come now Mum, if you don't it'll be too late for all of us. Cary's waiting.'

Tilly couldn't understand what was so wrong with trying to help people who had no idea where they belonged. She was stunned to realise that Beth and Cary couldn't sympathise with this fact. Beth left and she resumed her search.

The house was quiet, Tilly was intent on only one thing and didn't hear her visitor until she stood right in front of her. So shocked by the strong and vital presence of Krista she was unable to gather her thoughts. This just wasn't possible. Krista had drowned five weeks ago. Yet somehow here she was.

'Hi Tilly.'

Tilly was afraid of this girl. She was dangerously unstable. She had to play along. 'Krista! We've been so worried about you.'

''Cos you didn't find my body?' She leaned close.

Tilly could see her own face in the deep empty darkness of Krista's brown eyes and could only nod.

She moved away, wandering around the studio, picking bits of this and that up, examining them with a careless interest, as if she had seen them many times. 'I decided to come back and put you all out of your misery. Mai was good to me and the last thing she told me was that I must show all of you what she'd been trying to tell you for years. Of course I worked it out, but you lot never had the savvy.' She sat on Mia's stool and fiddled with a sharp scalpel.

'What? What did she want us to know?'

Krista looked about at the mess Tilly had made pulling papers and rubbish from boxes and shelves. She laughed. 'You really don't have a clue even though she told you time and time again. I've always known Lena was my mother because we have the same mermaid. You and Beth do. Mai never made them for the men, none except Cary and his is identical to yours and Beth's and Mai made this for the baby, she said it'll be a girl.' From her necklace she unhooked a tiny silver mermaid and handed to Tilly. 'It's in the markings, the scales on the tails are slightly different for each couple or group of people who belong together.'

Tilly reached out and took the pendant from Krista, staring at the minute markings on the tail. They were barely noticeable. She compared it with her own and they were identical. The fog in her brain cleared, she looked around at the devastation she'd caused when all along the thing she was searching for was hanging around her neck. 'Krista?'

But the mysterious girl who had come back from the sea was gone.

Tilly ran downstairs and along the quay. On the *Brigantia* she told everyone what had happened. They all examined their pendants. Beth and she and the one intended for the baby matched the one in Cary's ear.

'We should have just asked, seemed like she got it right.'

'And presumably Krista's is identical to mine,' Lena said. She looked at her sister, hopefully.

'Mai never gave me a mermaid.' Yvonne admitted. 'I suppose she knew that I'd never be a part of your lives.'

'Mai didn't know everything.' Jazzy had entered quietly. She walked over to Lena and kissed her cheek. She smiled. 'We're going to need new crew?'

Lena nodded and kissed her back. 'Thanks girl.' She turned to Yvonne. 'You could come with us. It's not too late.' She looked to Jazzy and was rewarded with a smile.

'Yea, it's time to face the facts and move on.'

'I've never been on a sailing boat.'

'Everyone has to learn; up to you.' Lena told her.

They all watched as Yvonne smiled and nodded.

'The heels need to go.' Lena told her.

They all laughed, but Yvonne still looked worried. She turned to Tilly. 'Where is she? Where's my girl?'

'I don't know Yvonne, but she is alive.'

'I think that girl will turn up one day when you're least expecting her.' From the top of the stairs where he'd been lounging for the last ten minutes, Cary voiced what they were all thinking.

Lena nodded. 'I know I've been a cow, but I'll try. And when she does get in touch we'll deal with it together. Despite what Mai thought Krista's your daughter, not mine, she was never mine.'

Yvonne smiled. 'What about Mam?'

Lena glowered. 'Don't push it.'

They laughed again and under the hubbub Cary pulled Tilly up the companion way to stand at the rail on the curved stern. Next to them a new boat was tied up. 'Meet my darlin', this is the *Genista*.'

'Your boat?' So much had happened and Tilly wasn't sure she understood what this new development meant. 'You're going away?'

'We're going away; all of us, you and Beth and Sean and Harry too if they want. I'm fully crewed and ready to go.'

'I can't just take off like that and Beth's pregnant!'

'Women have been giving birth in all parts of the world for centuries, in huts and palaces, hospitals and ships and when it's near her time I'll make sure we're near a fully staffed and equipped maternity unit, in the sun.'

'In the sun.' Tilly knew she was repeating him, but she couldn't take in the full implications of his words. 'There's so much to do. I have to find the babies.'

'You'll never find them. Maybe somewhere someone will notice that their old silver pendant is the same as someone else's, but it won't change their lives. The past is gone Tilly and we can have a wonderful future. What do you say? We'll head for the Caribbean islands and pick up a couple of charters, stay there until the babe is born then who knows? We can go wherever we please. You can learn the charts, be our navigator.'

'But the house? I've got things to sort out.'

'Say yes Mum, let Dad sort things out. We've all got computers to keep in touch and the boys will adore being back on board, you know they were born to the sea and maybe this one will be too and you can be a navigator, you love organising things and marking charts.' Behind them Beth hung over the rail of the companionway stairs, hugging her little rounding belly, her eyes shining hopefully.

A new life for all of them? Was it that simple? And Tilly realised that it was. 'Zander can rent the brew house and he'll have a home for Daisy and a studio for his work and be independent.'

'Now you're making sense.' Beth whooped with joy. 'Can I tell Lena?'

'No.' Tilly said.

'Yes.' Cary replied. 'Yes my dear. Yes and yes again. Try it on for size.'

Tentatively Tilly formed the word. 'Er, yer, yes?'

'Say it again Mum.' Beth told her with a peal of the purest laughter Tilly had heard from her since before they packed for Mallorca.

'Yes.' Tilly shouted. 'Yes.'

Whooping with excitement Beth ran back to the cabin, but all the yelling and cheering was drowned out by the merest whisper from Cary's lips as he kissed her. 'I love you.'

Tilly sank into his arms and knew that it was right. This was the unplanned life Mai had always wanted for her. She turned to look out through the piers at the deep, deep sea. 'And I'll watch out for the mermaids,' she whispered to her mother.

'That's my girl,' said Cary.